"A well-written portrait, not just of grief but also of the pain of realizing you didn't really know someone you thought were close to… A heavy but powerful read that tackles big topics."

—*Booklist* on *The Sister Pact*

"The story reads like *Go Ask Alice*… As Allie learns the many sordid secrets of her sister's concealed life, she begins to understand the powerful influence her sister had on her and struggles to find her own voice."

—*Kirkus Reviews* on *The Sister Pact*

"A powerful story of redemption, forgiveness, love, and the ability to persevere."

—*VOYA* on *The Sister Pact*

"A stirring close-up of a family haunted by emotional trauma."

—*Kirkus Reviews* on *The Homecoming*

"The overall message of relying on family and friends for support is clear, and John's pain and confusion are palpable."

—*School Library Journal* on *The Homecoming*

"This engaging story will appeal to all readers and will help troubled teens realize that there can be help out there for what's going on in their lives."

—*School Library Connection* on *The Homecoming*

"Ramey has penned a rare, raw, emotion-packed romance from a male perspective, with themes of empowerment and self-actualization."

—*Booklist* on *The Homecoming*

"A sensitive, funny, and sometimes awkwardly romantic story of survival and self-awareness."

—*Kirkus Reviews* on *The Secrets We Bury*

"A gripping novel that will tug on readers' heartstrings until the very end."

—*Booklist* on *The Secrets We Bury*

IT'S MY LIFE

STACIE RAMEY

sourcebooks
fire

Copyright © 2020 by Stacie Ramey
Cover and internal design © 2020 by Sourcebooks
Cover design by Kerri Resnick
Cover image © Piyapong89/Shutterstock
Internal design by Jillian Rahn

Sourcebooks and the colophon are registered trademarks of Sourcebooks.

All rights reserved. No part of this book may be reproduced in any form or by any electronic or mechanical
means including information storage and retrieval systems—except in the case of brief quotations
embodied in critical articles or reviews—without permission in writing from its publisher, Sourcebooks.

The characters and events portrayed in this book are fictitious or are used fictitiously. Any similarity to real
persons, living or dead, is purely coincidental and not intended by the author.

All brand names and product names used in this book are trademarks, registered trademarks, or trade names
of their respective holders. Sourcebooks, Inc., is not associated with any product or vendor in this book.

Published by Sourcebooks Fire, an imprint of Sourcebooks
P.O. Box 4410, Naperville, Illinois 60567-4410
(630) 961-3900
sourcebooks.com

Library of Congress Cataloging-in-Publication Data

Names: Ramey, Stacie, author.
Title: It's my life / Stacie Ramey.
Other titles: It is my life
Description: Naperville, Illinois : Sourcebooks Fire, [2020] | Summary:
    While facing disturbing revelations about the cause of her disability, a
    high school junior with cerebral palsy is on the verge of giving up on
    herself until her childhood crush moves back into town.
Identifiers: LCCN 2019024129 | (trade paperback)
Subjects: CYAC: Cerebral palsy--Fiction. | People with
    disabilities--Fiction. | Love--Fiction. | High schools--Fiction. |
    Schools--Fiction. | Jews--United States--Fiction.
Classification: LCC PZ7.1.R36 It 2020 | DDC [Fic]--dc23
LC record available at https://lccn.loc.gov/2019024129

Printed and bound in Canada.
MBP 10 9 8 7 6 5 4 3 2 1

For Bonnie and Mark,
because they keep me tethered to this world

ONE

Everything's different for girls like me.

My younger sister, Rena, would say I'm being dramatic. As in, "Stop being so dramatic, Jenna. Having CP doesn't make you the star of a telethon."

I always laugh when she says it, which is the whole point.

But right now, Rena and my best friend, Ben, are both at school, living their lives, while I'm lying on a cold MRI table, bare-assed and covered in a skimpy hospital gown. See? Different.

And also maybe a little dramatic. I get that.

The door swings open. I hold my breath, hoping for Gary as my nurse today. I cannot deal with my yearly MRI with anyone else.

"How's my favorite girl?" Gary's voice reaches me, and I let my breath go, turning my head to shoot him my best I'm-not-feeling-*too*-sorry-for-myself smile.

Gary's tall and lean. Muscular, though. I can see those peeking out of his scrubs. He's always changing his overall look, but now he's blond with a soul patch under his lip. He is dressed in his usual blue-gray hospital scrubs—no dorky Disney scrubs for him, despite this being the pediatric wing. We've known each other far too long, Gary and me. He was there for most of my surgeries and even the time I smashed Mom's Waterford glass into my forehead during a muscle spasm, effectively ruining Passover. So, all the good times.

He's wearing a Tree of Life necklace on a silver beaded chain and some other charm I can't make out. They clink together as he leans over me to prepare the straps they need to hold me in place. The sound is comforting, like church bells or something. I've always been a sucker for spiritual stuff. "You need anything?" he asks.

"I wouldn't turn down a trip to Florida and a good book," I joke.

"Let's run away. We can leave out the back door," Gary says. This is one of our things. "I'm thinking North Carolina. I'm sort of into mountains these days."

"Good plan. I'm pretty sure my body would terrify the beach-goers." I pull down my gown that's ridden up from all of his fiddling with the table, uncovering the most recent scars from my surgeries. If I was here with anyone but Gary, I'd feel pretty exposed. With him I don't have to worry.

Gary scoffs. "Girl, scars are sexy now. Totally in. Like tattoos and body piercings."

I laugh so hard I snort. "Are snorts sexy now, too?"

My left leg starts to spasm, pulling away from the straps. Gary launches into a story about his current boyfriend, Bryan, as he runs my leg through its range of motion, massages it, and puts it back into place.

"Bryan is very pretty to look at, but is a diva to the nth degree," Gary tells me as he adjusts a pillow under my arm and cleans the area for the needle. I barely feel the IV line going in.

"It's bad enough he's into all that new age, no-caffeine lifestyle for himself." Gary pauses for effect, his hand over his heart. "But when he buys *me* coffee, it's decaf!"

I fake a gasp.

"I know. You don't mess with a person's caffeine." Gary tapes my IV line in place. "I'm just going to inject the sedative now, then the contrast; it may feel a little cold."

This is one of the reasons I don't want these stupid tests. For normal people, it doesn't even hurt. For me, it's liquid ice snaking through my veins, slow enough that the rebound pain is there at the same time as the first burn. I tense, and Gary squeezes my hand. I do not want to cry. It's a deal I made with myself years ago, back when I pretended I was Daddy's little warrior.

Gary loads up a new playlist that Rena made for me called *Songs for Enduring Stupid Pain*, and he catches my gaze. "Going to start now. You just close your eyes and go someplace better than this, baby girl. See you on the other side."

He pushes the button, and I slide into the tube. I close my eyes and try to breathe easy. The drugs in the IV help my muscles relax, but they aren't enough to make me sleep—which would make this entire deal easier.

As I wait for the first song to play, I try to guess which one Rena started with. Let's see, pain as the motif? So many choices. But instead of a song, her voice pipes in. "Stay cool, Jenna. It's going to be fine."

That's my sister being all Zen like usual.

Then my big brother Eric chimes in, "Go get it!" I've got no idea how they managed that with him away at college.

"Kick its ass," Rena says.

"Stay out of the woods," Eric adds. It's an inside joke from when we were little—the three of us and our neighbor Julian used to go to the nearby woods to look for animals and trees and mythical things, because I convinced them all if they were around us, that's where they'd be.

Rena laughs, and then the soulful sound of Michael Stipe singing "Everybody Hurts" fills my ears. I can't help but appreciate Rena's choice on so many levels. The MRI clicks and thrums as the sedatives start to unclench the muscles in my head. Everything feels softer. Gary told me to leave my body, and in this tube I feel like I can. And I do. Soon I'm flying through the air, through the clouds, feeling what it's like to move free and easy, way above the hurt. Away from this body, to someplace better.

A familiar voice inside my head whispers, "It's so easy." It's me, but it's not—I call this voice person Jennifer, and she's like the one I could have been. Free. Easy. Strong. Clear. I want to be her someday, and that possibility fills me until my head feels all light and my mind expands until I'm flying even higher. And higher. And then I get a little queasy. My stomach backs up in my throat, and I swallow to get rid of the taste.

"Jenna?" Gary calls through the speakers. "Stay with us, okay? A few more minutes."

More clicks. More gongs. More time in the tube. I close my eyes and slow my breathing.

I wonder how he knows I feel sick—how he always knows. The rational part of me realizes it's because of the monitors I'm hooked

up to, but I also partly believe it's because of our bond. A bond I wish
I had with a boy.

And just like that, my focus shifts again. To Julian. Julian Van
Beck. The kid I've had a thing for since kindergarten.

Almost like the universe hears me, the next song is "Fix You"
by Coldplay. The first time I heard this song was at one of Eric's rec
hockey games. Eric was twelve. I was ten, but a very cool ten. Or at
least I thought I was. I was sitting on the bench next to the hockey
players—a perk of being Eric's sister, since he was the captain of the
team. I had one earbud in, and as the song started, Julian came off the
ice and sat down next to me. The little smoke of breath that sprouted
from his lips in the icy rink air was so soft, like a flower petal. If I
closed my eyes now, I could still feel the puff of breath, could reach
out and touch it with my fingertips, just before it dissipated.

"Try to stay still, Jenna." Gary's voice reminds me I am not on
the bench at a hockey game. I am here, stuck inside this tube. Stuck
inside my body.

A tear rolls down my face, but secretly I'm glad. Even if it's pain,
it's wonderful anguish. I am, simply, a girl who loves a boy. A boy
who will never know, since Julian moved away in middle school. But,
the point is, all of this longing is so strong and, in some way, the most
beautiful thing I've ever felt.

Right now, in this electric cage, I let my mind ride the waves of
sedatives. The song shifts, and I'm floating again. Flying over a lush
field. The grass under me looks spongy and fresh and so real that
it makes me want to walk on it. Want to feel it spring up under my
bare feet.

"Hold still, hon. Just a few minutes more. You're doing great."

I hold still. A breeze blows my hair back, which I know is impossible, but it still feels so real. And I've got that voice hovering next to me again, a small breath in my ear, like how I saw Julian's breath that day on the bench. "It's so easy," the voice says. Only the *e* part is stretched so it sounds like *eeeeasy*.

A strand of hair comes loose and tickles my cheek. I wish I could move it. I try not to think about it, try not to obsess, but it's killing me. Then it's blown back, off my face. "You're okay now. It's all done," Jennifer tells me.

"All done," Gary says. "Be right there."

And, just like that, I have to prepare myself for reentry. Into the harsh light of the room. Into the harsh vibe of this life. I leave that other version of me, the one that could move freely and easily, in that MRI tube. And I wonder if I could have been that girl all along, if only Dr. Jacoby hadn't screwed up.

TWO

Looking back on it now, I feel pretty stupid for not figuring any of it out way earlier. It was my own version of believing in Santa—I was told the story so often that I never thought to question it. (We didn't have to deal with the Santa fallout; I'm Jewish. Mom used to go on and on about how proud she was that they never lied to us, as if the worst crime ever perpetrated on a kid was the invention of a benevolent old dude in a red suit who distributes presents. It isn't.)

Dr. Jacoby—or Dr. Jerkoby, as Ben refers to him when we discuss the subject—is probably a good guy. He had a really strong history leading up to my delivery. He's a Harvard Medical School graduate who did his OB/GYN residency at Johns Hopkins. From what I could find online, there were no complaints filed against him. No lawsuits. Very small percentage of C-sections. I'm sure his kids and grandkids love him. He probably volunteers at his church, or cleans stretches of the woods so that animals don't choke on litter strewn by inconsiderate campers. Maybe he builds houses for Habitat for Humanity or serves soup to the homeless.

He may do a hundred million nice things, but nothing he does now will make up for the day he delivered me.

Because the thing is, I wasn't supposed to be like this. I wasn't supposed to have cerebral palsy. That day, something *he* did caused it.

But I didn't realize that until this past summer.

Ben and I were taking an SAT study course—his idea—and we were in the midst of a vocabulary practice test. I came to a fill-in-the-blank question: "The doctor was accused of…so they settled the claim in court."

My eyes danced over the choices. The root of all of the words was *mal*, as in bad. Maleficent, malevolence, malfeasance, malignancy, maliciousness. Maleficent was the bad fairy in the movie, and that word in particular meant mischievous. I knew the answer wasn't maleficent, because a doctor wouldn't be evil or mischievous. The other options—malevolence, malignancy, maliciousness—weren't the right ones, either.

But a doctor *could* be blameworthy. As in, "The doctor was accused of malfeasance…"

I started to sweat even though it was freezing in the classroom, my eyes locked on the word *malfeasance*. I bubbled the answer, so sure of my response, but that word stuck with me. That sentence. A doctor could be accused of malfeasance and *settle*. The combination of the words, the phrasing, made my mind race.

And everything around me became suspended in time. The air. The sounds of pencils scratching and my classmates breathing. My own breath caught in my chest. Suddenly, I remembered why the phrase sounded so familiar.

The other time I'd heard it, I was six, and we were visiting my Aunt Flora in Florida. Even back then I was obsessed with language and with words. Mom said it was like I inhaled them.

Aunt Flora took us to see these wild parrots that had been

released by their owners and had all found each other, forming a parrot community. There were some other little kids there, and we were all being so careful not to spook the beautiful birds. But then I moved and my crutch made a sound, and the birds flew away.

A sour-faced little kid said, "You chased them away with your silver thing."

"Crutch," I told him. "It's called a crutch."

The kid didn't seem impressed by the new word I just gave him. "How did you get like that? What's wrong with you?"

In my mind, it was a ridiculous question. I was born this way, just like he was born short and with weird spiky hair, and I told him as much. I saw my Aunt Flora and my mom exchange a look, and they took us back to Aunt Flora's.

That night, I had trouble sleeping. It's not like no one had ever asked me that question before. But this time it sort of got inside me. After tossing and turning for a while, I gave up on sleep, and I snuck into the hallway to listen to the adults.

They were sitting at the kitchen table, and Mom was drinking red wine. She looked really sad.

Aunt Flora was holding her hands and said, "You're doing fine. She's doing fine. Look at her, I mean…she's so smart and so pretty and so confident."

"I know. She is. I just can't help but think…"

"Look, Steve got enough money for her settlement. For the… what did the judge call it?"

"Medical malfeasance." Mom took a sip of wine. Put the glass back on the table. I could see from my perch that Mom was crying and Aunt Flora was rubbing her back.

Eric found me, put his finger over his lip, and walked me back to bed.

"Mom's crying," I told him.

"Yeah. She always does when Dad doesn't come with us for these vacations." It seemed like a big brother lie to make me feel better; I had a sense the entire thing was about me, even if I couldn't understand why. *Medical malfeasance*. I stored those toxic little words away for later, but forgot about them.

Back in the SAT classroom, I put those words together: malfeasance, settlement. As smart as I am, I'd never considered that when I was born, something maybe happened to make me like this.

I put my pencil down, got my crutches, and got out of there. The classroom doors slammed behind me like an audible exclamation point. Mom had been waiting outside for me. Ben followed. I told them I felt like I was going to have a seizure, even though usually those came without warning. We went home right away. Mom kept stealing looks at me in the mirror. I closed my eyes, trying not to think of those words, but they dive-bombed me like mosquitos in the summer. *Medical. Malfeasance. Settlement.*

Mom asked, "Are you okay, Jenna?"

I said, "No. I need to go home. I need to go home. I need to go home."

"We're going, baby. We'll be there soon."

When we got there, Mom unloaded me from the van and helped me to the bathroom and then to bed. I pulled up the browser on my iPad and typed my name, plus my Uncle Steve's name, plus medical malfeasance, then settlement.

I tried to tell myself whatever I found wouldn't change anything. Wouldn't change me.

Then I pressed search. The results loaded, and I saw it. My name. The doctor's name, Dr. Jacoby. Settlement. Steve Cohen, my Uncle Steve. The rest was hidden. I could pay money and find out how much we got, but there was no point.

I finally knew the truth: I wasn't supposed to be born like this.

The world shifted under me. Mom knew. Dad knew. Uncle Steve knew. This was worse than the Santa deception. I wanted to scream at Mom and Dad. I wanted to yell at Uncle Steve. I wanted to find them and shake them and make them fear me.

I sat there for a long time, staring at the screen until my vision felt painted with the blue-light glow. How could they all have lied to me?

"Do something," a voice inside me whispered, sounding braver than I felt. "Do something." The voice sounded familiar. Like it belonged inside me. Because it did. It was Jennifer, the girl who I could have been, would have been, if only a doctor hadn't messed up sixteen years ago. I beat my tears back. She was right. I needed answers. I would get them.

And the first person I was going to start with was Uncle Steve. He had been part of the betrayal, so he was going to spill his guts. He owed me.

I sent him an email with the settlement information attached and one simple line.

We need to talk.

He texted back.

In a meeting. Can't call now. But
can text. How did you find that?

Does it matter?

No. I guess not. This was all for you.
To be sure you were cared for.

Cared for? Like an abandoned
kitten? Like an orphaned child?

No. Like my niece.

So you did one of these for Rena?

Do you want to meet up after I'm
out of work? Talk about this?

No. Not now. Right now I want you
to keep this between you and me.

I don't think that's the right thing.
For you or your parents.

As your client I expect you
to respect my wishes.

My client?

Uncle Steve has always joked with us that he'd represent us against our parents if we ever needed him—as long as we paid him a dollar, he was our legal knight in shining armor. But if we really wanted to make it sacrosanct, we'd pay eighteen, the Jewish number that meant good luck. He was teasing, of course, but I pull up Venmo and send Uncle Steve a fast eighteen dollars.

Fine, we'll keep this between us for now.
But this doesn't change anything. You're
still the same girl.

That's where he was wrong. This changed everything. It changed *me*. Every decision I'd made before this finding became suspect. I rethought my classes, my life's plans, my participation in therapy. In short, I rethought my world.

THREE

The morning after the MRI, I wake up with my body throbbing from the abusive tests. But for some reason today, I feel pulled toward some kind of magic. Like something exciting is about to happen. Jennifer's voice finds me and whispers in my ear that I need to get up, go to school. But my head is woozy, my eyes are glued shut, and I want to sleep for days.

I hear Rena's alarm go off. Then Mom's steps down the hall. "You up?"

She means Rena, not me. No one expects me to go to school today.

The drugs they put in my IV for contrast are still sloshing around inside me, making me dizzy and nauseous, but I'm not down for a sick day. Not with Jennifer's voice in my head telling me there's a reason I need to get up.

Jennifer's voice comes to me, and it's like magic. The kind I've always believed in. The truth is, I have always had this weird obsession with magic. And while that doesn't make me unique or anything, because I'm sure everyone believed in magic when they were little, the thing is, sometimes I still do.

Practical magic, at least.

When I was twelve going on thirteen I started going to see

the rabbi to study for my Bat Mitzvah. As I waited in the library outside the rabbi's study for my turn, I'd walk by the bookcases, my crutches making the tiniest sound as they tapped the floor. My eyes fell on the beautiful gold lettering on the spines. Tikkun Olam. Jewish Mysticism. The World of Wonder. Malakim. "Malakim," I whispered the word written in Hebrew, like a secret code. When I looked that word up later, I saw it meant angels or messengers. Man, was I bought in.

But one day I picked up one of the books and read through it as I listened to the rabbi helping Eric Lisben recite his Haftorah. The combination of his soulful singing and the words on those pages got inside me, into that place that wanted magic. As I read, the letters seemed to rise off the page and swirl around in the air.

"Ah. That's a good one," Rabbi Goldman said, emerging from his study and eyeing the book I was skimming on Jewish Mysticism. "Have you read the part about the thirty-six saints?"

I shook my head.

"They say that in every generation there are thirty-six saints who keep the world in balance. No one knows who these saints are. Not even the saints know. When one of these saints die, another is born to replace them."

"Wow," I said, following him into the study. It was sort of like the *Buffy the Vampire Slayer* deal, though that's not the kind of thing you can say to your rabbi.

Rabbi Goldman sat on the side of the desk, his one leg hanging off. He laughed, and when he did, the soft wrinkles around his eyes creased even more. He had gray hair and a deep voice. "Yes, wow."

He rested his cheek in his beefy hand. "Some believe that these saints remind us of the divine inside of each of us. Any one of us can be one of the thirty-six, Jenna."

It was then I decided what I really wanted to be when I grew up. I wanted to be like one of those saints. I knew I could be important. I could be righteous. I could be free.

Anyway, after the Dr. Jerkoby debacle, I'd told myself it was time to grow up and ditch the fantasies, but this still felt real to me, somehow. Like hidden inside any one of us could be the power to save the world. Our little corner of it, at least. And wouldn't that be cool?

I pull myself up on the edge of my bed. My head pounds, and I can't help but make an awful noise. This makes Mom poke her head in my room.

"What are you doing, Jenna? You need pain meds?"

She means for the pain the dye caused. The headache, the body aches. The ache from cramping, which happens every time I have to do these tests.

"I need to go to school," I say.

Mom makes a face. She marches into my room and puts her hand on my head. I want to throw her palm off my forehead, but she pulls it back. "No fever."

"I can't keep missing days."

"Mrs. Wilson is getting your stuff for you. I'll swing by and pick it up today if you like."

I take a breath and sit up taller, a small feat that sends a shock of pain through my spine and blasts my head. "I feel like I'm forgetting something. You know that feeling?"

Mom looks at me like she wants to give me what I want. I shift forward, getting ready to stand, and wince at the pain.

Mom shakes her head. "Whatever you're forgetting will wait."

Maybe she's right. Maybe it could wait, whatever it is.

Before I can argue, Dad bellows from the other side of the house, "Sharon? Where is my cell? I've got that meeting in an hour..."

"I'll be right back." Mom holds her finger in front of my face. "You stay here."

The door closes partway, and I push myself to my feet. These tests are required to determine the next surgery or procedure that's supposed to help me, but the irony—that they temporarily make things harder—isn't lost on me.

The pain in my head is insane. It's like my body is a bottle of seltzer that someone shook up and my head is the cap that's holding off the eruption. Maybe Mom is right. After all, one of the reasons I switched to regular classes was to make my school life easier, so it would be okay when I missed days like this.

And yet, here I am working double time to get my sorry ass to school.

A knock on my door. "Jenna?"

"Yeah."

Rena lets herself in my room. "You okay? You need anything?"

"I'm going to school."

Rena makes a face. "You don't look so good."

"Thanks." I push myself up and try to stand with my elbow crutches, but they scoot out from under me, and I buckle. Rena wraps my arms around her shoulder and holds me up.

"What's so important at school? I'd give anything for a day in bed."

"Everyone says that until…"

"Yeah. Sorry. That was pretty crappy of me."

"You're fine. I just need to get ready."

Rena helps me limp forward.

I groan.

"Is this about the text I sent you?"

Then all of a sudden, the fog clears. The text. Rena sent me a text, and *that's* why I want to go to school. But my memory still needs to be jogged. I make a weird noise that Rena interprets as the question I'm too ill to ask. *What text?*

"About Julian," she says.

The ground shifts under me, and I stumble on my stupid rug. The one Mom says I shouldn't have in my room because it's the kind of thing I'll trip on, but I insisted because I loved the fake white fur and how fluffy and puffy it looked. Glamorous. Annoyingly, Mom was right about this. I lean against Rena with all of my body weight, and she should be pissed but we both kind of laugh, because that's what we do. When I've got my legs under me again, I move forward.

"Distract me," I say, only my tongue is kind of bunched, because right now it's acting like an anchor for the rest of my body. I'm aiming for mobility on top of stability. Coordinated movement is the name of the game. Most people don't have to think of it every time they move something or stabilize something, but I do.

"Closet or bathroom?" Rena asks.

"Closet."

She loops her arm under my armpit and braces me. "Julian's back in town. Back in school. I saw him yesterday."

A tiny bud of hope forms inside me. Then something replaces it. Annoyance. If I'd been at school yesterday I would have seen him, too.

We shuffle forward a few more steps. "Eric says the hockey team could really use him," Rena adds.

Julian. My Julian, with everyone but me. Rena saw him. Eric, who is away at college and not even at our school anymore, knew he was coming and has already planned how Julian was going to save the season. And me? I was busy getting injected with dye and lit up like a Christmas tree.

We reach the opening to my closet. Rena balances me using her hip and throws the door open, jamming the switch to turn on the light.

I breathe out, hard.

"You okay?"

"Ish," I say. One of our jokes.

My walk-in-closet houses three faux-fur jackets Rena insisted I needed this winter (one with a faux-fur-lined hood that she said was just delicious) and rows of Converse and ankle boots, because they add stability and also passed Rena's cute-enough-to-wear test. But there are also skeletons in my closet—my abandoned mobility equipment. My closet is a graveyard of stuff too expensive to get rid of.

A state-of-the-art electric wheelchair is parked underneath my spring clothes as if it's waiting for its turn to become useful again.

My Hoyer lift, the contraption we had to use after surgeries, when I couldn't get up by myself, hovers in the back. Its metal chains and swing-seat—made of ballistic material—loom large and frightening like a character from a Stephen King novel.

I glance at Rena. "I'm going to need my scooter, I think, but it's not charged."

"It might be. You know how on top of things Mom is about your stuff." My stuff. The stuff that I used to love because it helped me go places and do things. Since finding out about the settlement this past summer, my mobility equipment has become just another reminder of the entire birth injury lie. But I am aware that if I'm going to go to school, it will only be with the help of one of these little lovelies. So be it.

My head pounds, a sign that I should probably just go back to bed. What does it matter if I see Julian today or any day after this? But there's no reasoning with me when I set my mind on doing something. Dad used to say I got my hardheaded stubbornness from him, but he said it as a source of pride. Eric said it was my middle-child syndrome that made me so relentless. But I'm not sure either one of them would think my current drive to make it to school today is either cute or admirable.

Rena bends down and turns on the scooter. "It's got a little life, but not enough for an entire day."

I groan. "The full-on wheelchair it is."

She helps me back to the bed to sit, then returns to the closet and backs the wheelchair out of its corner, running it over her foot in the process. "Damn!"

"Sorry," I call out.

"It's cool." She blows the hair off her face. "After you're done with this contraption, I might have to exact some kind of revenge on it."

I lay back on the bed. "I get that." My legs ache. My back throbs. My head feels way too heavy for my neck to hold.

Mom throws the door open. "Oh, Jenna," she says as she sits next to me on the bed. "Are you sure you want to do this?"

"Yeah."

"Okay." She looks at Rena. "Just grab some clothes for her and get ready yourself. I'll take care of your sister." Then she turns back to me. "Let me just call the school and make certain they've got an aide ready for you."

And now my head hurts even more. "Not Mrs. Wilson."

"You'll take what you get, deciding to go into school after a procedure with no notice." Mom's in full-swing planning mode now. I want to argue. I want to remind her I told her I'd go last night, but it's not worth it. If it's Mrs. Wilson, it's Mrs. Wilson. I'll just have to deal.

* * *

Mom works the lift on the van and straps my wheelchair in. She hands me my shake. My hands tremble a little as I reach for it, and I'm almost positive Mom's going to abort the mission. Instead, her face softens, and she cups her hand under mine, bringing the straw to my mouth. "You need some nutrition in you."

"Thanks," I say, and I hope she knows it's for everything. A big part of me is still upset with Mom after my discovery this summer. But then Mom does so much for me—my whole family does—and I can't help but feel grateful for that.

Rena hops to the car, pulling her boots on, a toasted waffle hanging from her mouth. She opens the front passenger door. Rena only sits up front when she wants something. Mom eyes her, waiting for Rena to click her seat belt on, and then backs out of the driveway.

It doesn't take long for Rena to start making her case. "I've got to stay after today."

Mom harrumphs and drums her fingers on the steering wheel.

Rena puts her foot on the dashboard and ties the laces on her boots, talking around the waffle. "It's just today. I'll come home at the normal time tomorrow."

We get stuck at a stoplight, and Mom swats at Rena's foot, then wipes the mark her boot made. She edges us forward in the traffic that is already backing up even before 7:00 a.m. "I need your help."

"I've got to finish my design for the fashion show. You want me to fail?" Rena gestures wildly, and the waving of her arms sort of pulls my eyes in a car-sick-inducing way. I don't need that today, so I glance away. The drama is strong with the girls in my family.

The auxiliary cord is hooked to my car iPod, so I toggle until I get to a song I want to hear. Now tracking in the van? "It's Alright" by Weekend.

Rena grabs the coffee mug Mom loaded for her, takes a swig, and then salutes me with it. "Great song, Jenna."

Mom's eyes flit to Rena, then to me. A tiny smile forms on her lips because as annoyed as she gets with us all, she's always happy about how close we are. "All right," she tells Rena, "but when you get home, you're mine."

"Drama queen much, Mom?" Rena twists to wink at me.

Mom swats at Rena half-heartedly. The mood in the van magically shifts from cranky to light as Rena sings. "Sings sweet. Walks tall. Holds me upright."

The lyrics reach inside me and squeeze my heart. Will I ever bring sunshine or hold someone upright? I will never sing sweet, that's for sure. But now I know what doing those things would sound like and feel like. Music and stories do that to me. Slay me and heal me all with the same sword.

Rena chews, slurps her coffee, and does the hipster head bob to the music. Like the voice said in my head yesterday, it's so easy. She means life. My life. And anything I want to do. Jennifer is the eternal optimist.

As Mom pulls into the school driveway, she says, "Your brother is coming in for your birthday weekend. We're having a ton of family."

"He is?" I ask from the cheap seats in the back.

"Yup. In two weeks. He'll stay through the weekend."

And suddenly nothing feels bad. Eric's coming home. Eric. Rena. Me. They need a song for how great *that* feels. There may be no making me not have CP. There may be no rom-com happy ending for me. But when I'm with Eric and Rena, everything feels exactly the way it's supposed to.

Mom swings the van up to the curb where my school aide stands ready to retrieve me. It's Mrs. Wilson. I do my level best not to scowl.

Rena swivels around to face me. "See you at lunch." She gives me a two-finger salute, and I try to return it. My fingers are slightly squashed together, because it's morning, and my hands need a little time to wake up, but I make a decent attempt. Rena doesn't acknowledge how sloppy I am, just blows me a kiss and picks up speed as she joins the ranks of the able-bodied.

Mom unloads me onto the sidewalk next to the handicapped space in the parking lot. "You call if you want to come home, okay?" she pats her pocket. "I've got my cell on, and I'm just a few minutes away."

"Thanks, Mom."

She looks at me one more time, her breath fogging out in front of her. October in Connecticut can serve up some cold days, for sure, but this one feels particularly cool.

"It's going to snow," Mrs. Wilson says, stepping forward, her arms wrapped around her chest. "Mark my word. Hi, Jenna." Her voice is loud and grating on my already frayed nerves, but I smile and throw her a small wave.

Mom gives Mrs. Wilson a list of things to look for if I push too hard today. "Seizure, migraine…" she drones on while the wind blows, and I shrug into my coat. "Try to get her to eat something. She hasn't been able to keep anything down."

"I've got it," Mrs. Wilson says. "Let's get her out of the cold."

For once, I agree with her.

FOUR

I drive my wheelchair down the halls of Harrington High, and Mrs. Wilson trails behind me. The sound of her boots on the cold floors propels me forward.

I'm closing in on the guidance office. Ben usually meets me in this hallway, but he's nowhere in sight. I pull my phone out and check for messages. Sure enough.

Running late. Marketing Academy stuff.

Ben is big with the Marketing Academy. Marketing kids are like student government kids on a lot of energy drinks. Marketing kids don't plan dances. They plan marketing strategy and compete in state and national competitions. They aren't just preparing to win; they are preparing to rule the world. To find jobs in finance or any of the management careers. But in high school, the end goal is simple: the nationals in California. Ben says it's THE BIGS—his ticket to big business, world domination, and season's passes to Disney. Ben's a weird combo of things—some Machiavellian, some pretty mainstream.

I'm so busy musing about my bestie that I almost miss spotting him: Julian Van Beck. *My Julian.* It's been years since I've seen him, seven to be exact, but I'd know him anywhere. Wavy red hair that used to be cute, but is now downright sexy in a Prince Harry way. He's gotten tall, and even with his hoodie and baseball jacket, I can make out broad shoulders and what I have to assume is a pretty ripped body.

Part of me doesn't want to run into him. Most of me doesn't. I mean, here he is looking all grown up, and here I am, looking weak and worn out.

He leans against the wall in front of the guidance office, hands hanging loosely at his side. One foot is pressed against the wall, completely flat, and he gazes toward the ceiling. The look he always wore when he was avoiding something. Or someone. He's got earbuds in and a piece of paper hanging out of his mouth, half chewed. He used to do that, chew paper, when he was nervous. I've got this sudden need to see if he's okay, but I don't get a chance. One of the girls in my class, super-flirty Tori Zimmer, saunters up to him. Tori is kind of an expert saunterer. I wait to see how he responds, my breath stuck inside me. Who could resist her siren call? But Julian barely manages a polite smile. Tori walks off, and I want to celebrate in my head. Even if he's not mine, he's not hers, either.

And then it hits me. Maybe he won't recognize me. He probably doesn't even remember me. Ben's got this story of this guy he was friends with all through elementary school, in Washington, DC, where he grew up before he moved here. They were always together. Always. And then when he went back last summer, the dude acted like they'd never met. And when Ben forced the issue (because that's the way he is), he acted like Ben was nuts. He ran his hand through his hair, look around at his new crew of friends, and said, "You've lost it, man. I don't know you." Like the guy was embarrassed to be around Ben. Like he couldn't get away from him fast enough. Which pissed me off so much, I'd told myself I'd gladly give up my chance to be one of the thirty-six saints in order to open a can of whoop ass all over that idiot.

But now I'm wondering, is this going to be one of those situations?

I reverse my chair and aim toward my locker, hoping that Julian doesn't see me.

"I've already got your things," Mrs. Wilson says.

This is exactly why I can't stand her. Just when I'm trying to stay on the down low, she's throwing a big spotlight on me. Besides, she's simply here for standby assist, not to treat me like a kid.

"Jenna, wait," she says, persisting, and I wish I could run her over with my wheelchair. I would actually do it, make it look like an accident, if it wouldn't draw even more attention to me. How could she possibly know what I need from my locker? Has she been in my locker? She holds up the books for my first three classes. "See? We're all set."

I glare at her.

"The administration let me into your locker so I could get your books. We want you all set to catch up, right?"

Is she kidding? I can't turn away from her fast enough. Meanwhile my fingers feel sort of uncoordinated, which makes my lock that much harder to work. Mrs. Wilson takes my fumbling as a signal to hover over me. I hold up my hand. "I've got this."

Out of the corner of my eye, I can see Julian. Farther away now. Far enough away, I hope. I realize I came to school so I could see him, but now I just wish I could disappear. What was I thinking?

Kids pass by me. Lockers open and shut, Mrs. Wilson's annoying presence hangs heavy over me. Then there's a break in the clouds—Ben. I see his brown dress shoes, the ones he wears when he's presenting a big campaign in class. And they are moving toward me. Thank God.

"Hey, girl." He aims his books in the general direction of Julian's departure. Then back at me. "Who's that new kid?"

Ben is the only one who knows how I feel about Julian. How I've always felt. But when I told him, I admit, it felt safe, because Julian had moved away and was never coming back. My face gets hot. "Julian."

He cranes his neck toward the boy and then turns back to me, an approving look on his face. "*Your* Julian?" He says it quietly, but in my mind his voice is amplified so loud that everyone can hear.

"Could you not…"

He leans against the locker next to mine and says in a much quieter tone, "That's kind of cool, no?"

"Sure," I manage. "I guess."

"Tough crowd," he says.

Mrs. Wilson jumps in. "Come on, she's got to get going,"

The bell starts ringing.

Ben points at me. "Debrief later." Then he's off like a shot toward the 200 building, where the AP classes are held, like the rest of the go-getters. Where I should be going.

All of the sights and sounds in this hallway, coupled with the feelings of seeing Julian, make my head feel like it's expanding. The throbbing that nested there earlier intensifies, and a darkness fills the corners of my eyes. I hear a song in my head. The words and music seem so familiar, but I can't seem to place them. The song mixes with the sounds of a flock of birds screeching as they take flight. I can feel the wind blowing, and I know that's not right. It can't be. The lights crackle and flash and I brace for rain. Only that's not right, either.

I feel myself being lifted, and then I know a seizure is coming. I know. But I can't do anything to get out of its way.

. . .

I'm in the nurse's office waiting for Mom to come get me, and my head is pounding.

My body is transmitting so many sensations that I can't wrap my head around a single one of them, except for the dizzying nausea settled deep inside me.

The lights are low, and there's music playing in the background. I think I hear Twenty One Pilots. Normally I would say something about how much I love this song, but right this second I am full of disdain for so many things, including all of the things I love. Embarrassed tears coat my cheeks, and it's all I can do not to shake with how much I hate myself.

Did he see me? Did I pee myself? I can't even tell. How screwed up is that? My body is slick with sweat, so I won't actually know how bad this is until I get home and get changed.

The door opens. "Oh, Jenna," Mom says, her voice soft and shaky, like I feel. And it makes me wonder if you can ever completely remove yourself from the person who created you, and the body you were created in. Maybe when you're typical, you can adequately detach from your mother and carve out your own place in the world, but when you're the girl with cerebral palsy who has so many regressions, maybe there's a tiny ethereal tether that keeps you tied together. I don't know, but I feel like there is. When I was little, that tie felt special. Now it feels confining and childish. I don't have to tell you no teen really wants to be that.

Mom is quiet as she loads me into the van, but I can feel her heart cracked wide open, and I know she understands the entirety of my humiliation. We ride home encased in silence. I feel like a failure. I failed to make it through a day at school. Just like Mom said I would. I should have listened. I know Mom's mind is working overtime as well, as she maneuvers the van through the drizzly day, so we both sort of jump when Dad calls.

"How is she?" The Bluetooth in the car broadcasts his voice, etched with concern.

Mom steals a glance in the rearview. "I've got her. We're going home."

"Pick up."

I can see Mom's neck and shoulders tense as she holds the phone to her ear, the phone call private now. I know that he's telling her he wants me to get more tests done at Summit Children's Hospital. That's Dad's answer to everything. As if my body and brain is a stubborn motherboard on one of those supersmart computers he writes code for. Tests mean the hospital. More IVs filled with that horrible liquid slicing through my veins so that the contrast can light up my insides like the branches on my twisted tree. Just thinking about the pain from the dye and the discomfort from the procedures reminds me that my body does not like medical procedures. It rebels and rejects any attempt to see inside it. That's a lesson Mom and Dad haven't quite understood, but I live it.

I tap my head against the car window, a tiny bump that does nothing to soothe my building angst. Mom tries to tell Dad this is not a good time to talk. Dad and I share the same fiery outrage and stubbornness when things are unfair. Mom's always saying I'm his daughter.

My phone beeps. It's Rena.

You OK?

News travels fast. I palm my enormous phone and aim my fingers. Sometimes they're pliable and responsive to my commands, but at present, they're stiff and fixed in place, so I have to bat at the letters.

M OK

Nobody saw anything. I asked.

I lean my head against the window and let the tears stream down my face.

I swear. They cleared the hall right away.

Rena knows the dark thoughts that plague me after one of my episodes, even if she doesn't know about my lingering crush on that boy. Julian had always been part of our all-kid band. But he moved away before my crush could become real enough to share with Rena. Which means I can't ask the most important question: Did *he* see me? Does *he* know? Of course he does, everyone does by now. Everyone at school is talking about *poor Jenna*. Even though they mean no harm, the fact that I'm the topic of conversation makes all of this worse.

It was just because of the dye, right? It's
all going to be ok. You are going to be ok.

More and more she feeds me the lines I want to hear, but even though I believe in magic, I'm not stupid. I am going to have to deal with stuff like this my entire life. I close my eyes and let my mind drift to my own fantasy. Not about getting better, but about being someone else. I pretend I am with him, Julian. We bump into each other in the hall. I'm the new girl in town, Jennifer. The full name, because in my fantasy, my tongue isn't bunched and torqued. It's long and loose and able to leisurely slip over the r sounds—slow and seductive, sweet and sure. No reason to cut it short to Jenna. I am Jennifer. I am here. I am her. I've got long, straight, shiny brown hair that I curl sometimes. Today I have it totally straight, and when we run into each other I almost drop my books, but Julian catches them.

I'm annoyed at first. But Julian says, "Sorry. I should look where I'm going."

I straighten the papers that fell on the floor.

"Will you let me make it up to you? Buy you coffee?"

I'd turn away from him, just slightly. "I'm late."

"For what?" he says.

But I'm gone now, walking down the hallway onto my SGA meeting. I'm not the president or an officer or anything, but that's cool because, in my fantasy, I've got way too many other things on my plate to commit to just one club.

"We're home," Mom announces, shaking me from my daydream. "Let's get you cleaned up and then you can spend the day Netflix bingeing if you like."

I tell myself I was smart to dumb down my classes. If I was in the AP or honors classes, I'd have to spend this time catching up on all the classroom stuff I missed. Gen Ed English is ridiculously easy for a girl like me. I tell myself that I'm happy with my choice, even though I know I've already read all of the novels we're doing this year. Not having to sit through kids struggling with the end of *Of Mice and Men* today should feel like a gift, but it doesn't. It's not about the books. It's not about the teachers. It's about me being separated from Ben and everyone else. Almost myself. So close, but not quite there.

In bed, under the covers, my Netflix account loaded, I think about that appointment that's looming where we'll go over the results of the tests we just ran. And who knows what kind of plan they will come up with. It's always the *they*s that come up with the plans. Mom. Dad. The doctors. Not me. And that's got to change. I pull up my email. Uncle Steve was there at the beginning. He needs to be here now. For me this time.

I hit the compose button and type:

Uncle Steve,

We need to talk.

Jenna

I hit send, my fingers hesitating only for a second. He knew this was coming. I'd told him during Rosh Hashanah, when we were alone in the living room and Rena was fighting with Mom and Dad about not wanting to miss another day of school, that I wanted his help with a little lawyering. That's exactly what I called it.

"Whatcha need, niece-y?" he had asked.

"I've been doing some research."

He'd taken a bite of Mom's famous chocolate torte. "And?"

"Two words: medical emancipation."

He choked a little on his torte, which would have been comical if all wasn't so critical. He stared at the door. When we couldn't hear anyone talking anymore, he said, "That's a really big step. Are you sure?"

"Maybe," I'd said.

"Well, tell me when you're sure and we'll talk."

Just then Dad popped in the room. "Talk about what?"

Uncle Steve made some sort of cover story. I was too busy staring straight ahead and not wanting to be seen.

Now, I chew on my knuckle, a habit I know I've got to stop, but I worry about what Uncle Steve will say. Am I more nervous that he'll say yes or he'll say no?

Uncle Steve texts me back right away.

I'm always here for my favorite niece-y!

Should I tell Rena you said that?

No!

Seriously. I'm ready to talk
about the...you know...

If you can't say it...

I can say it. Medical emancipation.
It's time. You owe me.

I will help you talk with your parents.
I am not promising anything else.

You have to use your lawyer voice.

Your dad is not intimidated by that.

See that he is. I'm serious about this.

The law is on your side, Jenna. And
so am I. But you should listen to what
your parents and the doctors say.

That sounds like an equivocation.

I am at your service. Unless your
mom offers me chocolate torte.

I'll see that she only serves honey cake.

Where's the gag emoji? Now
you've made me cry.

I smile and text back.

I'm counting on you.

This is going to be a fun family weekend.
Just so it blows over by Hanukkah.

I wanna MaccaBEE in charge of my life!

I am not going to Latke
you push me around.

groan

Let's not make light of what you're doing.

I'm feeling gelt-y over all of this.

Jew-wish there was another
way...but there isn't.

And that's how we end the email thread about the most serious
campaign I've ever waged against my parents.

FIVE

An unseasonably warm Sunday lands Ben and me on the porch swing, his foot controlling how slow we rock. I've got two big pillows propped under me, holding me up. My hand winds around the chain and my legs are in Ben's lap.

He's naming the guys he thinks are cute enough for me to date.

"Todd Stein."

"Not bad. A little SGA for my tastes."

"I don't mind the student government part," Ben says as he stops the swing and dramatically pauses. "Those shorts, though."

I smack my thigh. "I know. Every time the thermometer goes north of sixty degrees, he's gotta show his knees off."

Ben nods. "That boy's in love with his knees."

"I don't have to see it all." My hands do a flourish. "Leave a little to the imagination!"

He puts his hands up like he's testifying. "Preach it."

This is what we do. What we've always done. We pick a subject and evaluate it. Like the night we first met at one of the youth group's sleep-ins. Boys and girls were supposed to be separate, but we hit it off immediately. We bonded over candy choice during the movie, M&M's, original only. And our opinion of *Avatar: The*

Last Airbender (best animated TV show ever), how disappointing M. Night Shyamalan's version of it was, and how much we wished we could have a flying bison like Appa.

The wind picks up and I shiver. Ben reaches behind me for the wool blanket Mom left. I'm about to argue that I don't need a blanket, that I enjoy a little chill every once in a while, when the blanket settles around my lap and my legs get warm. It's a soft kind of warm that wraps around my heart; he put the blanket on me because he loves me, not because I'm disabled.

Ben waves his hand in front of my eyes. "So? Todd?"

"Oh, right. I give him a solid B plus."

"B plus? I've got him down as an A minus at worst."

"I feel he's going to blossom in college, so I have to leave room for improvement."

"Hank Stevens."

"We're doing the esses now?"

Ben smiles and his eyes go a little dreamy. "So much beauty at the end of the alphabet, don't you think?"

I reach for one of the big sugar cookies Mom put out for us, hoping the pause in the conversation will keep Ben from venturing further down the alphabet. They're soft and easy to break into small bites, which is essential for my eating to be controllable. Tiny little infant bites. "Why are we doing this anyway?"

"Rating guys? Because we always do?" Ben laughs. "We've got to be proactive. We have to narrow the field, select our victim—I mean, target—and go for it."

I take another bite. Chew slowly.

"The field for me is wide open," Ben says, "but you know there's only one guy you're interested in…the one the only…"

I can't let him say it. I won't let him say it. I lean forward and smack him on the arm. He puts his hands up. Which makes me go bigger. I hit him again and again.

"Stop getting violent, girl!"

"You started it."

"So why not Julian?"

"He probably doesn't even remember me."

"How could anyone forget you?"

My eyes wander to Julian's old house. I close them, and it's like I can remember everything. The sights, sounds, and feels of our childhood together. My mind drifts to the time we were playing our version of street Marco Polo, one of my favorite memories. I was in my wheelchair then, having just had a muscle-lengthening surgery in my legs. I was supposed to be taking it easy, which means I was zipping up and down the street in my new electric wheelchair.

It was the year before he moved away. There was a little grass field at the end of our street and a small gravel area where Eric often played street hockey with some of the neighborhood kids. But that day, the street was ours alone—Eric, Rena, me…and Julian.

It was my turn to be blindfolded so Rena pulled the bandanna down, and I reached my hands in front of me. Marco Polo is ridiculously hard to play in a wheelchair, but it's made easier when your brother and sister and friend can't keep from laughing at your attempts to catch them.

"So close," Eric's voice was filled with happiness. "Almost, baby sister."

My thumb on the joystick of my wheelchair, I made it career forward. I could hear little bits of gravel kick up under my wheels.

"Uh oh," Rena's voice was muffled like she had her hand over her mouth. I felt her brush by me, heard her feet slide through the tiny pebbles.

"Ha!" I shouted and made my chair lurch forward. "Ha!" I inched forward. "Ha!"

The air was clear and crisp. I could hear steps, sure and solid while Eric's were quick and light. Julian. I was sure of it. I zoomed forward. My fingertips brushed his shirt. His laugh was high pitched while Eric's had already turned deeper.

"You have a license for that thing?" Eric joked as I lurched forward.

"Reckless driver coming through!" called Rena. I laughed, too, that uncontrollable, choke-on-your-own-happy-tears kind of laugh.

The front door banged open. "You've got to be kidding," Mom yelled from the porch. We could hear her all the way down the street.

"Here comes the mom-ologue," Rena said, joking. Mom's voice got louder as she approached us, but I wasn't about to stop. "Your sister can't even see you, how's she supposed to…"

I could hear Eric's feet skid to a stop on the gravel. "She's doing fine…" My ears locked on to his location. I leaned on the joystick, my wheelchair speeding up in time to grab his shirt. Rena took the blindfold off me. I shot my hands in the air in victory.

Eric fell backward onto the ground, doing an amazing job of faking it. "Did you have to help her, Mom? She's already got the wheelchair advantage. Jeez."

Rena wrapped her arms around my shoulders. "And she's won the last ten times!"

Julian shot me a look of complete approval, which made me blush.

Eric pushed himself to his feet in one swift move, climbed on the back of my wheelchair, and pointed forward. "Onward."

"You're such a dork," Rena said.

"Dork!" I agreed, but we zoomed toward Mom, who was now standing in front of us.

"You're going to break that…" Mom started running the other way, aware now how close we were to catching her. "Very expensive…"

I remember Julian's laughter. "Go, Jenna," he'd said, his hazel eyes lit up the whole time.

I must be smiling, because Ben says, "Hey, where'd you go?"

"Oh yeah. I was just remembering…"

"Julian…" He puts his hands over his heart. "Oh, Julian…"

"Gee, I wonder why I don't want to talk with you about the boy."

Ben laughs. "Look, no judgment here. I mean, you remember how moony I was over that Kevin guy…shudder."

"We were friends. Best friends. That was before you moved here."

"I know the timetable. What I don't know is what happened between you two."

I lie back and sigh. "It doesn't matter." I pull my legs out of Ben's lap. Sit up. He puts his hand on my arm. "I'm undateable."

"That's not true."

I take another bite of cookie. "Maybe I'm going to blossom in college, like Todd Stein."

Ben leans me against his chest. He brushes the hair off my forehead. "You've got classic beauty. Gorgeous blue eyes. Sultry lips. Wavy curls."

"You mean frizzy hair, and lips that get stuck. Not to mention how sexy it is when I have a severe spasm."

"Just makes you *you*." Ben rubs my head in the most mesmerizing movement. It's the kind of caress that makes you feel loved and safe. "You are a great beauty."

I stop the swing. Sit up again. "You mean a terrible beauty."

He makes me face him. Ben's eyes get all sweet and fierce. "No. I said what I mean. Listen to your dad. Go see those other doctors. See what they can do."

My mood nose-dives. "They can't do anything. My body is impossible."

He pulls me against him again, and we swing. Back and forth. Back and forth. "For a girl who loves stories, you seem kind of oblivious."

"Meaning?"

"Meaning you're at the point of the story when everything changes. And this year happens to fall at the denouement. Kind of convenient, no?"

"Are you throwing story at me, Ben? You may have to stick to business."

"How so?"

"If anything, we are at the inciting incident of my story. It is certainly not the denouement. You just like to throw around French words!"

"They roll off my tongue, don't they? The point is, you need to live your story, not fantasize about it."

"Is that even possible?"

"Anything is possible in your story."

I close my eyes and let Ben swing me to sleep, my mind filled with his soft voice and sweet promises.

SIX

Sunday night leads to Monday, and I wake up in the morning, just me—no voices, no besties, no nothing. No feelings of impending wonder. Just a normal day. And maybe that is for the best. We all need a break from drama.

In the van on the way to school, it feels like there's this silence hanging over us as we all hold our collective breath. This is how it always is after I return to the scene of my last seizure. Mom's not superstitious in general, other than writing checks for cousins' bar and bat mitzvahs in increments of eighteen, but even she is exceedingly careful after a biggie.

When I've missed school, I feel like everyone else knows things that went on. And I don't. I feel like I'm coming back to a place that has been saved for me by a spacer or something, and I wonder if it's worth trying to fit in there when everyone else has undoubtedly moved on.

The radio is on low and I hear "R.E.M." Rena takes my hand, because we both love Ariana Grande. She sings the melody, and I hum the harmony inside my head where all of the notes are perfect and full-bodied.

We pull in front of the school, and there are a few girls walking with leather jackets and scarves and wool beanies—the girls in the AP classes. I pretend I am one of them, a college in the Northeast in my future, carrying a Dunkin' coffee cup, pausing my conversation to take small sips. In a fair world, I'd be one of those girls, walking like they do, stride for stride, living my best life. We would be inseparable. If only I had a body that worked and a doctor who hadn't screwed up. Even when I was in the AP classes with them, before I dropped down to classes that don't take any effort, I was never truly one of them. I am so into my fantasy, the one where I'm an able-bodied AP girl, that in real life, I can't make myself move forward. I'm not in my wheelchair today but have a brace on my knee and my elbow crutches, and I'm stuck like my chair when it runs out of battery.

Mom gets out of the car. "You okay, honey?"

Rena says, "I'll walk her in."

"No. I'm fine."

I collect myself, put my crutches squarely on the ground. The sound they make is so loud to me, but a quick glance around tells me that no one else seems to notice.

"Jenna?" Mom asks, demanding my attention. Mom leans forward, her face in front of mine. She whispers, "Jenna?"

"Yeah. Sorry."

"Listen, Mrs. Wilson is going to walk you around today."

My face automatically sets into resting pissed face.

"Give me a break, Jenna. It's just for today."

"One break coming up." Eric's joke.

Mom waves one hand over her head as if to say "good one" as she heads back to her car. I watch her drive away, a tiny speck of regret in my stomach. I *should* give her a break. I want to. It's just I can't help thinking that she gave Dr. Jerkoby too many breaks. I often fantasize about how the entire thing played out. Like maybe he was out playing pool with his buddies and pounding shots of Bacardi the night before I was born. Or maybe he'd spent all night playing video games like a huge dork. Who knows? The point is, he didn't bring his A game for me, did he?

Our high school consists of four buildings, all connected by a courtyard. I'm stopped in front of the one hundred building. Mrs. Wilson opens the door for me.

All of a sudden, there's an influx of bodies. Hockey players, throwing their arms around the AP girls' shoulders. One girl says, "Watch it! Don't spill the coffee. Respect the coffee."

My stomach tightens. I hope Julian isn't in that crowd, his arm around another girl. Please.

But now I'm staring at the guys' backs. Their butts, really, and I'm relieved because none of them are Julian. And just like that I've become a total stalker.

But who could blame me? Julian's back.

Maybe that *does* means something in my story. I'm not saying he's going to see me, drop to his knees, and profess his love for me— although that would be cool if he did. I mean, maybe we can go back to being friends. Of the close variety.

Mrs. Wilson walks me to my first-period English III class. She opens the door as I approach, and a bunch of the other kids in my class say, "Thank you," as they scooch under her arm into the classroom, which makes her scowl. One of them, Tommy Luca, turns around and flashes me a grin. Solidarity. They get how annoying Mrs. Wilson can be, and this is one way to be on my side.

So I'm smiling a little as I make my way into the room. I walk to my desk—the special one they have for me in all of my classes, the one that can be adjusted to suit my wheelchair as needed—and put my backpack on my chair, all while Mrs. Wilson stands by, ready to help me. My backpack falls, and Mrs. Wilson makes a face and goes to retrieve it—but not before Tommy gets there.

He rehangs it on my chair. "Glad you're back, Jenna," he says. I shoot him a very grateful smile.

But as I do, something happens that illustrates the presence of a divine power: The door opens, and Julian strolls into my English class. My English class. Mine. He walks with his head down, red wavy curls trailing over his eyes the tiniest bit. Hockey players get to wear their hair long and outrageous. I am definitely a fan.

I'm surprised to see him at first. The hockey players here are part jock, all student. Most of them are in AP classes. That makes their team even sexier than some of the meathead jocks, I've heard girls say before—they're athletic and smart to boot.

But then I remember that Julian's always had trouble in school. His intensity on the ice is absent in all academic pursuits, so he used to tell me, as in, when he was grounded for the two longest weeks in fifth grade because of his report card. Then again in sixth grade. And seventh.

But Julian's brain doesn't make him less sexy. And his inability to get his brain moving at lightning speed doesn't make him less datable, either. He just needs someone to help him.

Someone whose mind works better than her body.

You know, someone like me.

His eyes crawl across the room as he searches for his seat. As he sees me, Tommy's handing me a notebook, saying, "This is what you missed."

"Thanks, Tommy."

I can feel the heat of Julian's stare, so I make my eyes meet his. It's two seconds of delicious eye contact. Eye contact that tells me everything I need to know. First, he remembers me. So that horrible fantasy is off the table. Thank God. And second, there is no way that gorgeous piece of hockey player is ever going to be into me. I only got a quick glimpse of him the other day. Now I can see him full on. He's *way* out of my league these days.

"Jenna." His face lights up. At least he's glad to see me. But it lights up in a way that is not romantic. He waves, and I wave back. It's all so innocent, but even this tiny dose of the boy is enough to make me momentarily happy. I start to doodle on my notebook, and I swear I have to make a conscious effort not to draw his name.

Julian sits down. I work hard not to breathe out a big sigh. My head is filled with so many possibilities and one big certainty. Julian is in my English class, two rows ahead of me and at perfect staring position. So that means I am guaranteed a front-row seat. Even now, instead of listening to Mr. S., I'm gazing at Julian, wondering if he's feeling like I am—or even in the zip code of how I'm feeling. Which is why I am caught completely unaware when Mr. Stechshulte asks, "Who wants to get our new student caught up after class today?"

Julian gives me a look like he wants me to save him from this embarrassment, and I so want to raise my hand, but my hand isn't cooperating. My arm is stubbornly pasted at my side, and, without my arm on board, my hand is not going to make the show. So I shout at my brain to get this done. To make my hand and arm lift. To open my hand. But by the time my arm lifts the tiniest bit, Tori says, "I'll do it, Mr. S."

And I want to die. I want the floor to open up and swallow me whole. I want to disappear. More than that, I want to yell at myself. I should be the one helping Julian. I should be his class buddy.

"In the meantime, it's time for one of our SAT prep quizzes."

There are groans all around, but it's not the hardest SAT prep quiz ever given. It's standard vocab plus analogies. That stuff doesn't trip me up. I take a quick glance at Julian, and I see his shoulders are slumped and he's chewing on his eraser.

If I was sitting next to him, I could say something to make him feel better.

"Exchange papers," Mr. S. says.

Tommy takes mine and gives me his.

As Mr. S. starts to go over the answers, I steal a look at Julian. He's rubbing his hands against his legs and that kills me a little, because I know he's feeling bad about how he did. Julian was never a scholar. He always had to be pulled out and get extra help with reading and stuff.

Tommy passes my paper back, a big "100%" written at the top. He makes pretend explosions with his hands. "You are off-the-charts smart!"

I slide his paper back—only five wrong. Not too shabby for him. I try to think of something nice to say but can only come up with a weak "'Adulation' and 'benevolent' are toughies." Which earns me a big, goofy Tommy grin.

"I'm no genius, but I'm getting better, right?"

If he means compared to the paper I graded for him last week where he got all of them wrong, then, well, sure. "Yup."

I give him a thumbs-up, and he laughs. "You're funny, Jenna."

Mr. S. does a walk around the room, glancing at people's papers, answering questions. As he passes by Julian's desk, he puts his hand on Julian's shoulder and points to the paper that Tori graded for him. He clicks his pen open. "Actually, this is the correct answer for this one."

I can practically feel the heat coming off Julian, and can picture how the tips of his ears have turned red. I may be way too focused on the boy's physiology. Most girls in my position would consider his anatomy. His strong shoulders. His cute smile. It's not that I don't get all of that, I do. It's just that I remember so much about him. How he looks when he's interested in something. Like hockey, of course, but also birds and trees, actual specific trees—the names and where you find them and all.

Mr. S. turns around and looks at me. "Jenna might be a good person for you to team up with. You both missed a bunch of assignments, and she's pretty great at getting caught up."

Now it's my turn for my ears to go red.

Tori grabs Julian's phone right out of his hand. "We already exchanged numbers and set study dates, Mr. S."

And it's not that they already exchanged numbers that bursts my dream bubble. It's that she's holding his phone and he's not objecting—to anything she's doing.

Mr. S. puts his hands up like he's surrendering.

I can feel Julian try to catch my attention, but I make myself busy looking over my paper even though all I'm doing is wishing like mad that I was the one who got to hold his phone and make study dates with him.

· · ·

Every once in a while, a bear straggles out of the woods on the north of town and goes into someone's back yard. It makes everyone talk about how we are depleting their habitat. Everyone gives their best bear advice, as in how to avoid getting eaten by one. Me? I worry about the bear. Will somebody shoot it? Can it find its way home?

Today, a bear sighting has everyone in school all worked up. Kids have their phones out at lunch. They're doing some kind of GPS thing that tracks the bear. I'm sitting with Ben and his group of marketing kids, who are all talking about fund-raisers and price points, and I scowl at my phone.

Ben puts his palm in front of Simon Newsome's face as Simon tries to talk him into carrying condoms in the school store. "It would definitely drive sales," Simon says.

Ben looks super annoyed. "No. No way," he says, then he swivels to face me, his shoulder bumping mine. "What's up? Aside from not being able to contend with the stupidity of our peers?"

Simon leans across the table. "It's not stupid. It's brilliant…"

Ben ignores Simon completely now, just shuts the dude down. He turns to face me full on. "Tell me what's got you down, sweets."

"You'll laugh."

"Probably. But that's our thing, isn't it?"

"I'm worried about the bear." I show him my phone. "They're tracking him, and it's not like it's his fault. He's just being a bear."

Ben takes a sweet potato fry off my plate, dips it in ketchup, and chews on it slowly. He looks like a movie star from the old days, only back then the fry would have been a cigarette. He watches the bear live-action tracking cam. "I think he got away," he says, showing me.

"Really?"

He puts his arm around me and gives me a squeeze. "That's why I love you, Jenna. You have the sweetest heart."

"Or I'm a big dork."

"Those things are not mutually exclusive, you know."

Julian walks into the cafeteria, and my eyes zoom in. I immediately feel worried for him, like the bear. No, this high school isn't hostile exactly. Most people are fairly chill, and I don't worry he won't find a table. I mean, theoretically he's already found one, since he's been back a while already. It's just, if he sits with Tori, that would kill me.

Simon snaps his fingers in front of Ben's face. "Are you going to address the condom issue?"

Ben cracks up and puts on one of his this-is-going-to-be-fun smiles, which distracts me for a second from the where-will-Julian-sit situation. "Should I give it to him?" he asks me.

"Uh, yeah…"

Ben shifts his attention back to Simon. I half listen while I watch

Julian exit the food line. "We are not going to pursue your useless idea. Final decision."

Julian starts walking down my row. The hockey team sits just to the left of us, so that's probably where he's headed. I breathe out. No girls sit at the hockey table. Eric says it's practically forbidden.

"Give me one good reason," Simon demands.

Ben's smile gets more wry, if that's possible. "I'll give you three reasons." He holds up one finger. "First of all, because the guidance counselors and the nurses give the things away for free." Another finger goes up. "Second, I do not want to know who is doing who here on campus." Ben looks at me. We both pretend to shudder. "Third. You know what, we don't really need a third reason because the first two were so good. But if you must have a third reason to be satisfied, it is simply this: I am the Marketing Academy president, and what I say, goes."

"That's right." I snap my fingers in front of Simon's face.

Ben turns to me. "Girl, you've got a mean streak." Everyone gets silent. His dimples show. "And I like it."

"That's what he said," Simon chimes in.

Ben's eyes go wide for the tiniest second before streamlining to pissed. He points away from our table. "Out. Out of my sight."

"You can't throw me out!"

"No one talks about Jenna like that in front of me."

Julian stops directly behind Simon. "There a problem?"

Chip, one of the hockey players, claps Julian on the back. "Keep cool, man."

Julian turns, hands Chip his tray. "The coolest." Then he

rotates back to face Simon and puts his strong hands under Simon's armpits.

"What the… I didn't do anything."

Julian lifts him to his feet, where Simon stands gaping. Julian pushes him forward. "Keep not doing anything away from Jenna."

My face heats. Embarrassment is one of those things my body can process right away.

"You okay, Jenna?" Julian asks.

My tongue is anchored right to the bottom of my mouth. *Get it together, Jenna,* Jennifer's voice bites at me, and somehow I manage to spit out a very weak "Sure, sure."

Chip gives Julian a "what's up?" look.

"She's Eric's little sister."

"Just don't get suspended for fighting. You're practically on probation already for grades. We need you, man."

It's Julian's turn to blush, and I wish I could help him like he helped me. His hazel eyes fall on mine. Kind, sweet eyes. "It's been a while, huh?" he says.

For a split second it feels like how it used to between us when we'd shoot baskets at the hoop Dad put up in our driveway for me to practice my balance. I had a decent free throw back then, and sometimes that would make Julian look at me like I was special.

Ben grabs my hand under the table. Squeezes it to remind me that the boy actually said something to me and politeness dictates that I answer him.

"Yeah." Could I be more articulate?

"We just moved back," he says. "Different house. Across town."

The boy is saying all of these short choppy sentences, and I can't decide if that means he's uncomfortable, shy, or just hoping to end this convo quickly. Ben squeezes my hand again, this time pretty hard, and I almost cry out, but instead I say. "It's nice having you…back."

Oh my God, I did not just say that.

Chip puts his hand on Julian's neck. "Say goodbye, man." Julian waves weakly while Chip forces him forward. "You gotta get focused on two things, grades and hockey. That's it."

The sounds of the lunchroom pick back up as if they had been paused for that nerve racking exchange with Julian and someone somewhere hit play. I still can't breathe or focus or deal with anything. My mind desperately goes over every single moment of the last few minutes. Ben lets go of my hand and takes out his phone.

"We still need to plan our big three," Ben talks above the roar. "Freshman Tours. Trunk or Treat. Homecoming. Who's ready to take lead?"

I usually love watching all the game play and politics of the marketing kids' table. Watching sophomores try to upstage juniors. Everyone hoping their pet project will make it into the showcase and eventually move on to competition and hopefully regionals, states, and then nationals. Today, I could care less about all the machinations. I only care about what's going on at Julian's table…or more importantly, inside his head.

From where I'm sitting I can see Julian pull out his phone. How I wish I could zoom into his screen. He's texting someone. Who? I watch as his face stays even, no lighting up for whoever is texting him. Crisis averted. For now.

Although, at some point, Tori will be texting him. Helping him with English even though Mr. S. made a point of saying I'm the one who should be helping him. Me. Not her.

So…why don't I? I mean, I could anonymously text him. He doesn't have my number, because I didn't get my phone until after he moved away, but I have his.

I stare at my cell.

I've always been good at memorizing things; it's how my brain works. So when Eric was team captain for the rec hockey team, he tacked the team list to the front of the refrigerator in case he had to call someone after practice or get them to volunteer for a car wash fund-raiser or something.

And I'd play this game. I'd make my eyes linger on the shapes of the names of the boys as if Julian, teammate number six, was just a part of a group. Like his number meant nothing to me. But each time my gaze landed on his listing, my face would burn with the knowledge that I was singling him out.

At the hockey games I pretended to watch the entire team, but from my perch in the box, I stared at him. I may have tolerated their strong, musky athlete smell and endured their awful jokes—but I was there for the eye candy.

I always tried to laugh or say something smart back, but around the team my tongue knotted, and the air I desperately tried to control, a small part of the incoordination of CP, raced through my nose just at the same time our team scored. So maybe there was a God after all, because he didn't want me to snort in front of Julian.

I think about Julian's number stored on my phone, just waiting for me to use it. The knowledge lights a fire inside me. I think of all the ways texting would be to my advantage.

First of all, there's wait time. I am almost always able to get a message out of my mouth, in the right order, pronouncing each word separately and like a pearl strung on a beautiful necklace. Most times, that's exactly how it works. Most times, I'm pretty clear. But sometimes, like when Julian was getting rid of Simon earlier, the electric wiring in my brain goes all loopy, and my muscles tense and slack, or slack and tense, and that means I'd sound like I was talking around a bunch of marbles, drooling, and choking as I tried to speak. Also there are the things I want to say to him but can't. That, of course, has nothing to do with motor control.

At the hockey table, Chip puts his arm around Julian and brings him into the impromptu huddle that's happening at his table. Hockey talk. Grades talk. This is how the year starts. Most hockey teams don't even start practicing until November—it's a winter sport. But our hockey players are all in for just the one sport. No fall ball for them. It's hockey, or it's nothing. So they start early, which means Julian's already behind. I wonder if that's weighing on him. I bet it is.

Julian nods to whatever they are saying. He's taking the vow, but his shoulders are still slumped. I want so much to reach out to him and tell him not to worry. It's like I can hear him feeling how he's not smart enough or fast enough or good enough. And I wish I could find a way to show him he's more than enough.

For me.

SEVEN

B edtime means I'm perched in my bed, surrounded by pillows, and with the head of the bed raised. I remember how as a little girl I used to feel like a princess as Mom and Dad kissed me good night and I slowly lowered my bed to the perfect position. Now, years later, still propped and surrounded by fluffy bedding, I feel trapped. It's weird how that happens.

I take my iPad that's set up next to my bed and swipe through a few messages from Ben, some random emails, and finally, the latest email from Uncle Steve.

I put together emancipation documents for you to look at and see what they're all about. We can talk soon.

Dread creeps into me, followed by guilt and, finally, sadness. I picture how Mom and Dad will feel when Uncle Steve and I make our big stand. Do I really want to do this?

I write back to Uncle Steve.

Ok. Thanks.

Mom's knock on the door makes me jump. My cheeks heat.

Guilt-ridden and unsure, I face Mom, who doesn't miss a single thing. "I was going to say good night, but you look sort of flushed. You feeling okay?"

"Yes, Mom." I close my screen, covering up my treacherous little email exchange. "I'm fine."

She comes within two steps of putting her hand on my forehead, but I throw a "Mom!" at her, which makes her pull her hand back. Just like that, I've won a minuscule victory.

"I wanted to tell you we have a doctor's appointment on Thursday. Dr. Rodriguez."

"Awesome." I'm suddenly glad that Uncle Steve and I are looking into this emancipation thing. I need to be in control of all of this.

"We'll just listen to what he has to say, Jenna. Let's keep an open mind."

I face her down with an icy stare. "Really? Like I haven't been keeping an open mind all this time? Like I haven't listened to you and Dad and all the doctors. The *army* of doctors." Doctors who could be just as "good" as Dr. Jacoby. My parents couldn't protect me from malfeasance then, so could they really do it now?

Mom's hands come out in front of her. "I know you have, Jenna, but this time might be different."

I breathe out. Breathe in. Try to calm the wild storm raging inside me. "My mind *is* open, Mom. It always has been. I'm not the one who lied this whole time. I'm not the one who…settled."

Direct hit. Mom deflates like a balloon. "Settled?"

"Come on Mom…the settlement…"

I've been sitting on this information since I found out about it, not sure how to broach the subject with my parents. Go figure it would come out in a fit of anger.

"You know about the settlement? How?" She asks. Her face pales and her hands shake, but at least she's not crying. Yet.

"I found it online."

"Oh." She looks at her hands, clasps them together, and looks back up at me, her face a mix of despondence and resignation. "I knew we'd have to have this talk one day."

"If you knew that, why didn't you tell me?"

"I don't know." She wipes her eyes. "It was all so scary, the day you were born. Your father and I were so…" She looks at the ceiling. "So scared."

"Because of the CP?"

"No. We didn't know about that right away. Because your birth was difficult. We were afraid we'd lose you." Now she's full-on crying.

"Mom. I'm fine."

She smooths down my hair, straight today, because Rena did it over the weekend. "I know you are."

"But this is exactly what I'm talking about. I have a right to know. *Everything* about me and my condition." And now I'm crying, too, which is awesome, because I'm trying to be all in charge and stuff.

She nods. Grabs a tissue off my night table. "I know you do. I know. It's just, it was such a scary thing, and you have no idea what it feels like to almost lose a child." She sits, her face completely drained of color now.

"So…medical malfeasance," I say, pushing.

"It's the term they used for the lawsuit, so we could set up a trust fund for you. The same fund that pays for all of your mobility aids and therapies."

"And the doctor?"

Mom looks at me funny. "What about the doctor?"

"He just gets away with it?"

"It's not that simple. No one knows exactly—"

"*I* know. He screwed up, and I'm paying for it."

"Jenna…it's not like that." She stands up. She waves her arm. "And you're doing fine."

"You call this fine? In bed at seven, because today exhausted me? Seizures? Surgeries? What part of any of that is fine?"

Mom pulls back as if I hit her. She tents her fingers under her nose. Looks up. "This isn't helping. None of this is helping, Jenna."

So that's where this ends. This is the extent of the conversation. "Tell me about when you found out about my CP. What did you do? What did you think? Were you scared?"

"Of course we were scared, Jenna. But you were fine. You are fine. You were so little, and we were worried, but you're fine now."

"Yes, I'm perfect, just the way I am."

"You have a lot to be grateful for. We all have a lot to be grateful for."

"Forgive me for not being grateful that I have these crutches and these messed-up muscles and these…"

"Stop it!" Mom waves her arm around. "Just stop it. I know things are harder for you. I understand all of that, but you have to keep going." She puts her hand on her head. "Oh my God, that's why you wanted to be moved into all of those classes."

My face burns, but I pretend like I don't know what she means. "What classes?"

"The ones that are too easy for you. The Gen Ed ones."

"There's nothing wrong with regular English."

"No, there isn't. But not for an English buff like you. I can't believe I didn't even think to ask. I'm so stupid." She walks around my room in wide circles that become tighter as she walks.

"No one would consider you stupid, Mom."

She stops to launch another doozy. "Perfect. Genius. Way to go, Jenna."

"Why are *you* mad now?"

"You want us to talk to you about things? It goes both ways." Her hands are on her hips now.

"What are you talking about?"

"When you found out about the lawsuit, did you come talk with us about it? No." Mom paces again, only now her hands can't decide where to be. On her mouth. On her hip. On her head. In the air, waving around. I don't think I've ever seen her this mad. "You just went ahead and got angry and did stupid, stupid things. And we let you."

"Let me? I don't get a say in my education?"

"Well, obviously you do, since you've dropped all of your AP classes." She wraps her arms around herself. "Is it too late to transfer classes?"

"Yes. It is. And I'm not doing it. I need a break from everything. Studying included." It's true. After I found out about the settlement, I felt exhausted. I'd been trying at everything, so hard, for so long. I just needed to…*not* try for a while.

"Well, you got it. Hope you like your break." With that, she walks out of my room without even asking if I want my light on or off.

Good thing I've got this state-of-the-art system. The entire house is wireless, and I can control every single thing. Want the door open? Press a button. Television on? Same. Awesome, except for the price I had to pay for this tiny bit of magic. The door shuts, and I swipe my way back to Uncle Steve's email. I bring up the documents, e-sign my name, and hit send before I can talk myself out of it.

Mom and Dad are never going to get over their need to control me.

But as soon as the email is sent, I feel like a total jerk. I realize in my own twisted story, I am the evil thing that gets her comeuppance. I reek of betrayal and misery and all bad things. Mom's right. I should have gone to them when I found out about the settlement. Instead I got angry and acted out. I suck. It's not Mom's fault I need these tests. The same tests I get every year. It's that idiot Jerkoby's fault. Dude was probably overdosing on energy drinks, doppios from Starbucks—whatever it took to get him going after his wild night at the casino or something. No wonder he got the shakes.

The point is, I get these tests every year. Then we meet with the doctors and we see what's what. Have I grown? Is my spine torqued more than usual? Have my hips dislocated? Are my nerves being impinged? And what can we do about my spasticity? That's the biggie. But year after year, there's no good option for me. Which is why I'm sick of going through it all. I'm sick of getting my hopes up. I'm sick of being offered the same old solutions. Drugs that make me sick. More surgery.

A massive weight is on my chest, and I feel like I can't breathe. I chew my knuckle—a habit Mom hates, which weirdly feels like me getting back at her a little bit. I press the heels of my hands into my eyes. Tears run freely, and I let them.

I just can't do this right now. I can't. I need relief.

Then I pick up my phone and pull up my contacts. I stare at Julian's number and let myself believe for a second that I could text him. That I could send him a nice little message, and he'd be glad to hear from me. And just imagining it is enough to lift my spirits.

I pretend that I am Jennifer, the better version of me. And as Jennifer, I would text Julian, for sure. To help him, maybe. Because Jennifer is happy to help people.

Julian Van Beck could definitely use some helping. And who better to help him than his former best friend, me? I stare at his phone number. His name lights up my mind, and I can see a Julian montage flash before my eyes. Julian with Rena and Eric and me tramping through the woods all those times. Julian playing hockey with Eric on our street, looking to me for approval when he scored. Julian that day when we went into the woods together, just the two of us. Julian in English class, head down, his body almost curling into itself.

Yes. I will help this boy. And I can be Jennifer when I do. That's kind of cool. I tell myself that the best kind of giving is when the receiver doesn't know the one giving the help, like I learned about from those books in the rabbi's study. It wasn't only the thirty-six saints. It was also Maimonides's levels of charity. Apparently, it's even nobler when the giver doesn't know the recipient, but I figure

I've got half the equation for the ideal selfless act here, and I'm disabled, so I'm feeling pretty good about the whole situation. I mean, I'm not saying I'm one of the thirty-six or anything, but...

I want Julian to feel special. That's the point. I can do that for him. Because I know his heart.

My finger lands on his name and sticks there along with my eyes. I do the trick of staring so long, the numbers float around and appear to lift from my phone. Like that time in the rabbi's study. I stare longer. I stare at it until it feels the number is burned into my retinas, like it's been in my mind since I memorized it. Hadn't I told myself one day I'd tell Julian how I still feel about him? Why not now?

I think about my first text. Me, not Jennifer. Or me as Jennifer. We are entwined with each other, each of us the positive or negative image of the other. I could speak to Julian. And he doesn't have to know it's me.

I construct my first text: You probably don't remember me, but I remember you.

Satisfied with my message, since it hits on so many levels and still doesn't give me away, I hit send. But then I am instantly hit with a wave of regret. My face heats, and my chest feels tight. Little beads of perspiration dot my neck and my upper lip. Lovely. And just like that I'm back to being Jenna. Stupid Jenna, staring at the screen wondering if he can trace this back to me.

But then he writes back. Who is this?

It's weird. For a smart girl, I really hadn't given this whole thing much thought.

What am I supposed to tell him now? I'm the girl who's been in love with you since kindergarten? Or, I'm the person who knows so many things about you. Like how you look down when you don't know the answer to a question in class. Or how you fidget when you're nervous, the movements starting with your hands and progressing down to your legs. How you are always chewing gum, which makes me wonder what it would be like to kiss you. No! I'm definitely not going to say that last one. How about, I know how sad you looked in school today when Chip reminded you of your little grades problem.

I want to help you.

Is it that obvious that I need help?

No! I mean I want to help you adjust to your new school.

Oh. Right. So you knew me before?

A little.

Okay, so that's an actual lie, but…

And I knew you?

Maybe.

We were friends?

Now that's a hard one to answer. So I don't.

How's your schedule?

So we're not in classes together.

Do you like your teachers?

You're not going to answer any
personal questions, are you?

Nope. Not one that will tell you who I am.

Why?

It's an experiment.

See, I knew you were pranking me.

No. Not pranking you. A friend once
told me that anyone can help someone
else, but it's most effective if it's
anonymous. I want to try that out.

I just totally riffed on Maimonides, but…

But you know who I am.

                                   Yeah, there's no way around that.

So how does this work, exactly?

                                   Easy. If you have a school-
                                   related question, ask me.

Any question?

                                   Except who I am, yeah.

Ok. Why is Mr. Fishborn such a tool?

                                   You have Fishborn? Sorry. His
                                   wife left him last year.

Oh. That's too bad. So he
used to be nicer?

                                   Nah. That's why she left, I guess.
                                   But her leaving has made him
                                   meaner. If that's possible.

Perfect.

Just be sure to turn in your
packets on time. He does
not let due dates slide.

Got it.

He's a huuuge Georgia
Bulldogs fan, if that helps.

Now to just find a way to work
that into the conversation.

I'd be subtle. Wear a Bulldogs
shirt or bracelet. Don't mention
it. Let him notice.

Great idea! Thx.

My body tingles with the thought that I am making Julian feel
good. I swear, that's how this starts. Good intentions. Mostly. It
also doesn't suck that I've got his undivided attention again. God,
I missed him.

Who is this? Really?

I consider telling him my name is Jennifer. But that seems way too close for comfort.

> I told you. Someone who
> wants to help you.

Like my guardian angel?

> Sure.

Or my fairy godmother?

> Even better. Anyway. GTG. TTYL.

No. Stay.

My heart beats like a happy little emoji doing a happy emoji dance. This. Is. Awesome. This is how we used to be.

> I'm here.

Thanks for taking time to talk with me.

I want to reach out to him. I want to stretch my fingers through my phone, let them come out the other side, and touch his. I picture how it would feel to touch his hand.

It's been fun.

Hey. You're not some idiot on the team
trying to get me all worked up?

No. Promise. This is not a joke.

I don't want to be played.

I'm not playing you. I wouldn't.

Just so you know, I'm not going to
do anything stupid, so if this is a
game, you'll be pretty bored.

Even though I'm not playing him, I *am* sort of tricking him. But
I push that feeling down. So I type.

It's not a game. I like you.
I want to help you.

Why?

I start to panic. This is getting too messy. I've got to stop this
before it goes too far. I think about just closing out of my app, but I
can't. Not yet because I see those three dots on my phone that mean
that Julian is texting me back. That he's waiting for me.

You there?

I can't walk away from him and leave him hanging. So I become Jennifer again. Jennifer can handle this, I'm sure.

I like you. You seem like a good guy.

As long as you don't get your
hopes up too high.

That makes me laugh. So like him. Never feeling like he was smart enough. His older brother is a graduate of Harvard Law. Also one hell of a hockey player. But Julian's smart, too. I remember. When we used to go into the woods, just the two of us, he was always the leader. Every tree looked exactly the same to me, and I felt like we were going in circles. But Julian led us. Calmly. He pointed out each kind of tree. Told me each of the trees' stories. He bent low and pulled the bushes back, revealing purple berries. "You can't eat these." He must have named ten different types of trees. Another seven kinds of bushes. I felt so safe with him. And I knew if anyone could see his knowledge of the forest that they would never question his intelligence.

Hello? Where'd you go?

Just figuring out how low I should aim...

Maybe aim middle-ish?

Gotcha.

What do I call you?

For some reason this question slays me. Because I'd love for Julian to call me anything he wants.

Instead I simply write:

GTG.

And with that, I close the scene effectively. I get my chapter out and leave the reader hanging. You know, if Julian is the reader. It's my job to get him to keep wanting to read. So I go to bed imagining his face as he read my texts. His perfectly symmetrical lips would turn up slightly. He'd put his hand over his mouth to hide his smile. That's how I picture him now. Looking back at my texts, rereading them, reading into them, too.

Just then my phone jumps to life.

You said you like me. You. Like. Me.

Laughter pours out of me, and I have to lean back. I breathe in. Breathe out. I think of Julian's face. His messy hair. His deep hazel eyes. The outer ring, light golden brown, with a ring of chocolate around the outside. I wish I was that other person I could have been.

The girl who isn't stuck in her stupid body. The sophisticated and self-assured me I should have been. Jennifer. I think of what that me would say. I let *her* take the wheel.

I always have, I type. Then I close my eyes and hope my world doesn't explode along with my heart. My body is now thrumming with the drumbeat I've been moving to for years—his name. *Julian. Julian. Julian.* But then I think about what I'm doing. I mean, what am I thinking? And I backspace, erasing one letter at a time until I'm left with an empty message box.

So now there's this sad-looking blank space where my heart just was.

Another message from Julian comes through.

You there?

Oh yeah. Julian. He's waiting. What can I say to him that wouldn't seem too pushy or sketchy?

So instead I write. Going to sleep. I chew on my finger, deciding if this next part is too much, but then I type it anyway. Good night.

Friends can say good night to each other. It's totally fine.

But then my phone lights up with his message back.

Sweet Dreams.

And I know that I'll be up half the night thinking of him.

· · ·

7:00 A.M.

whose bright idea was it to
make school start so early.

No idea. Idiots.

Ha! I didn't know you could be so salty.

Me before coffee.

Me before hockey.

lol.

Hey, what's your hockey?

Hmmm. I guess books. I'm a
pretty big book nerd.

You're a smarty-pants. Cool.

12:02 P.M.

Do you eat in the cafeteria?

That's not an allowable question.

You're tough.

You know it!

2:34 P.M.

Do you text in school?

I guess that's a no.

EIGHT

Two days later. Two days of delicious texts from the boy. Two English classes. Two lunchtimes of catching glimpses of him in the cafeteria. I'm staring at my phone, specifically at his texts, as Mom drives us to my doctor's appointment. This time I'm riding shotgun, but when I'm not looking at my texts, I'm staring out the window.

"Put on what you want." Mom points to the radio as if I need permission. As if Rena and I don't usually take over the minute we get in the car. I consider scrolling through my phone for a good playlist, but I'm just not feeling it.

Mom drums her fingers on the steering wheel.

I stare at the world passing by around me and think about how all the time, I feel separate from everyone else. Okay, so I'm giving into a moody little spiral. I think about Dr. Jacoby. About all the things I imagine he did wrong the night before I was born. Was he up all night shooting darts and listening to a Rolling Stones tribute band? Is that why he didn't pay attention when my poor little body went into distress?

I'll never know. But I do know some things. I know that it's time for me to get right with all of this. Somehow. Will that happen today during my doctor's visit? Don't think so, but it's not like that will stop the train wreck that's about to happen. The one I set in motion.

So here I sit in Dr. Rodriguez's office with Mom and Dad, going over this very serious situation: my pain-in-the-ass body and what we are going to do about it.

"According to the films, Jenna's at baseline. No changes." Dr. Rodriguez stares at my chart as if he didn't know off the top of his head that I'm just as afflicted as I used to be. What did he think? I'd suddenly grow out of my CP? That's not really a thing. "As for trying the baclofen pump, I don't love that she's had some bad reactions to medications in general."

"She has?" I can't resist a little sarcasm.

Dad throws me a look. "Like?" He knows the answers, but he likes to be kept up-to-date on what everyone's thinking.

"Well, last year when we tried the oral version of the meds we'd put in her pump, she experienced extreme nausea, dizziness, seizures, and—"

"You make it sound like the Ten Plagues or something. Seriously, someone pass the wine," I say, cutting in, which makes Dr. Rodriguez smile and Dad scowl slightly.

"Honestly, Jenna, can we hear what the doctor has to say?"

Who am I to interject a little humor into the situation? I guess Dad's used to me being his obedient little daughter in matters and appointments like this. Times change, dude. People change. I definitely have.

Dr. Rodriguez clears his throat and looks back in my chart. "I think it's worth trying out the baclofen pump anyway. We can schedule a screening test for her. Take it slow and easy."

Mom's hand tightens around the chair while she stretches the other one out toward me. I give her a look and she withdraws it. Not trying to be mean, but I can't do this. I just can't. And yet, here I am in another doctor's visit with Mom crying. Everyone is making plans for me that I don't want to be part of.

"Maybe we should ask *her* what *she* thinks?" I say.

Dad ignores my outburst and leans forward, his hands clasped together so it's like he's having a private convo with the doctor. Dr. Rodriguez flips a page in my chart, reads, and flips it again. Reads some more. His finger starts at his mouth, but makes its way to something in my chart. He looks at me.

"My concern is that you won't be able to tolerate the baclofen. Even in the pump." He leans back. Rubs the area over his eye.

Dad says, "But don't we all feel that's Jenna's best chance at gaining better muscular control?"

Mom nods.

So does Dr. Rodriguez. "Yes. If she tolerates it, it's the best course for her."

Are they talking my doctor into this? They can't actually think that's a good idea, right? All of my sass and my bravado disappears; this is just nuts. I stare at the ceiling. It's got an ugly water stain in the corner, which detracts from the "healing green" color of the office.

Dad asks, "What are our options?"

"*Our* options?" I ask—obviously from the cheap seats.

"We could put her in the hospital for a few days. That would allow us the flexibility to run some tests. Find out if we can make this thing happen."

"How long?" I ask.

"Two days. Three at most."

Tears burn the back of my eyelids. I shake my head without even meaning to.

Mom looks at me, and I'm glad she caught my response to all of this.

Dr. Rodriguez addresses just me this time. "I know you are not in favor of a hospital stay, Jenna. But the protocol calls for tests before surgery. Let's see how those tests go before we go any further. And let's keep you are under medical care for a little while after so we can help alleviate any potential side effects." He looks to both Mom and Dad and sweeps across the room with an open-palmed gesture, which sickens me. "We all believe it's in your best interest."

"Talk to my lawyer," I say.

Dr. Rodriguez smiles. Patronizing me. Trying to be a good guy, maybe. I smirk back. Because I know all I have to do is snap my fingers and Uncle Steve will serve the papers. But then what will happen? I mean, if left to my own decisions, what would I want the doctors to do? I haven't figured that part out yet.

"When?" Dad asks.

"Well…" Dr. Rodriguez shifts his attention to his computer. "Schedule is open for next Thursday."

"That's right before her birthday." Mom's voice sounds choked up.

"Maybe figuring out how we can finally give her the baclofen pump and give her the best chance at normal mobility would be the best birthday present ever," Dad says.

Oh my God, he said it. He said "normal." We have outlawed, banned, and forever exiled that word from our vocabulary.

Mom stares at him. He crosses his arms.

I want to scream at him. I want to shriek. I want to blast him for being so effing insensitive. But I get where he's coming from. If I become "normal," then he can let himself off the hook for not picking up at his first meeting with Dr. Jacoby what a d-bag of a doctor he was.

My cell vibrates. I almost pull it out, but I need to stay strong.

Mom dries her eyes. "I'm not so sure…"

"She will be able to participate fully in birthday activities by Sunday at the latest."

Around me the conversation starts up again, as if they never really expected me to participate.

"Jenna? Are you even listening? Honestly, I wish you'd try to care about these next steps," Mom asks.

I turn to her, anger coursing through me. "What I want doesn't matter. You know I don't want this. You know I don't want the surgery. You know all of this, and yet you keep going."

Mom's expression goes from annoyed to incredibly sad. She brings a tissue to her nose. "We just want to help you."

Her sadness breaks through my wall of anger, and I see past all of my shit and straight into her heart. When this all started—my life, I mean—I was just a kid she wanted. I mean, she didn't ask for me to be so much work, did she? She probably envisioned a normal kid. There's that word again. Even after being banished from our house as if the word alone is responsible for all of this.

"Jenna?" Mom moves my hair away from my eyes. "You here?"

"I'm here," I say.

"So you'll try?"

"You're not exactly giving me a choice, are you?" I stare into her eyes, will her to see me, really see me, to understand that my gripe is not with them, or even with Dr. Jacoby. It's with this situation, the one that means I've got to relegate my care to people who feel justified in deciding things for me. For. Me. Like I'm an infant still and dependent on them.

Dad turns to me. "Jenna, we've given in to you about your classes, which both your mother and most of your teachers feel is a bad decision."

For the millionth time I think about who I could have been. But this time I get all mystical about it. I think about me—the preborn, soul of Jenna—who became mixed with the human person with the messed-up body.

I swallow the rage that brews inside me.

"David..." Mom tries to defuse this nasty situation.

"And...after this semester is over, we are definitely going to have another discussion about that."

My stomach drops. If he moves me out of my classes, I won't be with Julian anymore. So I throw my hands up. "You win. I will do this. But I am *not* changing classes." It occurs to me that Uncle Steve might need to help me with a few school-related things.

There's a lot of murmuring and a bunch of wrap-up words, but I remove myself from all of them.

When we exit the office, the day is nasty gray, and the fake light-blue siding on the building we just left pisses me the eff off. The hospital is the same kind of phony. All bright on the outside with tons of windows. Painted and designed to look like a nice place, a happy place, a making-dreams-come-true sort of place, but I know the truth. It's no castle. It's a prison. At least for me. But then again, everything's different for girls like me.

5:00 P.M.

Are you over me already?

No. Sorry. Had a bunch of stuff after school.

You worried me.

Sorry. I had a pretty suckish day, TBH.

You want to talk about it?

Nah. Thx. How was your day?

Crapped out on a Geometry test.

Who do you have?

Bartoletti.

He's a softie. He'll let you correct all of
your answers to bring your grade up.

Really?

Yeah. And he'll tell you you'll get
half of the points back, but most
times he gives you more than that.

You had him?

No. Know someone who did.

Thanks. You save the day again.

Have to go for my superhero
costume fitting now. ☺

Send pics!

As if.

What? You can cut off your
head so I can't see it.

Not. Going. To. Happen.

I happen to be an expert at
superheroes and their costumes
so you might need my help.

> There are literally
> thousands of comic books
> to use as models.

Uh oh. Big question. Might
be a deal breaker for us.

> ?

Marvel or DC?

> DC. Of course.

So glad you're not an Avengers
fan or something.

> Are you kidding? With Khal
> Drogo playing Aquaman?

Whatever it takes to keep
you in my universe.

Don't you mean the DC universe?

That too.

☺

NINE

B en drives Rena and me to school this morning, which already makes it a better day than yesterday's suck fest. Once Rena's bounced out of the car and onto the pavement, I turn to Ben.

"I've got a confession."

Ben stops sipping his Dunkin' iced latte long enough to raise an eyebrow.

"I'm sort of…" I look at my phone. "Well, I inadvertently…"

"Spit it out, girl. You're not on trial."

"I'm kind of catfishing someone."

He chokes. He puts his hand on his throat and leans forward. I pound him on the back. When he's fully recovered, he says, "You're what?"

"I guess that's what you call it." I flash my phone at him.

He takes it. "I better have a look."

I put my hands over my face. Peek between my fingers. This is going to be bad.

"Wait…what? You're not catfishing *someone*—you're catfishing Julian."

My hand goes out, but Ben doesn't return my phone. "It's not as bad as it looks."

"Mm-hmm." He scrolls backward. I guess I didn't realize how

many texts Julian and I have exchanged because he's still scrolling minutes later. He puts his hand on his forehead. Looks at me. "I have so many questions. So many. So. So. Many."

"I get it. Just ask."

He steeples his fingers and drums them against one another. "Which to choose, which to choose."

I smack him.

"Okay. I guess my first question is why?"

My turn to take a sip of my drink. "Ummmm. I wanted to?"

"Okay. I can see that." Ben puts on his careful tone, like the way you'd talk to a wild animal or something. Not the kind of tone he usually uses on me. "So you're not worried about being found out?"

"I'm being careful."

"Honey. No. This is not careful. This is playing with fire. No. This is playing with fire and a big can of gasoline. This is playing with fire, a big can of gasoline, and kerosene as backup. This is…"

I put my hands in the air. "I get it. I get it. I'm an idiot. But honestly, it's a fun distraction." I take another sip. Try to act nonchalant. "And it'll be fine as long as I never give him my cell number."

Ben raises his eyebrow. "You two are in class together. You used to be friends. For some reason, he'll need something. He'll ask you for your number, and what are you going to say?"

I chew on my straw. "I don't know. Ugh. You're right. I'm screwed. *Oh my God.*"

Ben plays with his eyebrow, which he only does if he's super-stressed. "We'll figure something out. But man, Jenna, when you go, you go big."

"Yes, I do."

"Speaking of going, let's move. I think the cool fall air might calm me down." He fans himself.

We open our doors almost on cue. He races around to meet me with my crutches. His car's a bit low for me, and I need a little boost. "You're a little savage, aren't ya, girl?"

"Savage and stupid."

"Nah. I think you're just moved by love."

"Who do we love?" Chip comes up behind us, and I want to die.

"Who don't we love?" Ben quips, his arm slung around me so that I don't faint right there in front of Julian's friend.

Chip cracks up, then jogs ahead of us.

I jab Ben in the ribs. "That was close."

"Too close for comfort. We will discuss this more when it's safe." Ben walks me to my hallway. "If only you were in my classes."

"I know."

"Is this revenge plan against your parents worth our being separated?"

"No. But bonus? Guess who's in my English class."

Ben kisses me on my cheek. "You're playing with fire in all areas of your life. You know that, don't you?"

"I like to be consistent."

"Yes. Yes. Consistency. So important." He points at me. "See you at lunch. Don't you do anything ridiculous until then."

I watch him walk away and wonder if he's right that I've bitten off way more than I can chew. The bell rings, and it feels like a warning.

And a warning I will most likely disregard as I practically sashay into my English class. Julian comes in at the echo of the bell, and I'm sitting in the back of the room so that I can see everything that happens in front of me, including his entrance.

My seat allows me to gawk as Julian lowers himself into his chair with careful deliberateness. Mr. Stechshulte gives him a smile that's half pained. I've seen Julian move on the ice, where he flies. If he's late to this class, it's on purpose.

Mr. Stechshulte starts, "Class, I am on the verge of making a terrible decision. Please talk me out of it."

Everyone sits up straighter. Tori holds up her new iPhone. "Should I get it on Snapchat?"

The class laughs. So does Mr. Stechshulte. Also Julian. He leans toward Tori, his chin in his hand, and looks at her like she's something special. It feels like someone punched me in the stomach.

"I'm going to let you guys choose the next book we read."

"*Captain Underpants*," Steve Maxwell, with his thick neck and meathead body, yells out.

The class laughs some more until Mr. Stechshulte holds up a copy of *Great Expectations* and one of *The Great Gatsby*. Needless to say, I've read both of them. Twice. But with this class, no matter what the book is about, they are going to vote with their eyes. Gatsby is a much thinner book, by more than half.

"Show of hands." Mr. Stechshulte holds each book up, moving them forward one at a time and collecting votes. Like I thought, not even close. "Okay," Mr. S. says, "we've got our next book."

Out of the corner of my eye, I see Julian slump lower in his chair. I remember he said he hated to read. *The Great Gatsby* is a great read.

It's filled with really cool symbolism and incredible scenes. But most of all, it's about a guy who loves a girl who, even though she loves him back, is unable to act on that love. She's this little bird trapped in her gilded cage, and, even though Gatsby gives her a way to break out of that cage, she doesn't do it in the end because she needs its protection. This book feels so close to my reality sometimes. That's the thing with stories—when you can see yourself in them, it's easier to remember the details.

Julian runs a finger over his spiral notebook, where he's written the names of bands. Blink-182. Mumford & Sons. Red Hot Chili Peppers. Imagine Dragons. There's something about that list that gets to me and makes me feel porous and open in the best possible way. Like he's showing me who he is inside.

Suddenly I imagine myself as Jennifer. I've gone over to his house to help him, and we spent three hours going over Gatsby. I am equal parts exhausted and really happy, because he really seems to be getting it. I'm wearing a red flannel shirt. His. And super comfy jeans. My legs are stretched out, long and lean. We are the image of teenage perfection, me in my Jennifer body, him in his hot hockey player one. He reaches up and moves a piece of hair behind my ear, staring into my eyes, then searching my face. His gaze reconnects with mine. He looks happy, wearing the little smirk that he usually covers with one hand. But this time, he doesn't cover it, and that tiny bit of intimacy makes my body light up like a candle. I let him inspect me, but then the heat of his attention gets to be too much, so I defuse it.

"I'm a mess, really. So not ready for viewing."

He puts three fingers over my lips. "Shhh."

His bed is so soft and the covers are so inviting and he's so damned cute, I just want to lie back and let him follow me.

"You're perfect," he whispers. I am perfect. I am good enough and smart enough to deserve the best. I let him kiss my neck and behind my ear. Rascal Flatts is playing in the background. I'm not a huge country music fan, but something about its lazy twang softens my resolve further, and I let Julian kiss me. My hands frame his face. He called me perfect, but he's the one who's perfect. He smells musty and salty, and I feel his body pressed against mine—his strong legs and his tight frame. I feel the weight of him on me, and it makes me feel so grounded and alive. So alive.

"Jenna." Mr. Stechshulte waves his hand in my face. "You okay? You with us?"

I blink. I'm back in class. Facing forward, thank God, and not staring at Julian. Sweat dots the back of my neck. I sweep my hair back because that's a normal girl thing to do, but really because I need to cool off.

"I'm fine." I reach for my water bottle and almost knock it over, but Mr. Stechshulte catches it. Everything is going in slo-mo. I feel myself fading away, becoming farther and farther from this world, and I wonder if this is a start of a seizure. But then the lights snap back into focus.

Mr. Stechshulte hesitates for a fraction of a second, then nods and strides back to the front of the room. "Okay. So we decided." He turns on the projector and focuses it on the screen at the front. "Here is the reading schedule."

Everyone laughs, because he had obviously predicted which book we'd choose.

I grab my water bottle and take a slow drink, but then my hand releases, and I drop the water bottle, sending it spilling all over the floor.

Mrs. Wilson, who is popping in on me today to make sure I'm okay, chooses this exact moment to stop in. "Oh, Jenna."

"It's no big deal." Mr. Stechshulte pushes the button on the wall. "We need a mop in room 1–153. Just water." Then to me. "Nothing too tragic, right, Jenna?"

I nod.

"You're all right?" he asks.

"I'm fine," I say, though I burn with embarrassment.

"Good." He does one of those old-man, good-guy winks. "Now where were we?" Mr. S. does a motion with his hands directing the class' attention back to him, and I breathe out.

Mrs. Wilson takes out her cell and types in some sort of text. I'm sure it's about me. And I'm also sure it's not something I'm going to like. "I think we better get you a wheelchair for the rest of the day, just in case."

I seethe with anger at Mrs. Wilson, even though she's really just doing her job. And I don't exactly want to get into it with her in front of everyone, so yeah. I'm stuck.

"Remember to stick to the schedule, people. Do not fall behind." Mr. S. pauses to scan the class. "I know what you're thinking. It's just a few pages. But *trust* me. You don't want to have to play catch up."

"Do you want me to copy down your assignments?" Mrs. Wilson

reaches for my backpack, which must really annoy Mr. S., because he shoots her one hell of a withering look. Then he scratches the area over his eyebrow, and I can practically hear him sigh heavily.

"It'll be in Google Classroom for everyone to access later. You should all do that." He points to the class. "Now would be good."

Mrs. Wilson withdraws her hand from my chair.

He winks at me again, and I know for sure Mr. S. is trying to help me. I'm reminded why Mr. S. is just about everyone's favorite teacher.

I steal a look at Julian, who must feel my eyes on him, because he turns to face me. He nods at Mr. Stechshulte like he's a good guy. Like he's glad that our teacher was nice to me. Julian's always been a little protective. I smile back. Then I look at my computer and pretend I'm typing something important when really I'm just biding time until the classroom door opens and some aide brings in a wheelchair for me to borrow. Luckily the bell rings just as the chair gets here. Life is good.

* * *

My strategy for going to lunch in a wheelchair is to hang back and let everyone else get there first. I pack my lunch and have a seat at Ben's table guaranteed, so there's no point in taking on the crowds. But Mrs. Wilson doesn't like to wait. After the bell rings, she wheels over my small electric wheelchair, the one they keep at school for me in case of things like this.

"Just for the rest of today," she says, and I forget that most of the time she's a condescending pain in the butt. Maybe I'm projecting my feelings on her, a concept of transference—something they're learning about in Ben's AP Psych class, which I know because I read his AP textbook online using his PIN. I'm that dorky.

I start to work the toggle and maneuver through the masses, a feat that would be way easier if I had my better chair or even my electric scooter. That thing can pivot on a dime, but this old thing feels clunky.

"Can I drive for you, Jenna?" Mrs. Wilson checks her watch. "I've got a call to make."

"I've got it," I say as I jerk forward a few more feet.

She stops and looks at the path being forged to the cafeteria. "You sure?"

"Yeah. It's fine."

"Okay." She smiles at me, hesitates, and looks at her watch, which is flashing a bunch of messages that she must feel compelled to answer.

She nods one last time and turns around.

A breeze blows, too cold for middle of October. I shiver and pause my movement, not ready to go forward. I feel almost like I'm a little seasick. But then some kids open the cafeteria door for me, and I let them give me that courtesy. Another cold wind blows, and suddenly I can't manage moving my chair and holding my coat around me. The cafeteria is blindingly bright and buzzing. There's so much talking. Laughing. It's all too much for my senses. I push forward some more, trying to avoid knocking someone over, but the round tables look like they are spinning. I start to get panicked.

Hands come down on my armrests. I can't see who it is.

"May I help you?"

It's Julian.

My heart melts. In the melee, his question sounds so gallant that I almost forget he's just being kind.

"You usually sit over here, right?" he asks.

I don't even answer, my voice locked in my throat from the fugue-like feeling I'm working through right now. But I clock that Julian knows where I sit. He wheels me up to Ben, who jumps up to move the cafeteria chair out of the way and make room.

"It's about damn time, girl." Ben gives me a side-eye, taking in the wheelchair situation, but he knows better than to ask why I'm using it with all of these people around. He's got his fake glasses on, the ones he wears when he's trying to look especially smart. "You're missing everything."

"Mostly I'm missing you," I manage to say, because it's one of our things.

Ben tilts his head a tiny bit. "Let me have a look at your handsome escort."

Julian puts his hand on his over his heart.

And I melt again.

Julian leans his body against the arms of my wheelchair. "What are we missing?"

Those two letters light a fire in me. He said *we*, as is the two of us, as in how couples refer to each other. We. We. We. Wheeeee.

Ben smiles at me—a little too obvious for my taste—and that makes me want to beat him silent. Is he kidding me? He dips a fry in ketchup. "So," Ben says as he turns back to his crowd. "We need to get planning…"

I tune him out because this is his way of giving Julian and me space.

"Thanks for the ride," I say.

"No problem. I can take you to your next class if you need."

"Nah, I'll be fine." The words are out before I can stop myself.

"You sure?"

I can imagine Jennifer cringing at how inept I am at this flirting thing, but in for a dime, in for a dollar. "Going to ditch this chair after lunch. Don't need it."

"Okay. If you're sure." He salutes Ben and takes off.

When he leaves, Ben says, "Well, that was smooth."

"I know, I know. I am a complete idiot." Julian's trajectory to his table is intercepted by Tori, and I try not to watch her flirt with him, but it's like the universe wants me to have a front-row seat. "Perfect. Just perfect."

"Look at it this way, you've got the whole 'playing hard to get' thing totally down."

Julian ducks away to join his hockey friends, but it's pointless to get too excited about that. If it's not Tori, then it'll be somebody else. Someone who knows a thing or two about how to do the dating thing. Someone who doesn't fumble over her thoughts. Who doesn't mess everything up.

I nod and force my attention back to Ben and his friends and pretend as best as I can that I am not still feeling the sting from my stupid fantasies.

But the thing is, I remember.

I remember when we were little. When he hung out at our house. That time in first grade when the kids on the playground were playing who would you marry, and Julian didn't hesitate. He shined his smile my way. "Jenna," he said.

"Why her?" Elana Whaley pouted.

"Because she's not afraid of anything." He smiled at me, and I smiled back. I was pretty fierce back then; it's true.

Lucy, one of the queen bee girls in my class, told him, "You'll have to give her something. Or it doesn't count."

I thought that would end it right there, but with one hand he undid his prized Batman watch. He'd gotten it for his birthday and was never without it. He would never let anyone else touch it, much less hold it, but he took it right off and handed it over to me. My palm was stretched out, shaking a little. Even back then, he made me feel so important.

"A Batman watch? That's so stupid!" Lucy declared.

I closed my hand around it, a simple movement for most people, but hard for me to pull off sometimes, without clamping down too hard. "I think it's cool."

Julian's smile spread across his face and even filled his eyes. Then a couple of boys raced by with a kickball, and Julian ran off with them. He turned back and called, "Hold on to that for me, Jenna."

"He's kind of cute," Lucy said.

But I didn't need her approval. I already knew.

. . .

4:05 P.M.

Favorite Disney princess?

Who says I even like Disney princesses?

Please. Everyone does.

You do?

Of course. Mulan. She's badass.

I'm not sure I buy that.

Buy what?

The Mulan thing. Guys say they want a
badass, but when you were little, tell me
you weren't all swoony for Cinderella.

Ok. Guilty. I have two favorites. Mulan and
Cinderella. Buuut the new version of Cinderella
who doesn't need the prince to save her.

So the Into the Woods Cinderella. Cool.

Don't know her, but if you say so.

So you're saying you don't have a favorite?

Truth.

Ok. Belle.

I knew it!

Because of the books. And
because she's French.

Oh sure. Sure.

Would it interest you at all to know I am
like the Beast? At least on the ice!

The Beast is really the prince. So...

The prince who gets the girl
and scores all the goals.

Funny, I don't remember scoring goals
in any of the versions I've read.

You have to read between the lines.
It's called making inferences.

On second thought maybe I choose Elsa.

Because of the Beast comment?

Lol. No. I like that she goes off on her
own. Lives her best life. You know?

Yeah. But don't go moving to
one of those no wi-fi places.

Where is there no wi-fi?

Green Bank, WV, home to
national telescopes.

Interesting.

I'm full of useless info.

Not useless. Cool.

Yeah. Cool. But don't move. Promise?

Promise.

TEN

I aim to go straight to my room when I get home, but Mom steps in. "What's the big rush, Jenna?"

"Just want to get a start on my homework."

"You have a lot?"

"Some."

"Okay. Since it's just you and me for dinner, I revoke the 'no working at the table' rule." She plops my computer down in front of me, then moves herself to the recliner nearby, where she's got a book stashed and a TV tray ready for her soup. Moments like this seem almost perfect to me.

Mom smiles at me like I'm such a good kid, which is funny because really all I'm doing is researching ways to help Julian with *The Great Gatsby*. So far I've pulled up a bunch of summaries online. I've bought a few of them, then I'm combining the parts I like. Cut. Paste. Copy. I load them all into a file to send to him tonight. If he texts.

As I'm Googling teaching methods for high school English, I get an email notification from Uncle Steve.

Subject: Baclofen Pump Success Stories.

Subtle, isn't he?

It won't hurt to look. So I open the email and read his note.

Just so you're completely informed.

—Uncle Steve

I open the first one, a video of a girl a little older than I am. College-aged looking. Her story is pretty convincing. She used a wheelchair when she was little. Had some surgeries to stretch tendons. Still had spasms. Tried oral medications. They made her sick. This was her last-ditch effort. Had the pump placed last year and hasn't looked back. I rub my eyes. Given her experience, I'd have to be nuts not to try this.

So I decide to look for all of the reviews of the procedure. It's weird—every single thing from books to movies to medications all have good reviews and bad ones, but this pump only has positive reviews. Could that be accurate?

My cell pings, and there's a new text from Ben.

So? Still floating from your mini flirt fest
with Julian today?

I chew on my nail and almost send a question mark, but then I realize he's talking about when Julian pushed me to our lunch table. To be honest, it's not like I forgot about that. Or how it felt when he breathed on my neck. Or how casual he was when he leaned against my wheelchair. How he used the *we* word. I just don't want to think about how I mucked the whole thing up.

Hello???

That was cute.

Cute???? Sigh. You. Are. Too. Much.

He was just being nice.

So let him be nice some other way. ☺

☺ Bye.

Ok. But I am not done with this.

My cell beeps, but I shift my attention back to another baclofen success story. I'm sure Ben's final word is super amusing, but I'm drawn in now to YouTube and Brittany, who looks straight at the camera. She discusses how she had to use a wheelchair all through high school, which is way worse than my current situation. Now she's boasting she's chair-free and only uses a cane or a walker when she's tired. I detect a tiny muscle weakness on her right side, mainly around her mouth. Probably no one else picks up on it, but I do, because I've been there. I wish I could speak to this Brittany person. Could I? I scroll through the links at the end of the video. There's her picture with an email address to ask questions. Her email. Should I reach out? Ask to speak with her? If she's a real person and not just a paid actor…would she want to speak with me?

A feeling of extreme exhaustion sets in, like how your bones ache when it's too cold. This means my body's worn out for the day. I've spent too much time upright. Seven o'clock is too early to go to bed, but that's my body. It demands. I listen.

I am a mess of knots and spasms all of a sudden, primarily in my back and legs. The small of my back, as they say, even though I know the actual medical term for it. L3 and L4, which refers to the lumbar region of the back. Disc numbers three and four. Sometimes I can work that out by laying on a tennis ball where the point of biggest pain is and holding it there for two to three minutes.

"Mom?" I call.

"Hmm." She doesn't look up from the book she's reading.

"I'm going to bed."

Mom doesn't ask to finish the next part in the book. She doesn't sigh or anything. She simply closes the book and lowers the recliner and smiles at me. How come she doesn't resent me? I mean, my body, my needs, me. I am way too much. I wish it were different, but it isn't. Shouldn't it bother her? Isn't she as tired of my body as I am?

Mom's by my side in seconds. She pushes my soup to the side and closes my computer.

Her smile is the only indication that she saw I was watching a baclofen video, but she knows better than to say anything. "You need help?" she asks.

"I've got it," I say.

"Okay if I just stand by?"

Mom knows that when I get like this it doesn't take much for me to teeter and fall or twist something the wrong way.

"Maybe just turndown service," I say jokingly.

"So fancy." Mom's voice is all sweetness and light, as if it's her dream to wait on me.

She follows me to my room and busies herself as I change, wash up, go to the bathroom, and finally brush my teeth. Mom helps me into bed. I reach over my head to the shelf that holds a single tennis ball.

"Your back?"

I nod.

"You want a pain pill? Or a muscle relaxer?"

"I think I'm okay."

She opens my night table drawer and spills two pills into a little cup we keep there. "In case you change your mind later." She puts my water bottle next to my bed.

"Thanks, Mom."

"As you wish," she says. It's one of our things, and I'm glad she still wants to say such things to me after our arguments this week. After all of my defiance—whether warranted or not.

I push the tennis ball against my lower back, the right side, since that's the part that hurts the most. I settle under the covers. Mom hands me my computer and my phone, which beeps the minute I have it in my hands.

"Anybody interesting?"

"Just Ben. He's all pissy about some school store thing gone wrong."

"I like that Ben, though." She walks to the door. "Let me know if you need anything."

She means text her. So much more civilized than screaming or ringing a bell, like Colin in *The Secret Garden*. Mom actually got me a little bell one time, because I was fascinated with the concept. But now, technology.

Speaking of which, I guess I should answer my bestie. Only when I look at my phone, I see that it's not Ben who has been texting me. It's Julian.

6:58

Hey.

7:15

You there?

7:23

Oh. Was hoping you could help me.

My heart rate accelerates. Back when I participated in physical therapy, the therapist would always say "Make your heart beat as fast as someone who's in love," and there was a heart sticker on the monitor that he wanted me to shoot for. I'd laugh and think, "How would I ever know about love?" But here I am, texting the boy I adore. Adoration isn't love exactly. Also, he doesn't know it's me. But those are small details. Miniscule even.

I text back a very articulate, hey.

Oh, awesome. I was just going to give up
on you.

I rush to type back.

Don't do that!

I won't.

Man, Julian's gotten flirty. Not that I'm complaining. Even though part of me is annoyed he's flirting with someone else, even when that someone else is me.

So what do you need?

You ever read The Great Gatsby?

Of course! It's a classic!

It's probably going to kill me.

Yeah, but what a way to go!

Wow. You're really into this stuff,
huh. Ok that settles it, I'm going to
try to look at it through your eyes.

Good. Then you'll see it as
an incredible love story.

What color are they anyway?

I'm so confused. Is he talking about Daisy and Gatsby? Why
would that even matter? Then his next text comes in.

Your eyes, I mean?

I giggle. Yes. I actually giggle out loud. But I type back.

Better keep to the book, right?

Yeah. Just thought if I was going
to look through your eyes I'd need
to know what color they are.

Brown.

My fave.

You lie.

Yes. But never to you.

And for some reason it feels like he means it. Like he knows it's me and he's sending me a message, like that time he gave me his Batman watch.

Read the first two chapters
and then we'll talk.

Well, since you won't tell me your real
name, I'll have to have a nickname
for you. How about I call you Juliet?

Ok. Now all I have to do
is find my Romeo.

Wow talk about an arrow to the
heart. Would it be too much to
admit I'm slightly obsessed with
these conversations now?

Obsession is a word that means something to me.

Maybe not Juliet, maybe that's not
right. You told me you like Elsa.

Cold and removed! I like it.

No. Beautiful. Happy to be herself.

That's a little too close to home for me.

And we are losing focus. I found
things for you for Great Gatsby.

I pull up the study guide I put together from those online
sources earlier and paste them into our thread. Hit send.

Let me know if these help.

OMG This. Is. Awesome. You are
awesome. I started reading earlier,
and I didn't get all of this...stuff. I was
totally stuck. Thank you! Thank you!

That doesn't mean you can cheat and
not read the actual book, you know.

I don't cheat.

I laugh.

So tell me something
personal about you?

                              Like what?

Something no one else knows.

I think hard. What would sum me up?

                              I still believe in magic.

Who doesn't?

I release a breath. I didn't out myself. But then there's this weird feeling in the pit of my stomach, a disappointment that he didn't figure it out. Like I believed on some level that he has also just been waiting for us to have that mock wedding from first grade.

He texts again.

You mean like magicians?
I love magicians but I don't
think that's real magic.

Sorry if you're a magician.

I laugh.

                              I'm not a magician. I mean
                              like mysticism, I guess.

There's the kind of magic when I take the
ice and I've got the puck and I know I'm
going to score. Everything falls away.
Nothing matters. Just me and the net.

That's what I mean. Finding things that
are bigger than just you. You know?

Yes! What do you have?

I guess I have stories.

Tell me one.

I swear I feel my heart swell and crack at the same time. Man,
this is stupid. It's not even real, but it feels so perfect. So personal.

Have you ever heard of the 36 saints?

No. Are they DC or Marvel?

☺ They are a myth, maybe. A belief
that at any given time there are 36
saints that serve to keep the world
in balance. If one of them dies,
another is born to replace them.

Wow.

Wait. Like Buffy the Vampire Slayer?

☺ kinda

That's very cool. And you
believe in these saints?

I think so. I want to.

Are you one of these saints?

☺

Can I tell you something? Without
you thinking I'm an idiot?

?

I have dyslexia.

That's no big deal. A lot
of people have that.

It sucks. But I deal with it. It's different
for everybody, but for me it makes it
hard to tell the difference between
some of the emojis, especially the faces.
The smiley face ones, the crying ones,
the winky face ones, I can't always
reliably tell the difference between
them, and I'm worried I'm going to send
the wrong one at the wrong time.

I didn't even know that was a thing.
How about this—from now on, we'll use
the words. Like smiley face. Sad face.
Laughing my ass off face. That work?

Yeah. Def. You don't mind?

Not at all. It'll be our thing.

Our thing?

Every superhero team needs
a thing. This will be ours.

So we're a team now?

Yup. Smiley face emoji.

You really are a saint. Smiley face emoji.

As he says that I can feel that breeze against my cheek. I hear the
birds in the forest that day. I feel his hand in mine.

You've helped me so much. I'm here for
you if you need. Ok? Any time. I never turn
my phone off. Keep it right next to me.
Day and night. So if you need to talk...

I laugh.

Thanks, I'll keep that in mind.

So tell me about Gatsby.
Will it end happy?

No! You have to read it. And no fair
skipping to the end. That's for cheaters.

I told you. I never cheat. Don't ride
dirty. Don't crease the paint. Don't...

Like a hero. Going to sleep now.

Gnite Sweet Dreams.

I put my phone down and stare at the ceiling. After the tests, I've got to get real. The next few days are the last ones I can live as this Jennifer. I've got to face it. I promise myself I will. Which is why I do actually send an email to that Brittany Cox person. A simple one.

To: BritCox_36@Umass.edu
Subject: Baclofen pump question

Hello,

I'm sorry to write you out of nowhere like a creeper, but I saw your baclofen pump success story video and wondered if I could ask you some questions. I have CP and am in high school, and I'm really not sure about doing the pump. The doctors are all go for it and my parents agree, but I kind of want to talk with someone who's done it. No BS. Just straight talk. I hope you don't mind I wrote.

Here's how to get me.

JenConeof3@yahoo.com

ELEVEN

T he following Monday is when the Uncle Steve stuff starts getting real. As I get out of school, I see him parked in the parent pickup lane in front. He beeps at me. Ben's walking next to me, but stops when he spots my uncle. "What's that about?"

"Welp, I may or may not be working with my uncle to get control of my medical rights."

I twist my fingers as I tell him.

He puts his hands over mine. "You aren't!"

"I might be."

He grabs my hands. "Don't get me wrong, I am always on Team Jenna. I mean always. But this seems kind of extreme."

"I know."

"Are you sure this is what you want?"

"No."

Ben moves my bangs off my forehead. "Just be sure, okay? This is one of those bombs you can't unexplode."

"Is that even a word?"

"Not the point. You don't think you could just speak with your parents?" Ben asks.

"I don't know." I hold a finger up for Uncle Steve so he knows I'll be right there. "I just know that I need to feel in control of my life."

"Jenna, nobody's in control of their life."

I laugh. "As much as I can be."

"Don't you think changing classes was enough? And by the way, other than having Julian in your class, how has that little experiment played out?"

"Fine," I say, but I know I don't sound confident.

"Riiiiight. That's why you keep logging into my AP textbooks."

I blush.

"I gotta go, sweets. But just be careful. This is the real world, you know? Not some story or fantasy." He kisses me on the forehead and then bounds off.

My hands go to my mouth. Ben's right. I've got to be careful. I shield my eyes with my hand and walk toward Uncle Steve's matte black Jeep. Yeah, he's that kind of cool uncle.

Uncle Steve gets out when I make it to the Jeep and stands by as I lift myself into his car. "Sorry," he says. "This thing is stupid."

"Stupid awesome," I say.

He grins, runs his hand across his beard. "Yeah."

I point to his facial hair. "No court dates lately?"

"I make my junior partner do most of those these days. You know, so I can look scruffy."

"Living your best life," I say. Then, "Does Dad know you are here?"

"Yes. But not why."

"How'd you play it this time?"

"Your mother has her book club tonight. Rena has drama rehearsal. Your father is out of town. I told them I'd take you to dinner."

I point to my temple. "Smart."

"I know, right?"

"Although it is slightly annoying that they feel the need to have coverage for me when they go out."

"Listen, you have every right to be outraged by many things. The fact that the dress code is stricter for girls than boys. The unfairness of gender inequality when it comes to pay. The fact that Panic! At the Disco is now only Brendon Urie. Dinner with your best uncle is not one of them. Also, we have to talk strategy."

"Brendon Urie is a god."

I hijack his Bluetooth and play one of my favorite playlists. The one that starts with "Crazy=Genius." You know, an oldie but a goodie.

He feigns indignation. "I never said you could…"

"I didn't ask."

Uncle Steve turns onto the highway, and I lay my head back and let the music take me somewhere else.

It's not until we've ordered—eggplant parmigiana for Uncle Steve, pappardelle with mushroom marinara sauce and broccoli with garlic for me—that Uncle Steve gets to the point. "So, have you made a decision?"

"Still thinking."

"Good. But these tests that are coming up? How do we feel about those?"

"Not great." I hadn't heard back from Brittany yet, and so I was sticking to my gut feelings about all of this.

"So you want to file the paperwork before them?"

I take a tiny bite of pasta. Chew. Swallow. Think. Regardless of when I time it, filling out the paperwork—and everything that will come after—will suck.

"Have you considered having a sit-down with them to talk to them honestly before filing emancipation paperwork?"

"Definitely," I say. "Mostly."

"So are you going to?"

"Not sure." I cover my face with my hands. This is all too much.

Uncle Steve pulls my hands away and looks me in the eyes. "I'm not trying to make you uncomfortable with all of this, but as your lawyer, I have to advise you."

"And as my uncle?"

"I say try to speak with them one more time. See how you feel. The paperwork is all ready to go."

"Okay. Am I the worst, wishy-washiest client you've ever had?"

Uncle Steve smiles warmly at me. "This is a very hard line to draw, and I'm glad you are thinking twice about it."

I breathe out.

"These tests are coming up in just a few days, and you should know how you feel before they happen."

"I don't know how I feel. I mean, I hate the tests, but maybe they would help. But also maybe they will be 'inconclusive.'" I make air quotes around that word. "And then it'll be all for nothing, and we'll have to jump into deciding to do the pump or not."

"I know. It's a very difficult choice, but, it's up to you to make it. And we don't have to decide anything tonight. I simply wanted you to know I'm ready with operation Free the Dove whenever you are."

"Operation Free the Dove? That is the dorkiest code name ever."

"Like you have a better suggestion?" He asks.

"Tons. Operation Phoenix Arises."

Uncle Steve nods. "That one's pretty good."

"Operation Persephone," I say.

"Not sure I buy that one."

"Operation Uncaged."

"Okay. Sure. But don't you want to eat your pasta?" Uncle Steve asks.

"Yeah." I take another bite. Lift my fork in the air. "Operation Lotus because I'm blooming like a flower. Operation Avatar because I'm becoming a parent-bender."

Uncle Steve winces. "May be pushing it a little. Hey, Operation Cloak and Dagger."

"Um…no on that one. Hard pass." I laugh, and this is how we spend the rest of dinner.

. . .

8:56 P.M.

Do you like Avatar: The Last Airbender?

How could you question that? Of course.

Best tv show ever.

So that leads me to…

Avatar or Death Note.

Both. Obv.

I think you have trouble committing.

Dude!

So commit. Tell me something you love.

I like rom-coms.

Don't all girls?

That is so patronizing! And misogynistic!

You're right. My confession? So do I.

Now you're just being a jerk.

No. I'm srs.

Ok name your favorites.

The Princess Bride.

You just like all the swordplay.

Ok. What about...To All the Boys I Loved
Before. Watched it with my little cousin.

You know it was a book first?

I'm not a heathen. Of course I know.

So did you read it?

Um...next question. Your favorites?

Ohh. This is hard. I love old
Hollywood ones. You know.

Sure. Sure.

I'm serious. Like Rear Window.

That was NOT a rom-com.

Says who?

What other ones?

10 Things I Hate About You. A Cinderella
Story. The live-action Cinderella.

Of course those. And...

To All the Boys I Loved Before.
Also, yes. I read the book, too.

Such an A+ student...

After I saw the movie. I'm
embarrassed to admit.

Wow. Mind blown.

Maybe you're rubbing off on me.

Well you're definitely rubbing off
on me. I'm ahead on my reading
for The Great Gatsby.

And?

I'm not hating it as much
as I thought I would.

I'll take it. Gnite.

Gnite. Sweet dreams.

Sweet dreams you too.

Smiley face emoji.

Back at you.

Tuesday

7:03 A.M.

Do you ever wish you could have
some control over your life?

All the time! What's up?

My parents are driving me batty.

What are they doing?

Trying to plan my summer for the
next three years. Trying to pick the
college I should go to. If I should play
hockey or not. They talk about all
of this as if I don't have a choice.

Parents take their plays from the

same books. Angry face emoji.

You're to blame for this recent siege, btw.

What did I do?

Well, apparently, I got an A on my last

Gatsby test, thanks to you. I maneuvered

my Algebra II grade to a decent B

and my parents think I'm a genius.

Woooohoooo!

Yeah, so now they have expectations

for me. Great Expectations.

That's the next book we'll read!

Don't get your hopes up too high, Elsa.

Remember, I'm aiming middle-

ish. It's not my fault you went

for the shorthanded goal.

Did you just use a hockey reference?

I might have done some studying myself.

Heart emoji.

TWELVE

B ye, guys." Rena races out the door and into the car of her best friend, Shayna. Apparently they've got a bunch of stuff to work out for this year's fashion show, which leaves me alone with Mom for the ride to school since Ben has a doctor's appointment. I figure I can use the one-on-one time to my advantage.

"So," I say as we pull away from the house. "I wanted to talk with you about the tests they've got planned."

Mom turns to look at me, a chipper smile on her face. "You have any questions about what we're going to do?"

"No, I'm pretty sure I understand what the tests entail. What I want to do is talk about the 'we' part. As in what 'we' are going to do. The thing is, Mom, I'm the one getting the tests. No 'we' about it."

"Honey, I know. But I have a really good feeling about it this time."

"Ha!" I say.

She turns to look at me again. "Ha?"

"Well, Mom, in the past, some of these tests or procedures or diets or therapies, well, they haven't always been the best choice. For *me*, that is. The only part of the *we* that is getting poked and prodded and medicated."

"I know, honey, but we have to keep trying."

We pass the old lady who does her morning walk every single day. Cold or hot, doesn't matter—this woman's out there with her flashlight when it's dark out and her water bottle when it's hot. The determined look on her face makes me feel all twisted inside, distracting me from all the things I want to tell Mom.

"Jenna?" Mom prods.

I sigh and glance back at her. "Let's take a little stroll down memory lane, shall we?"

"Don't be snippy." Mom gets a little too emphatic with the brakes at the stop sign at the end of our neighborhood, and we jolt forward. "Sorry."

"Do you remember when I was eight?" My voice shakes, so that doesn't help, but I have to say this next part. "We did the Botox treatments? Supposed to be easy, effective, and perfect for someone like me?"

Mom nods. "I know…"

"Major epic fail. Two weeks in the hospital. Incontinent for weeks after that."

She turns onto the through street but steals a glance at me as she does. The color has leached from her cheeks, leaving her pasty and pitiful. She holds one hand out to me. "Jenna, we are your parents. We only want what's right for you."

"Or how about that weird Feldenkrais lady who was also a psychic and said it was my past lives getting in the way of this one?"

Mom smirks a little. "She may have been a mistake. But that method is supposed to be supereffective and with no side effects."

"Was it effective?"

"Her psychic beliefs may have gotten in the way of a true Feldenkrais experience."

"How about the ketogenic diet that was just…" I struggle to try find a strong enough word and end up saying, "Disgusting. But we did it because you were convinced it would stop my seizures?"

"I realize not everything we've tried has been successful…but you aren't having seizures anymore, except after the contrast…"

"Mom. Come on. Every time we've tried to do things for my benefit, it has backfired."

Her voice gets sharper. She points at me. Not a good sign. "That's a wild overgeneralization."

We are stopped at the traffic light leading into school. I use this for my next argument. My biggest one. "Mom?"

She turns to face me.

"What if this is as good as my CP gets?"

Mom puts her hands on the top of my head, smooths down my hair, and leaves her palms cupping my face. "First of all, this was never about your CP. I don't even think of things that way. If I did, I'd lose my mind."

She'd lose *her* mind?

"It has always been about taking care of you, Jenna, whatever that meant. But, if this is the best it gets, then we'll take it. We'll figure out how to make it work for you. But it's not. I feel it in my bones, Jenna. We are going to figure out how to help with your pain and with your muscle spasms. But you have to trust us."

The light turns green and some idiot beeps at us. Mom waves a hand in the rearview mirror as if that will make the person behind us suddenly be patient. She's like that—the perfect combination of drill sergeant and big softie.

I know why she's worried. I know she goes on those blogs of older people with CP. I've caught her, reading over her shoulder before she knew I was there. The blogs are mostly people her age who pushed themselves too hard and now their bodies are deteriorating. Fast. Those who used to be ambulatory are using a wheelchair. And that sucks for them, I guess. But Mom doesn't get it. She doesn't understand that accepting a wheelchair or a walker, while it is not every girl's dream, is a hell of a lot better than not doing things you want. That a wheelchair can be a way to rest and get out from under the pain. Sort of wait it all out.

I've looked on some teen blogs, too. The college kids with CP. I hear them say that their bodies need more downtime. But they are living their lives. Aren't they? "It's not that I'm uninformed," I say. "I know what's possible, and I'm saying if I have to choose between terrible side effects and status quo, I'm thinking what I've got is not as bad as it could be."

Mom parks in the handicapped spot in the front of the school. I've got nowhere else to go with this conversation, so I climb out of the car.

"Ben's driving you home?" I can tell by the way she's looking at me she's just trying to say something to make everything right between us.

"Yeah," I say.

"Love you," Mom says, and I look away so I don't see her eyes—because I can tell by her voice that she's crying a little.

"For God's sake, Mom, I love you too. I just want to have a say."

She nods. I shut the door, a little too hard, which I feel kind of bad about, but not bad enough to walk back my stance. So I make myself move forward. When I get to class, I pull out my phone and text Uncle Steve.

Well, that went well.

You talked to your mom?

Yup.

And?

She cried.

Did she listen?

Not sure. Maybe a little. I think.

Baby steps, niece-y. Baby steps.

I want to tell him I'm too old for baby steps, but the bell rings, and that means that in the next few minutes I'll get to watch Julian enter my classroom. That knowledge pushes all the bad feelings away.

. . .

12:10 P.M.

Harry Potter or Lord of the Rings?

Um...both?

Hedwig or Dobby?

OMG you're evil! Who could
choose between those two?

You can't keep saying both!
You have to choose.

Ok then, chocolate chip or
sugar with sprinkles?

Both.

Smiley face emoji.

Favorite food?

Nah. It's weird.

Now I have to know.

Soup.

That is weird.

OMG I'm never confiding in you again.

Kidding!!! Who doesn't love a bowl
of Campbell's Chicken and Stars.

Gross. Also, I'm onto you.

What?

You're hoping that the type of food I like
will give you some clue as to who I am. As
in right now you're probably scanning the
room looking for some girl eating soup.

Ha!

Don't deny it.

I didn't.

THIRTEEN

When I get home, Mom's waiting for me, and I wonder if that's a good thing or a bad thing.

"Sweetie, sit down." She pats the couch next to her.

I let my backpack slide off my shoulder and onto the bench where we hang our coats and store our boots. "Sure thing," I say, but I admit that my mood nose-dives when Dad walks into the room.

Jewish households work this way. You see someone or something out of the ordinary, and you automatically start counting heads. It's like this: Rena? I just saw her like ten minutes ago as we passed each other. She was heading to rehearsal and stopped to hand me a cookie she'd made in culinary. So she's probably fine. Eric? Did something happen at his college? Did he fail out? Get hurt? Mom's not crying so that's probably not it. All of this goes through my mind, but all I manage is, "Everything okay?"

Dad smiles. "Yes. Everyone's fine." He sits in the chair opposite Mom.

Right. So this is about me.

Dad starts, "Mom said we needed to have a little talk." He holds up his hand in reaction to my balking at the term *little*. "I mean to say, we need to discuss how you'd like to proceed with the medical…" His hands grope for the words.

"Decisions. I would like to have a say in my medical decisions."

For Dad, there is always an element of pride when I assert myself. Even when it's against him. So I've got that in my favor.

"Yes. Your medical decisions. And while your mother and I feel that you do have a right to decide what happens to your body, we are worried that you will opt out of some treatment that in the end would be beneficial just because of some short-term pain."

I try not to answer right away. I try to let his words sink in, but it's so galling that they believe *they* should have any say in what happens to *my* body. I want to text Uncle Steve right then and there. I want to scream at them to speak to my lawyer. I want to shout that I am not shortsighted. I am simply the one these medical experiments are happening to.

Dad looks like he's going to say something else, but Mom puts her hand up. "Let's listen to her, David."

Hot tears spring to my eyes, and I work like mad not to let them fall, but I'm losing the battle. Sad tears, those I can hold back, but angry ones spill without my permission.

Mom turns to face me. "Oh, Jenna." She slips her arm around my shoulders, and I can hear her crying also.

Dad turns his face away, because one thing he can definitely not deal with is when any of us cry. "What do you want, Jenna?" he says with a softer voice. His *I'm trying to be reasonable* voice, and that's when I know I've got him. But I don't want to win because I cried. I don't want to win because Dad softened. I want to win because I'm strong and I'm right. Mom hands me a tissue—she always seems to have tissues with her—and I wipe my nose and try to sit up straighter.

"It's not fair for you to decide what's going to happen to me." I sniffle. "It's like I'm an animal or something."

"We make Eric and Rena get flu shots every year just like we make you. We made Rena get braces, and she didn't want them," Dad says.

"I was on Rena's side when she didn't want braces. But also, braces are not surgery. Neither are flu shots. If I had cancer…"

"God forbid, Jenna," Mom blurts.

"God forbid," I say to make Mom feel better. "But if I did, would you make me do chemo even if the doctors said it wouldn't change my long-term prognosis?"

"That's not the same thing at all," Dad argues. He shakes his head. "Not at all."

"It feels the same to me."

"We know that and we're sorry." Mom hands me a brochure while giving Dad a *calm down* look. "There's a class being offered at the hospital. It's all about the pump."

"We'd like you to take the class," Dad says.

I nod, processing this development.

"Then you can decide if you want to proceed and when," Mom adds.

Dad holds up his finger. "But we want a say also. Consider us as silent partners. Investors."

"The silent part sounds good," I say.

Dad laughs. "Take the brochure. Sign yourself up for a class. We will put the hospital pretests on hold until you've made your decision. But…moving forward, if you get more of a say in your medical decisions, we want more of a say in your academic ones." He lifts his chin a bit and stares down at me.

I'm feeling fragile when I want to be kick-ass, so I don't answer him with a smart remark.

"Deal?" Mom asks.

"Deal." I point to my room. "Am I excused now?"

"Yes, but I'm making kale lasagna for dinner, so you might want to join us for that."

Low blow. My favorite.

Dad smiles as Mom leaves. "Still friends?" he asks.

"You should've been the lawyer instead of your brother." An old joke.

"I'm thinking that's a career path you might want to explore," he says, "which is why you need to go back to the higher-level classes where you belong."

"I need to get some work done," I say, my eyes telegraphing my desire to go to my room. I've got the brochure they gave me clutched in my hand. I could open it and read it, but I already know what it'll say: I need to get the pump. I don't want to hear that right now, just when I've finally convinced my parents to let me have some say.

So instead I decide to indulge in one of my dorky guilty pleasures: reading the AP Psych textbook and pretending I'm in that class alongside Ben. According to the online syllabus, they are on unit 4 Sensation and Perception. I could seriously add to some of those class discussions. Part of me feels like trying to hack into them, you know, sort of hang out in the online classroom, but that would make me even more of a weirdo than I already am. It's not that I can't do this stuff. It's just that I don't want to have to reliably do it. Not when at any moment my muscles could make me a spasmodic example of what happens when the doctor who delivers you goes a little light in the head during the procedure.

Mom, Dad, and Ben think I'm making a big mistake taking these classes that are too easy for me. Are they right? Was I too reactive? I remember when I used to be so sure of things. When I listened to Mom and Dad, mostly before the big dramatic birth-accident reveal.

But that kind of knowledge, the belief that there was a Jenna before and a Jenna after, that kind of thing changes you. Just like the baby who is turned into a crow because her mother can't bear to have the baby she birthed, just like the swan princess that became something else because others needed her to be human or bird, I am part the thing I was supposed to be and part the one I became. My point is, I have been touched twice. Once by Dr. Jerkoby who jerked his hand as he delivered me, then again when I found out about the birth injury.

Part of me wishes I could go back to before, when I didn't know. When I stood solidly behind Mom and Dad's decisions for me.

I pick up one of my snow globes from the shelf above my desk. The ones Mom makes to commemorate family trips and exciting moments. The one I grab is of our last Florida vacation. We were in Boca Raton, Florida, to visit my mother's aunt Judy. Eight years ago in August.

Eric and Rena went swimming. Body surfing, Eric called it.

It came right when we were planning my surgeries to loosen the muscles in my legs. We'd gone to the doctor to see if we could schedule them, but my growth plates were still open, so we had to put it off. We'd gone straight from the doctor to the airport, practically, and I remember how stunned I'd been. Dad and I had been so sure we'd be able to get it all set up. He'd planned an entire recovery movie list. He'd bought a bunch of board games. He'd notified his work that he needed time off. It was going to be epic.

I'd done some swimming in a pool before, but never in the ocean. Dad would sometimes walk me out to where I could still stand but the waves were a little choppy, but since he was out with Eric and Rena, I was left to hang out in the wet sand with the little kids.

Mom took video of Eric and Rena and Dad. I tried not to get pouty, but it was hard. Dad must have seen me or sensed my mood, or maybe he was feeling the same way. The next thing I knew he strode out of the waves, his hands out in front of him like a zombie.

"Aaaah," I screamed.

He stopped directly over me and dripped on me on purpose.

"Hey," I called out. "You're drowning me!"

"I am?" He laughed, bent down. "You're made of sugar now and you melt?"

"Maybe," I said.

He turned to face Eric and Rena, then back to me. "So, want to try that?"

"Are you insane, David?" Mom put the video camera down. "No way. The water is way too rough today."

Dad ignored her and crouched lower. He turned around and pointed to his back. "Climb on."

I stared at him. Maybe he *was* insane. But then I remembered

Dad's face when the doctor said it wasn't time for the operation. It had looked like he'd been punched in the gut. Dad was not a wait-and-see kind of guy. And I wanted to try something that could distract us, make us both feel better.

As I climbed on Dad's back, Mom reached for his arm. "Don't take her in too far."

Dad turned to face her. There was a moment between them that I didn't understand. "She'll be fine, Sharon. She'll be fine."

Mom's hand went to her mouth, but she backed up. Her signal for backing down. Dad turned toward the ocean, and we moved forward. The waves lapped up my legs. It was so much warmer than I thought it would be. Much warmer than the ocean on the Cape. I'm not sure exactly what it was that day that caused the magic. Maybe it was Mom's worry for me; her constant fear of something happening to me made me want to prove that I was strong and brave and free. Maybe that was the catalyst that triggered my slacking muscles and got them ready to work.

All I know is something happened in the ocean that day. I closed my eyes to keep the salt water out. The sun was so warm on my face, and it made me safe feel. And so strong. I wanted to be free. Something made me want to let go of Dad. So I did.

It worked. I rose above the waves, Dad's hand reaching for me, but my body moving, bobbing, floating—swimming on its own.

Rena danced through the water next to me. "You're doing it!"

"Be careful with her, David!" Mom shrieked from the beach.

I used her fear that day, made it propel me forward. It made me try to balance on the water, prove to her that I could do this.

"She's fine," Rena yelled back. "She's like a mermaid."

I *was* like a mermaid, only with a little help from Dad, Eric, and Rena to stay afloat. My strong need to beat what was holding me back made me surge forward. I was trapped in this unwieldy body, but my props made me large.

In my room, here and now, I stare at the snow globe. Inside of it, encased in the glass sphere, is the picture that Mom took that day of me being a mermaid. I want that feeling back. The feeling of being fearless, knowing I have my family there to support me. We were always there for each other.

And I believed we always would be. I blow on the snow globe glass. It fogs. I wipe it clean. I breathe on the glass again. Let it fog over. Cover that scene.

The thing is, I don't want to be trapped in a crystal dome.

My cell pings.

Come see me play tomorrow.

Everyone in the school will be there. It's a
big one.

I'll even score a few for you.

As much as I'm enjoying being Julian's virtual confidant, it's just like that snow globe—fake. And that's starting to not be enough anymore.

The game is the start of something called the Connecticut

Cup, which happens every year at this time. It's a big deal for the senior hockey players, since it's their last hockey season. Hockey isn't as popular as football in our school, but it's my favorite sport. We celebrate the start of the Connecticut Cup with a week of dressing up, followed by the game, which is against Danbury High. We play them twice: once at the beginning of the season and once at the end. Whichever team wins the cup at the end of the season wears their hockey jerseys to the Hockey Homecoming Winter Formal, the dance commemorating the end of the Cup.

Eric was so proud to wear his, but Christina, the girl he took, was less than excited about the whole thing. Especially since Eric decided to "do it right" and wear his unwashed jersey, the one he'd worn on the ice to win the cup. Rena and I thought it was funny.

Eric's coming into town tomorrow night in time for the first big game, which makes this all feel like it's coming together for some weird reason. Like the universe is conspiring with me. Making magic.

I stare at all of the snow globes Mom made for me. There's one for my preschool graduation. Me on my hippotherapy horse, Midnight, and one for every first day of school. Lots of me with Eric and Rena. Some of me and Ben.

If I close my eyes, I can almost see my perfect worldview where we could see into the mystical realm and enter the secret garden where every person would have their own Tree of Life. Millions of trees, all filled with these glass globes documenting the best moments of their lives. How beautiful would that be? I tap on one of the globes. It makes the most comforting sound.

Julian said he wanted me to come to his game. I close my eyes and try to picture one of these globes with a picture of me and Julian in it. Now that's what I'd call magic.

FOURTEEN

Everyone acts like idiots in school this week. Truth be told, they like any excuse. But this year the hockey team has a hot prospect for the Ivy League, Daniel Beard, so the week leading up to the first game in the Connecticut Cup is bigger than ever. It's kind of cool. We've got "dress up like your favorite sports mascot" day. "Dress up as a rowdy hockey fan" day. And today, game day, is "dress up as a character from *Frozen*" day, because, you know, why the hell not? My classmates defy the rules and wear hats and gloves and scarves into the classroom.

As fun as this is, the hours are ticking away for me, like some deranged clock in a messed-up fairy tale. To start with, Julian and I have been put in the same book circle in English.

There are five of us in this group, each with our own particular job. Lorin is the group leader, I'm on quotes, Julian is on foreshadowing, and the rest—Karen Forester, Frank Dumante, and Bella Justice, who frequently bemoans that her parents obviously wanted her to be a stripper or a mixed martial arts fighter—are on facts. It's not looking good for the team.

Lorin, who is a serious book nerd like I am and who takes her role as leader very seriously, starts us off. "So how many of you have actually read the first two chapters as instructed?"

"Come on, man, I had two matches this weekend. I'm toast," Frank contributes from his completely reclined position in his chair. His posture must piss Mr. Stechshulte right the eff off, because he kicks the chair's leg and points to the papers in front of Frank, which makes him sit up straight and pretend to be on top of it.

Mr. Stechshulte hands out a few papers stapled together, and I'm surprised and disappointed to find that he's given us summaries on the first two chapters from Shmoop. My face must register my displeasure because he says, "Just in case you need a few reminders of what you read this weekend." And then he's gone.

Frank smiles stupidly and he points to our teacher, who has retreated to his desk. "That guy's got style."

"No," I surprise myself by saying. "He just knows you didn't read the book."

Julian smirks.

Frank balls up a piece of paper and tosses it at Julian's head. "Like you read it."

Julian holds up one hand like he's testifying. "First *three* chapters, as a matter of fact. Ask me anything."

I can't help the pride that fills me. Julian read the chapters. Because of me. Lorin rewards him with a grateful look and then she's back to business. "Okay so first thing, we've got to choose a theme to concentrate on. There's classism. Power. Money. Or love."

"Love," Karen says.

Frank snorts. "Always the same with you girls."

"Maybe why half of us are turning to girls ourselves."

"I'd like to see that."

Julian kicks his chair. "Enough." And his eyes slide to me to see if I'm offended. I know he's trying to be nice, but it irritates me that feels the need protect me.

"So love it is," Lorin says decisively, ignoring Frank. "What do we all think?"

"Well." Julian sits up a little taller in his chair and looks at the notes he took over the weekend. "It's clearly a riff on marriage versus love. I mean, Daisy is married to Tom, who claims to love her, but hurts her both physically and emotionally."

"Excellent analysis, Mr. Van Beck," says Mr. Stechshulte, who somehow managed to sneak up behind us again without any of us noticing. "This group is getting an A for today."

Lorin grins and makes a few marks on her paper. I'm mostly thrilled that Julian is feeling smart and confident. I smile at him and he gives me one back. A purely platonic *I'm glad to be in class with you* smile, but I'll take it anyway. Love is about making the other person feel special, isn't it?

. . .

Ben waits for me at our lunch table, dressed as a lumberjack with a collection bucket in front of him. One of his big fund-raisers is charging $1 for not dressing up on spirit days. He pushes a cinnamon roll across the table toward me. I rub my hands together, but just as I'm about to reach for it, Ben says, "Slow down, girl. We've got a lot to discuss first."

"Uh huh."

"Your outfit, for one." He slides his sunglasses down his nose. "Or lack thereof."

He points a fork at Simon, who is dressed as a reindeer.

"Yeah. About that," Simon chimes in.

"So disappointing." Ben shakes the container at me. "Pay up."

"I'm saving it for the game," I say.

"That's what he said," Ben says as he nods his head toward Julian, who is sitting with his friends, but is staring at his phone.

A little thrill goes through me. Julian is waiting for me.

Well for the pretend me, anyway.

. . .

Thursday
3:26 P.M.

So, this is the big game.

Yup.

That's all you've got?

Yup.

No words of encouragement? No telling
me to get it done, score, kick their butts?

You already know all of that stuff.

True.

So tell me something I don't know.

I'll be there, cheering you on.

Heart emoji.

So how exactly do I interpret
a heart emoji?

That's up to you.

OK. I think it means you're
happy I'm going to be there.

Sure.

I'm missing something?

Sometimes you've got to
read between the lines.

Heart emoji.

What does that one mean?

You used an English/reading term.

And that makes your heart beat fast?

Yup.

Good. To. Know. See what I did there?
Used punctuation as emphasis.

OH MY!

The ladies love a smarty-pants.

This one sure does.

Three heart emojis and a
smiley face emoji.

FIFTEEN

It's about two hours before we leave for the game and there's no sign of Rena or Eric yet. "Mom?" I call out.

"In here." Mom's in the kitchen, shoving a pan into the oven. She closes the oven door and looks up as I approach. "They'll be here soon."

"I need Rena to help me with my costume."

She wipes her hands on the dish towel and reaches under the sink for rubber gloves.

"Can you grab the beets?" she asks as she takes a cutting board out and sharpens one of her knives. "It's supposed to be really nasty out tonight. I can't believe how fast the weather turned this year."

"Don't even start. Rain or not, cold or not, I am going tonight." I plunk the bag of beets down next to her.

Her eyes go to my face in that worried Jewish mother look that makes me super uncomfortable.

"Stop, Mom. I'm fine. It'll be fine."

She holds the beets under the water and scrubs them clean. I take each beet from her and dry them with a paper towel and soon we've got this rhythm going so well that I don't even hear the door open. Or the approaching steps.

"Damn, what did those beets ever do to anybody?"

I turn to face Eric. Squeal. Drop everything and run straight for him.

He crushes me with his hug, but it's a good kind of crushing.

"How you doing, little sister?" he asks.

"Glad I'm not a beet!"

"Very funny, Jenna," Mom pushes past me and gets her own Eric hug. "How are you, sweetie?"

He puts his hand on his stomach. "Starved." Then he drops a big duffel bag on the ground. "Brought my laundry, but I'll do it myself."

Mom rolls her eyes. "Put it in the laundry room, and we'll battle that out later."

I walk with Eric as he deposits his laundry as directed. "I heard you got a little raucous with Mom and Dad?" he asks.

"Had to happen," I say. "Who told you? Mom, Dad, or Uncle Steve?"

"Rena. The ears of the house."

I put my hand on my forehead. "She's like a super spy. I didn't know she knew. She wasn't even home when the big talk happened!"

Eric checks the washer. "Should I actually be a grown-up and do my own laundry?"

I punch his arm. "Tell me how Rena knew."

He rubs his arm. "Man, you're getting strong." I wind up, threatening another assault. He puts his hands in the air. "Okay, okay. You know how our house is. Nothing's a secret."

We walk to the front of the house, where he finally takes his coat off and hangs it on the hook.

"So that means Mom and Dad have been talking about it." I chew on my finger. "I mean, that's the only way she could have heard."

"All I can say is never underestimate the curious nature of our baby sister."

Almost on cue, Rena pushes open the door, sees Eric, and slams into him. The two of them lurch toward me. And soon we are this blob of happiness. Limbs and bodies and hugs and smiles. I seriously missed my brother. I've definitely missed this. The three of us together here in the living room, threatening to knock over glass vases and picture frames. Mom approaches, arms outstretched, and we let her be part of the hug.

When we break apart, Mom says, "Dinner's in half an hour."

"We'll be late for the game."

Dad enters from the hallway off the garage. "Dinner is non-negotiable," he says to all of us, but catches my eye to make sure I've got the not-so-subtle double meaning. It's clearly a crack on our recent battles.

Then he smiles, and all of this feels so perfect.

. . .

"Hurry up, Eric," Rena calls over her shoulder after dinner, "we've got just enough time to make you Olaf and convince Jenna to go as Anna."

"Olaf? Hell no. I've got my own costume. Besides, shouldn't you be Anna, you know, the younger sister?"

"It's role playing, Eric. I can be the eldest for once."

"She's been trying to usurp you for years," Eric tells me in a conspiratorial tone.

"I don't mind. As long as she takes my place when it comes time for the hospital stays."

Rena's smile stretches. "Least I can do, big sister. We'll use some kind of magic or something to Freaky Friday that shit."

Mom shakes her head, but we can tell she's into all of this.

As Rena dresses me up, I sit and think about what's coming next. The hockey game with my favorite people. I'm excited and also nervous. I want Julian to do well. I want the team to win. I want so many things right now, and it feels so good.

Ready in ten minutes. Ben texts.

I send him a smiley emoji.

Rena paints my lips. "This color is called Lolita," she says breathily. "It's perfect for you."

"You mean for Anna?"

She plops a wig on my head. Then a ski hat with those fuzzy balls on the end. "Of course."

. . .

Ben's arrived, and we're ready to head to the game, but before I go anywhere, I've got to do an assessment.

Weather? Rainy and cold. That means extra layers, like everyone else, but it also means Eric has to start the car and warm it up for me. My body doesn't stay warm once it gets cold, and I have a real risk of respiratory infections. So that also means a blanket for me in the car and one for during the hockey game.

Next assessment? Mobility aids. It's going to be a long walk from the parking lot, unless we use my handicapped placard for the car.

"I'll drop the girls and park," Eric says.

Dad shakes his head. "They probably won't let you do that. Take this. Just in case." He hands over the placard, and Eric takes it.

Mom points to my walker and my electric scooter, waiting in the living room. "Which do you think for tonight?"

"Um…neither?" I counter.

"One or the other," Dad says. I can tell by his stance this is also nonnegotiable.

"Which is easier?" I ask Eric.

He fiddles with his keys. "Whichever one you want. We will make it work, no problem. I just ask that we make the decision and get going."

And here we are. Me facing down my beast, in the form of mobility aids. Which would be easiest to use? The scooter, definitely. But the walker would make it easier to get into the seats in the stands.

"We can bring your crutches for when we get inside," Rena offers, clearly reading my mind and my mood.

I think of all the accessibility issues with going to a game at Skate Zone. Over the years, with me attending Eric's games, the facility has improved its accessibility. Some issues were fixed thanks to my father's insistence and my uncle's legal intervention, plus a grant from an anonymous donor to put in ramps in a few different places. Still, it's a bear to make it work with a crowd and the frenzy. I can picture me tripping in my walker. That would be worse than using my scooter.

"Okay. Scooter."

Mom smiles, clearly glad I'm being reasonable. "All charged and ready to go."

As we all load into the car and start the drive to Skate Zone, I think about what this would be like if I was Jennifer—the girl who can race to the car in the cold and shiver as she waits for it to warm up. I'd take my gloves off and blow on my hands. The cold would feel good to me, make me feel alive. I'd look at my phone and see my boyfriend's texts to me. I'd wear the scarf he gave me for my birthday—delicate, baby-blue faux cashmere because he knows I'm cruelty-free when it comes to my food and my clothes. I'd wear it as our special signal—a reminder of how soft his arms are around me and how we'd celebrate his victory, just the two of us, in his comfy bed.

"Jenna?" Eric calls. "Jenna?"

The scene fades, and I stop being Jennifer and become the girl in the van with Panic! playing in the background. "Death of a Bachelor," to be precise.

"Yeah?"

"I asked if you were warm enough."

"I'm fine. Just thinking about the game."

"I'll bet," Ben adds. If I could reach him, I'd smack him silent. "As we all are."

Rena giggles. "You two are so weird."

Eric inspects me like people in my family always do—for signs of impending seizures and the like. I stick my tongue out, to which he says, "Real mature," but he moves the car forward. We've reached the superlong line to get into the parking lot.

Mr. Burrows, one of the hockey dads, is collecting tickets, wearing a fanny pack around his middle to store the $5 he gets from every driver who wants to park. We are considered the home team this time, so our team gets to keep the purse. These are all well-established traditions.

Eric puts the window down and reaches for his wallet, which is stuck in his Viking belt. The fact that he had packed a full Viking costume is not lost on me.

"Well look who it is. I might have heard you were coming." Mr. Burrow fist-bumps Eric, which makes Rena and I exchange amused looks. Eric may have graduated, but he will always be the champion. "How's college treating you?"

"Can't complain," Eric answers.

Mr. Burrow leans against our door, despite the long line of cars snaked into the street. "We're going to destroy them tonight," he says, smiling widely. Then he notices Eric's hand, waves away Eric's five-dollar bill. "No, no, put that away. No charge for you. Best scorer in three counties."

"Thanks, sir. I heard Matthew's having a hell of a season."

"Doesn't hurt that Daniel's the best goalie in the state."

"Never does."

Mr. Burrows steps back and waves us forward. "Glad you're here for the big game, Eric. Wouldn't be the same without you. Try up front, they might have saved a spot for you."

When we get to the first row of the parking lot, there's a cone in the center of the remaining parking space with one of Eric's old jerseys attached to it. "I'm guessing this is for us?" he says.

Rena throws her hands in the air. "Huzzah."

The sheer number of people already on the sidewalk reminds me of the performing arts theater where we saw *Wicked* for my birthday last year. Rena had wanted to see it forever, and Ben got me hooked on the idea. Dad finally took off work one Saturday and took us. I wanted to go into the city. I loved how New York was always filled with people walking in a big crowd, like everyone was moving toward something exciting. I loved how you could lose yourself in the mob and become a totally different person. But NYC is never easy with all of my mobility devices, so we went to a performing arts center in Hartford.

Mom used the opportunity to talk to me about that operation the doctors wanted to do. The baclofen pump. How much better I could be if only I let them slice me open and fix my broken parts with magic or that superglue stuff they use on cuts now. The thing is she bought the entire deal. Why shouldn't she? She wasn't the one who'd be ripped open and have that mess stitched inside of her.

Now driving through the crowd in my scooter, I wonder about the baclofen pump and if it could make my life better. And if so, wouldn't I be stupid not to try?

We get to the front of the rink, and Mrs. Jacobs, one of the senior boys' mothers, is taking tickets. Her face lights up as we wind our way forward. She wraps her arms around Eric. "So good to see you. Ian said to go straight in."

"Thanks, Mrs. Jacobs."

Eric leans on the handlebars of my scooter. "Pays to know people."

The hockey rink is super loud already. Our school is dressed up in *Frozen* costumes, and it's really funny to see the difference in the stands. Danbury's fans are dressed only in their boring blue and white garb. Ben points to a bunch of kids in his marketing classes standing at center ice but in the nosebleed section. They are all holding signs and blowing those cheapo horns you get at a party store. They are collecting donations from the crowd as they do. "I'm going to manage the peons. You mind?"

"No, go ahead," I tell him.

Eric points, and I park the scooter under a railing beneath the bleachers. I'm feeling slightly numb from the cold and my legs are pretty stiff from an entire day of, you know, existing. Also my hip is starting to complain. Eric puts his arm around me and holds up one side and Rena does the same on the other. Together they help me walk up the stairs and then down the other ones to the bench. In the background are the sounds of the players warming up—the swoosh of skates against the ice, the clacking sound of sticks hitting the puck, the boards vibrating. All of these things feel like my childhood, watching Eric play…and also Julian. I'm in heaven, and I mostly forget about the pain.

Julian gives me a sweet smile when I get to the bench, but then directs his attention to the opposing team. Eric hands me a blanket to put on my lap. Julian sees Eric, and man, do his eyes light up. The two of them do the bro-hug thing.

"Glad to have you back, man," Eric tells Julian.

He's got no idea.

The coach calls for the players. They crowd around him. Eric sits next to me. The game's about to start, and the feeling around me is electric.

Julian's got the first shift. I watch breathlessly as they drop the puck, and he chases after it. Chip wins the face-off. Julian skates parallel to him as they race to the opposing goal. Our fans are on their feet. Chip passes the puck to Julian. He shoots, and Danbury's goalie catches it in his big glove.

"Damn." Rena grabs my hand. "So close."

One of our defenders steals the puck and passes it back to Chip. Chip handles it, moving past Danbury's players.

Eric yells, "Center, center, center!"

A Danbury defender, huge guy, checks Chip into the boards and the puck flies center. Julian fights for possession, slamming his body against a crowd of Danbury players. There's a tight circle, and sticks fly. I hold my breath. Somehow Julian emerges, puck dancing in front of his stick. Rena squeezes my hand. The air changes around us, like everyone knows. Julian's got a breakaway. He handles the puck all the way down in the front of the goal. He winds his stick back, and it's like time stops and everything freezes. I watch Julian, stick raised, then sloping downward and back up, the puck whizzes past the goalie, over his right shoulder. Score!

Eric screams, "Yes! Yes! Yes!"

Our stands go wild. Rena and I jump around.

I feel the stands behind me thunder as our fans stomp and scream, and it's a slippery feeling. Slippery but exciting. Julian skates back to the bench. Sits with a thump. He's breathing hard and grabs his water. Chip pats him on the back. So does the coach.

Julian leans forward and watches until it's his line's time to get back on the ice.

The team is fired up, and so is Eric. He alternates between jumping on the bench and climbing the stands to help Ben and his friends lead the cheers. Rena stays sitting next to me, which is sort of unlike my social butterfly little sister, but I can't say I mind.

Three guys sit down on the bench next to us, leaving no more room for Julian when his line comes off the ice. He stands and scans the crowd. Looking for *her*, I guess. I don't bother to get jealous this time. Real me has spent all evening with the boy. It's Elsa's turn now.

When it's time to go, I'm weary and sore. A night in the bleachers after a full day at school makes my muscles scream, and even with the blanket, I am cold. Every freaking part of my body hurts, as if *I* was just on the ice playing and getting beaten up. So all I'm thinking is that I want to go home and go to bed.

But the hockey players are still celebrating, and that means Eric's not going anywhere. They run into the box, jump on him, he follows them out to the ice, even without skates.

"Idiot," Rena says, but she says it like she's envious. Who wouldn't want to be celebrating with our players? Turns out everyone would, which is why the stands on our side are emptying, people slipping and sliding all over the ice. I'm dizzy watching them, so cold it hurts, but also so wanting to be part of it.

"You can go," I tell Rena. If I was her, I would want to be where the action is.

"Are you kidding? I'd be taking my life in my hands. Those people are nuts." She leans against me, and her warmth feels so good.

But then Chip comes back into the box and grabs Rena by the hand and pulls her until she squeals and goes along.

I sit here watching all of this beautiful chaos. I don't want to be part of it, exactly, but I'm still sad I'm missing out. It reminds me that I'm separate from them. I pull the blanket around myself, bury my face in it, covering my nose. If my nose is warm, the rest of me is, too.

The intercom springs to life. "Everybody off the ice."

There's the sounds of skates zooming in then stopping, and a familiar voice says, "We did it, Jenna. We did it!"

I lift my head from the blanket and come face-to-face with Julian. His eyes are shining, and his smile is stretched wide. "I'm so glad you were here."

"Me too. You were amazing. Three goals!"

He nods. Happy. So alive. And so, so close to me. In that single moment, I feel like what Julian and I have now is enough. And I am as happy as I've ever been. Until I see him reach into his pocket and check his cell.

No matter how close I feel to him, Julian is elsewhere, with a version of myself that I'll never be.

. . .

8:06 P.M.

Did you see me?

Were you there?

Tell me you saw.

Yes!

You were amazing!

I'm so glad I'm back here.

Me too.

So now, that I am a conquering hero,
haven't I earned something special?

Like what???

Tell me something about you that will
help me figure out who you are.

Oh. Smiley face. We go
to the same school.

Cool. That narrows it down
to like 2,499 people.

I'm a girl.

Ok 1,754.

See? You're getting warmer.

Slightly annoyed emoji.

Crying while laughing emoji.

I'll figure it out one day. Just you wait.

Thumbs-up emoji.

Smiley face. Tonight nothing
can get me down. Not even not
knowing the identity of the girl who
inspired me to score three times!

I inspired you to do that?

It was for you.

Heart emoji.

Same.

SIXTEEN

I rest my head against the car window during the drive home. The heat is pouring out of the vent straight onto me, and I'm starting to feel less frozen. The sounds of the fans roaring still fills my head, but a small sadness I can't really name plants itself in my heart. In some weird way, I feel like Julian's cheating on one of me. With me.

When we get inside, Mom wraps me up, tight. "I left some pills on your dresser. Thought you might need something."

I nod.

Dad helps me to my room. "Maybe you should take tomorrow off from school? Let the other kids catch up." His favorite *Chitty Chitty Bang Bang* quote.

I'm too tired to argue. "Maybe."

I don't even get changed, just hit the toilet, then throw myself into bed. I reach over and take the Advil Mom's left for me, ignoring the prescription pain pill and muscle relaxer. My head feels weighed down and like it's filled with cotton. The room feels farther and farther away, and soon I'm falling asleep, floating and flying free.

And then there's a weird knocking trying to pull me back to earth.

"Jenna. Jenna."

It's not my Jennifer voice. It's familiar, but my head soup doesn't process it.

"Jenna. Wake up."

And then someone shakes my shoulders.

"Jenna," Rena says.

And I bolt awake. "What? Are you okay?"

She laughs. "Shh." She moves over to my window and opens it.

My brow furrows. "What's going on?"

Rena whirls and puts her fingers over her lips. "Shh," she says again.

My eyes work hard to adjust to the darkness, to make sense of the shapes around me. The night-light I always have on throws enough light that I can see Rena helping someone into my room. I grab my covers and pull them up, then remember I'm still fully dressed.

"Hey, Jenna," Chip says. I want to die. What do I look like? Was I snoring? Is there sleep drool all over me?

Rena comes back to me. I grab her hands. "What the hell is going on?" I whisper.

"Wait one second. And quiet down, Mom and Dad are just on the other side of the house."

"What are we doing?"

Rena grins conspiratorially. "Sibling field trip!"

"Where's our other sibling then?"

"In command central—so his bedroom, obviously," she says, as if that's a ridiculous question.

"Of course."

She turns to Chip. "You better wait outside."

"Gotcha. See ya in a few, Jenna," he says, climbing back out the window.

I salute him.

"What the hell was that?" I whisper as Rena helps me out of bed.

"Shh. It's cool. How are you feeling?"

"Tired. Sore. Fabulous." I do jazz hands to help *sell the sizzle*, as Ben always says.

"Come on, it'll be totally worth it." She drags me toward the bathroom, where I brush my teeth while she brushes my hair and pulls it up in a ponytail. She walks me back to my bed and hands me a sweatshirt.

"Hands up," she says, prompting, and on goes my sweatshirt. "Hold on. We probably need these." Rena puts my braces on my legs, the ones I only wear when I'm horseback riding or going on the stationary bike.

"Where are we going? And why do I need braces?"

"Trust me, you're going to love it."

Then, she helps me put on my short UGGs and hoists me to my feet. Next comes my short coat and hat and scarf, leaving me to wonder when these plans were made.

Soft steps creep closer to my door. Rena and I huddle in my room and wait for Eric's telltale knock. Rap tap rap. Rap tap rap.

Rena opens the door. Waves him in.

"You ready?" he asks.

"Coast clear?" Rena asks.

"They went to bed an hour ago. The television kicked off ten minutes ago. We are a go." He opens my window again and speaks to whoever has assembled there.

Eric climbs out first, avoiding the big shrub there. "Your turn,

Jenna," he says, his arms open wide to help me out. His body is hold-ing the shrub back, so I've got a pretty clear shot.

Good thing my bedroom's on the ground floor. The cold air shocks the breath out of me. My eyes tear. I cough.

"You okay?" he asks.

"I think so." My arms reach for him, and Rena helps feed me out the window, but my pants get caught on the sill.

"Wait," Rena says. "She's stuck."

For some reason, this makes Eric and me laugh hysterically. Which makes Rena go "Shhh! You'll wake them!"

Eric drags me away from the opening so Rena can climb out, my elbow crutches in a bag strapped to her back. Without someone to help her, she ends up flat on the ground. Which makes her laugh even harder.

Chip lifts her up. "Sorry."

There seems to be a lot of Chip in Rena's life lately, and I'm not sure how I feel about that. Eric seems to pick up on it as well since he's staring.

"Everything cool?" a voice calls from the side of the house. I can't place it, but it sounds familiar. I know it's one of the other hockey players. And if other hockey players are here…

"Yeah. We're coming," Eric answers. "Hold on." He turns to close the window. I'm sure that any minute Mom and Dad are going to bust us if people don't stop talking.

Rena and Eric put their arms around me and help me walk on the uneven ground—a peril in the light, but super dangerous in the dark. I don't want to fall and ruin the entire mission, whatever it is.

As we round the corner, I see there are two cars parked out on the street. I pray they won't slam the doors and wake our parents. But then a bunch of hockey players jump out, and I see Julian, and I suddenly don't care about waking Mom and Dad. Mostly I just care about my breath and wish I'd paid more attention to my hair and my face and all the girly things.

"Hey, Jenna, want to skate around with us?" Julian asks. He looks lit up—he's happy about the game, and he's glad Elsa texted him. With a heart-stopping shock, I realize that Julian might actually be falling in love. With her. With *me*. The sky is clear and a million stars shine down on us. "It's perfect, isn't it, Jenna?"

Everything seems to hinge on my next comment. Like the trees are standing by, the moon listens in, and the night birds stop making noise. It's like this one moment belongs to us. I know I should be more careful, but it's hard to keep my mind straight when it feels like the world is conspiring to give me everything I want.

"It's magical," I say. "Definitely."

Julian smiles with me, and then gets this weird look on his face like he's trying to remember something. I realize that I may have tipped my hand with that magical comment.

Rena steps between me and Julian. "The infamous skate-around, and we are crashing it."

The skate-around is a big secret to nonhockey players and most adults. The owner of the skating rink allows it—most of the hockey players work there, so he's close with them. It happens at different times during the year so no one can track it, try to crash it, or shut it down. Nobody brings dates or girls of any kind to the skate-around. We are breaking new ground right here. Eric made this happen.

Julian beams. "And I get to share it with my favorite family."

I want to throw up a little bit. *That's* how the boy feels about me. Like I'm just part of his favorite family.

I stumble a little bit on my way to Ian's van, but Rena helps me. There's a little fighting for seats, but Eric says, "Jenna gets the middle row, captain. No arguments." And no one does.

That's the easiest seat to get into. I wait for Julian to join us, but he jumps in the car behind us.

Rena sits next to me, the boys in the back. Rena grabs my hand and leans in. "This is pretty cool, huh?"

"Pretty cool," I agree.

Dylan, the guy driving, doesn't turn on the headlights until we are halfway down our street. I rub my hands together and blow on them. My nose is freezing again. So I tuck it into my coat.

Eric throws a worried glance my way and then cranks up the heat. "You feel that, kiddo?"

"Yeah. I'm good."

Rena unhooks her seat belt and moves next to me. "Scoot."

I do and she sits next to me, squished onto my seat.

"Hey," Eric says. "You need to get back in your own seat, Rena."

"It's like three miles. Chill." She wraps her arm around me and rubs my arms until I start to warm up, even though I'm also sort of worried the entire time about her not being in her seat belt. That's how my family rolls. Not happy unless we're worrying our heads off.

When we get to the rink, I relax a little. The guys from the back seat cruise past us to get out. They don't exactly bump into us, but they're still kind of awkward and brutish and I'm grateful I wasn't standing up when they did it.

"Take it easy, you hoodlums," Eric yells.

Rena helps me out of the car, and I hobble forward, strap on my crutches, then move more surely.

The other car pulls up behind us, and those guys race to the front door of the rink, waiting for Ian to get there with the keys and the security code. Once inside, Eric flicks on the lights and looks around. "Love this place."

He hands Rena my skates—I need special ones, of course—while he ducks behind the desk to pull out the right ones for her. Rena and I get ours on, and Eric bends down to tighten my laces and hers. "You gotta get this right or it won't work," he says.

The guys are already on the ice. It takes my breath away to watch them.

"You coming?" Rena asks.

"You go ahead."

I lean against the wall. Julian skates by, then turns around and stops in front of me, shaving ice as he does. There's something sexy about the way he moves, creating an ice pile out of nothing, and I realize I am officially lovesick. I mean, who thinks some shaved ice on an ice rink is romantic? I've got it bad.

"You ready?" Eric stops next to him, but says it to me.

I want to go out there, but my body is so tired. "I don't know..."

"Come on, Jenna, we need everyone on the ice," Julian says in an almost flirty way.

Someone jumps in the booth and flips on the music and some disco lights. It's a party now.

With Eric on one side and Julian on the other, I am pretty stable on my feet. We skate around the rink twice. Then there's a big screech and some laughter, and I see Rena on the floor. Eric breaks away to help her, leaving me with Julian.

"Love Shack" comes on. Julian laughs, but I start to stumble, so he glides in front of me, turns around, and starts skating backward as easily as he was skating forward. He slips across the ice, holding me up like we are dancing. "Beats English, huh?"

I laugh. "Yeah." I wish Ben could see this. Also, what would it be like to actually dance with Julian with a silky dress on, my body pressed against his?

"Can you keep a secret?" Julian asks.

"Sure." I look down, try to keep my feet from crossing over.

"I'm not going to school tomorrow. Skip day for hockey players."

The feeling of him trusting me is perfection. My heart wraps itself around that thought. He is confiding in me. Me, not Elsa.

I almost tell him I'm going to be out too, because after tonight I am for sure going to need a few days to recuperate. It feels like something friends should tell each other. The words present themselves to me, dance on the edge of my tongue, ready to be dispatched at my command. Then I stop myself. He doesn't want to hear about my drama. So I ask, "What do you guys do on skip day?"

His eyes twinkle as he meets my gaze. "I'll never tell." I laugh, and we keep skating.

"You're a pretty good skater, Jenna. Must be in your blood."

"Yeah, right."

"I mean it. You want to go a little faster?"

Of course I don't. I can barely keep my legs under me as it is. But he says it with that same little-boy fierceness, with the look that he wore when he said he wanted to marry me on the playground. It's hard to say no to that face.

Up close like this, his jaw looks so strong that I want to trace the line of it, feel the tension there. I analyze every single thing he does. I wonder if he ever thinks of me the same way.

Chip and David skate by us really fast, then circle back and come straight at us, stopping just short, throwing shaved ice everywhere.

"Hey, take it easy. Idiots." Julian wipes a piece of frost from my face. "It's fine. We can go slow."

"I just…"

"You want to go back?"

I shake my head, a vigorous no. I don't want this perfect moment to end. "Do you want to go skate with the guys? I mean, you don't have to keep skating with me."

"I skate with the guys all the time."

I blush. "Um, maybe we could go a little faster."

"You're sure?"

"Uh huh."

His arms reach around me, his hands clasped behind my back. My hands go on top of his arms. His body is so different from when we were kids. He's all muscles and bulk now. A firm place to land. His face is close to mine, but I've still got my coat as a layer. He's just in his jersey. So when he stops us, my body bumps into his.

"Sorry," I say.

"No worries," Julian smiles, but his eyes stare into mine, all hazel with earthy brown flecks—the kind that feels most at home on the ice or in the woods.

Eric skates by us, pulling Rena behind him. "No slow dancing, Van Beck. Not with my sister."

Julian chuckles then starts us skating again, medium fast.

"It's okay. I trust you," I say. "We can go faster."

"You're sure?" he asks.

I can scarcely breathe, but I say, "Yes."

"Okay. Hold on tight." He reaches down to straighten my legs like he's seen Eric do. His hands, even through my many layers, light a fire in me. "Ready?"

"Yeah."

I close my eyes, and Julian pulls us faster and faster.

I'm loving it, and I hear myself laugh. I feel myself fall forward and Julian catches me, straightens my legs, and pulls me right up against him. Right up against. And we are flying and the lights are blinking and I'm so happy. So completely happy. I want him to twirl me like in one of those dorky musicals that Rena and her friends love. I want him to do that. I want him to do more. And then it happens.

My hamstring spasms.

My body jerks.

I pull him down with me.

Eric screams, "Jenna!"

I fall forever, in slow motion. Julian tries to adjust us, tries to lift us, but I go into a full-blown hands-over-head extension pattern, and I'm like a rubber band that's been pulled taut and then released, and there's no amount of force that can stop that. Julian lands on top of me. Hard. His body on top of mine. My leg scissors behind me.

And I hear a snap.

SEVENTEEN

R ed and white lights flash outside, and there's the sound of
people walking on the ice. A gurney appears, pushing through
the crowd around me. Eric. Rena. Julian. The pain is as real as a
person sitting in front of me. More real than I am. The ice is cold
under me, and my body is drifting, pulling me down and into the
ocean. I'm swimming, and Dad is holding me above the waves.

That Jennifer voice finds me and whispers, "Stay up here with
me. The pain doesn't need you." I believe that voice. I throw myself
into that voice. "We are in the library studying," Jennifer says. "In
college. There are a group of cute guys at a table across the room." As
she talks, I can feel myself leaving my body, feel the wooden library
chair underneath me.

The sound of a scissor. Cutting. They are cutting my sleeve
and I should care about that, only I really don't. A blood pressure
cuff snaps around my arm and I don't feel it. I don't feel much of
anything. Numbers are called out. A needle goes in my arm. A
person I don't know talks to me like I should know them. Like I
should care. "Come on, Jenna, stay with us, sweetheart."

Rena scoots past the medical personnel somehow and wedges
herself into the tiniest spot, which is one of Rena's many gifts.
She can make herself fit. She holds my head, her tiny icy hands

around my head, and puts her face by mine. "I'm sorry, Jenna. I'm so sorry."

I want to talk to my sister. I want to tell how incredible it was to dance with Julian, even for just a minute. How it felt to press my body against his. To twirl. I was moving free and easy, just like that voice promised. But if I want to speak to my sister, I've got to leave Jennifer and my place in the library. I'd have to float down into the mess of my body on the ice right now, lying there, splayed like a bug that went splat on a windshield.

Hands go under me and I'm lifted. Lowered. Placed. Lifted again. Wheeled. We go over a bump. My body jumps. I hear myself cry out, the burst of air from my lungs more a result of the abrupt jostling than my desire to scream.

"Hey, take it easy with her." Eric's voice is laced with tears and anger. It's a weird kind of voice from my brother, and for a second that makes me shift back into my body. What a stupid idea. As soon as I am able, I rise into the mental library again.

My body bumps up and down again, this time with hands on me, holding me still. I am the center of this drama, but I'm so removed from it. I'm loaded into the back of an ambulance. It speeds up, and I close my eyes harder. So hard that I am not sure I'll ever be able to open them again. I don't. Not for days and weeks and months and years, because sleeping makes me not feel the pain.

◦ ◦ ◦

Before I open my eyes, the sound of a monitor greets me.

"I think she's waking up." Mom.

I blink, trying to be the dutiful daughter, trying to make up for what went down last night. Last night, right? "Hey," I manage.

Mom's face is tired and worn, but her eyes shine when I speak, and her lips turn upward. "Hey, sweetie, how are you feeling?"

"Thirsty." Just saying that word makes my mouth go dry. "I'm thirsty." It's an easy feeling to figure out, and gives Mom something to do while I try to piece together everything that happened.

"Let's raise her a little," Dad says as he mans the control that lifts the head of my bed.

Mom's got a straw sticking out of a cup and aims it at my face. I grab it before it can stab me or try to shove its way into my lips. I hold it still and take a drink. Choke. Mom pats me on the back while Dad shifts me forward.

They're making me feel like a porcelain doll, and not in a good way. More in a "OHMYGOD, I'm such a freak" kind of way. I feel like I'm going to choke again, this time on my parents' good intentions. It's like they are sucking the air out of the room. I hold my hands up. "Please," I say. "I can't breathe."

"You can't what?" Mom sounds panicked.

Dad laughs. Pulls on Mom's shoulders. "She needs room. Give her some space." The truth is, Mom handled all of our daily issues, but Dad was the one who took care of us when we were really sick or hurt. The time Eric broke his leg, the time Rena had pneumonia. Dad had a way of understanding what we needed and calming us down, just by being there. I'm busy waxing nostalgic when I notice the trapeze over the bed. And my leg stuck in it.

"No," I say.

Before anyone can respond, the door opens, and a woman dressed in scrubs walks in. Her hair is dark brown with grays layered through, and she's got it in a high ponytail. "Hello, Jenna," she says. "I'm Dr. Lukowski."

"What happened?" I ask. "I mean, obviously I broke my leg and all, and I remember it happening, but then…"

"You were pretty out of it when they got you here," Mom says.

"Pain will do that." The doctor stops to take my pulse. "You have a broken tibia. No major complications, I'm happy to say. Just your garden-variety leg break."

"Did I have surgery?"

"No. It was pretty simple. We did a ton of X-rays, and we put you in a cast, obviously, which you'll stay in for six to eight weeks, depending on how your body heals."

"How long have I been out?"

"Today is Friday. You got here last night. Not so bad. One full day with drug-induced sleep. I'm afraid you'll be enjoying our lovely accommodations for a few days, at least. Luckily there are a ton of movies at your disposal." She hands me a remote. "Try to relax and enjoy a few days off."

"When can I go back to school?"

"Next week. Why? You have a big project?"

I think of Elsa. And Julian. And the Hockey Homecoming dance. That's just weeks away, after the second game with Danbury.

It's not like I thought I'd out myself to Julian at that dance. Or that if I did, Julian would be happy and embrace me and we'd be a thing. It's not that I think that. I don't. I swear. But…if I'm holed up and in a cast, then there's no possible way that could happen. And that sucks.

"Whatever the project is, it'll have to wait a bit," Dr. Lukowski says.

There's a knock on the door, and then Eric and Rena come in, both of them quiet, eyes on the floor. Rena pushes her way past the doctor and grabs my hand. "Oh my God, Jenna, I'm so glad you're okay."

Her eyes are shiny and wet and I say, "I'm fine. Don't."

But it's too late, she's crying and Eric is also. "Sorry, sis," his eyes are hooded. "I…it was…"

"We'll talk about this later, Eric," Mom snaps.

"It's going to be a dark one," I say.

"What?" Mom demands.

"Your mom-ologue. I'm thinking dark. Like *Carrie*-the-musical dark," I say, knowing the reference will simultaneously make Mom irritated and Rena happy. Two birds, one stone sort of thing.

"Or *Repo!* dark!" Eric adds. *Repo!* is the musical Mom hates the most.

Dad is a fan, which makes him pump his fist. "Yes!"

"David, don't start…"

"*Sweeney Todd* dark," Eric adds, which makes Rena squeal like a little girl.

The doctor smiles and says, "I'll see you in the morning. No dancing tonight."

Such a funny exit line, but my smirk disappears.

"Jenna?"

"Yeah. I'm fine, Mom. I mean, I'm okay, considering."

"Okay."

I half expect her to start on her usual deal that this is a good thing. A perspective-building thing. Mom loves some perspective building. But she doesn't. She cups my chin in her hands and smiles a very Mom-like smile at me. "You rest now. Anything I can bring you?"

"My iPad. My computer." I think of Julian. "My phone!"

Eric slides a messenger bag toward me, and I grab for it, and he looks puzzled. "You seem pretty excited about your electronics all of a sudden."

"Yeah. Don't want to get behind in classes."

This time Dad scoffs. Mom smacks him. Rena laughs. "What?"

Mom grabs Dad's arm. "Nothing, sweetie, we just need to get home and let you rest. The nurse will be in soon with more pain meds. Take them, okay?"

Eric kisses me on the forehead. Dad on my cheek. Rena leans down and hugs me. "You scared the shit out of me."

I grab her shoulders, make her stay close. "I'm sorry. But, Rena did I…did anyone see me…"

"No. Nobody knows anything. I mean if you even… It wasn't like that," she whispers.

Relief and embarrassment compete for equal attention inside me.

"You went down. We all jumped up. You sort of passed out. But nothing else, I swear. We called the ambulance, and Julian and I waited with you while we let them in."

"Was I talking?"

"No. You were just lying there, being brave. So it was all fine. Promise." Rena moves a piece of my hair behind my ear, like I used to do for her when she was little and climbed in my bed and asked me to read her a fairy tale.

"Thanks."

Mom leans in to kiss me, and as soon as she does, a nurse pushes open the door. Not my usual nurse, Gary, but a stranger with a needle full of pain meds for my IV. And a sour look on her face. Perfect. "Best let her rest," she tells Mom.

"We're just leaving," Mom answers, and pushes the rest of my family toward the door.

Eric is the last to go. "Wait," I call.

He stops, his foot in midair. He keeps it dangling there for laughs.

My nurse is not amused. "Just for a minute. I need to grab a thermometer anyway. When I get back, you all go," she says, pushing back out through the door.

I have a hard time holding in my laughter until the door closes, and Eric lets his out at the exact moment I release mine.

He points toward the door. "She seems nice."

"I just wanted to thank you and Rena. Last night was magic."

"Until you broke your leg."

"I mean it. It was perfect, the best."

"Good because Mom is so pissed about the sneaking-out thing. Man, you'd think she wanted you to actually break your neck, the number of times she said you could've."

"Tell her I'm sorry to disappoint. When do you go to school?" I ask.

"Sunday. But the semester is almost over. So."

Sadness seeps in. I've messed up my weekend with my brother. Awesome.

"Okay. Going to sleep now." I close my eyes, even though I have no intention of sleeping. I need to check my phone. I need to speak to Julian. But not as me. Obviously.

His texts are so sad.

Thursday

10:07 P.M.

Are you there? I'm sort of freaking out.

10:15 P.M.

I did something terrible. Hurt
someone. Didn't mean to. But.

10:22 P.M.

I wish you were here so I
could talk to you.

Friday

9:43 A.M.

Maybe you've heard. And hate me.

11:05 A.M.

Hey. Sorry. I dropped my cell in a
puddle and it stopped working. Just
got a new phone. What's going on?

Hey. I thought maybe you were over me.

No. Of course not. What happened?

It was awful.

What?

I was skating with a girl and she
fell and broke her leg. She's in
the hospital now. Bc of me.

I'm sure it wasn't your fault.

It was. I talked her into skating and
now she's hurt. What can I do?

Just be sweet. I'm sure she
doesn't blame you anyway.

Should I go see her?

Not in the hospital. No one wants
to be seen in the hospital. No girl
anyway. Wait till she gets home.

She doesn't hate me, right?

Not a chance.

I hope so. Better go to sleep. Gnite, Elsa.

Gnite, Julian.

EIGHTEEN

It's Saturday morning, and I've been up since six. So fun. It's now nine o'clock. My phone buzzes, and I grab for it, hoping for messages from Julian, but instead I get birthday messages from Eric, Rena, and Uncle Steve. All with balloons flying around and that confetti thing the phone does. I'm busy feeling sorry for myself, because no text from Julian, but it's not like he knows that I'm his secret texter. I'm not even sure he knows it's my birthday, anyway.

We are on our way. From Eric.

Before I can message him back, my door bursts inward and my family crowds in. Not just Mom, Dad, Eric, Rena, and Uncle Steve, but also Mom's sister, Aunt Betty, and Uncle Bobby and my little cousins, Kevin and Whitney. Mom carries a big cake plate with what is no doubt my chocolate torte cake, the one Uncle Steve and I love.

Kevin and Whitney bounce on my bed, which makes me groan and Eric grabs them by the waists and lifts them off. "Settle down, you two, or no cake."

Rena opens her arms for Eric to place them in her lap. She starts whispering things in their ears that make them laugh and cry at the same time. I know my family is filled with dorks, and I realize we are not normal, that we are close and annoying and all too much, but I wouldn't trade us. Not for the world.

Mom pulls the tray table in front of me, and Dad helps me shift up in the bed, plumping the pillows behind me. Then, with a big flourish, Mom uncovers the cake and puts two candles in: a one and a six. She takes a lighter out of her purse.

Dad says, "You can't have candles in the hospital, it's dangerous."

She waves him off and lights each candle. Just as the singing is about to start, there's a knock on the door.

"Ruh roh," Eric says. "We're caught!"

The door opens. I don't look. I just keep staring at the light, until I hear, "Hey, man."

And then Rena says, "Julian! How nice."

My eyes shoot to the door as I wonder what kind of fresh hell this is, having him here, seeing me like this. What will Mom and Dad say? They can't be too happy with the boy.

Julian's carrying one of those flower arrangements with a get-well balloon floating above it. "I didn't mean to interrupt..."

Mom steps forward. "How nice."

I'm praying for him to stay across the room. Far from me and my hospital funk. I pull my covers up over my chest. It's then I remember I'm not wearing a bra. I'm not even wearing proper clothes, just a horrible hospital nightgown.

"Hey," Julian says with a wave. "I just wanted to bring... Oh, it's your birthday. I used to know that," he says, making this situation even more awkward, if that's possible. "Anyway, I won't stay. I just wanted to say I'm so sorry about—"

"Is that your boyfriend?" Whitney asks, making everyone laugh. She pouts. "Why is everyone laughing at me?"

Julian sidesteps the question and my little cousin and puts the flowers on the dresser across from my bed. He shoots me a look that's supposed to mean *little kids are ridiculous*. I return it. "How are you feeling?"

"Let's let Jenna have a minute with her friend while we go find cups," Mom says, ushering the crew out into the hall. "I forgot to pack those."

Kevin reaches into the bag Aunt Betty brought and says, "Mom has some right—"

"She doesn't have the right ones," Rena adds, rolling her eyes at me. "Come on, it'll be fun."

Everyone leaves except Dad, who stands next to my bed, arms crossed, as if he's daring Julian to try something. I couldn't be more mortified.

"Sir?" Julian extends his hand.

There's an uncomfortable silence. I want to hit Dad's arm, but I'm too busy holding my covers over myself.

Finally, he extends his hand. They shake. "Not too long. She needs her rest."

"Of course, Mr. Cohen."

The door shuts, and that's when Julian's eyes crawl from the floor to my face, which makes my hand fly there. It leaves my chest vulnerable, but dispatching my hand to the covers would make the entire situation even more uncomfortable.

"Hey," Julian says. "I feel really bad about the other night."

"It wasn't your fault," I say.

"I can't stop thinking about how it sounded when…" His face gets a little white.

I want to reach my hand out to him, but that seems too intimate. "It's okay," I say. "I'm okay. It wasn't your fault. It's just my stupid body."

His face gets red when I mention my body. And that makes me feel good in a weird way. "I was afraid you hated me." His eyes stay on mine. His voice gets shaky. "Please don't hate me."

"I could never hate you, Julian," I say.

"I just wanted to say I'm sorry. My friend told me that no girl wants—"

"You to see her in a hospital," I finish, then realize I'm a total idiot. "People say that all the time," I add, hoping to fix my major blunder.

His eyes narrow, and I try to read his expression. He might be suspicious. He might be figuring things out, or he might just be uncomfortable, but then there's a knock, and Mom pops her head in. "Okay to come back?"

And now I blush three shades of tomato because how embarrassing can she be?

Julian says, "I'm just leaving."

Mom says, "Stay for cake."

Julian looks to me.

"Sure," I say. "Stay."

He smiles and then Eric is back in the room and the two of them replay all the glory of the game. Rena corrals the kids. Mom slices the cake. I get the first piece, but no way am I going to eat chocolate cake in front of the boy.

After I've gotten all of my presents—a $50 iTunes card from Eric; a makeup set and cute little purse from Rena; a charm bracelet with books on it from Uncle Steve; and *Grimms' Fairy Tales*, a collection of Edgar Allan Poe's works, and a collection of Shakespeare from Aunt Betty and crew—the nurse comes in.

Mom offers her a piece of cake, and Dad hands me a little box. Rena helps me open it. It's a gold necklace with three charms: an oval with my name and birthday, a birthstone gem, and a Jewish star. I love it. Aunt Betty puts it around my neck, forcing me to shift forward so she can do the clasp.

The nurse gives me another dose of pain meds in my IV and they work so fast that soon I can only really think of one thing: sleep.

My eyes close.

I hear everyone pack up and leave. Mom kisses me on my forehead. "I love you, Jenna Cohen. You may be grown up, but you are still my little miracle."

. . .

Saturday

8:17 P.M.

This has been a hard week.

I know! How's your friend?

She's okay, I think. I'm not.

                                        I'm sorry.

I just can't stop thinking about it.

                        Think about Gatsby. You've
                            got a test coming up.

Hey, how did you know that?

                        There are always tests. Right?

True. True.

Gnite, Elsa.

                        Gnite, Julian. Sweet dreams.

I was hoping you'd say that.
Sweet dreams, you too.

NINETEEN

There are stories we tell ourselves to get through dark times. I'm no different. No matter what is going on in my life, I find consolation on the printed page. Stories prepare us for difficult times. Stories scare us away from dangerous choices. But most of all, stories distract us.

This morning, the stories I'm telling myself are distracting me from what's happening with my body. With my leg in a cast and me not being supercoordinated to begin with—and also having an extreme tendency toward muscular spasms, you know, because I have spastic CP—Mom's going to have to help me bathe. Hurrah.

Mom pulls out the Hoyer lift, and I can't help but groan.

"I'm sorry, Jenna, but we don't have a choice."

Rena used to dress my Hoyer lift with props from the drama department. Long, golden-haired wigs for the *Into the Woods* performance that won her Best Actor for our school at State. A sword from *Othello*. Eighties wedge heels underneath, as if it had feet. Fashion-forward feet, of course. We used to throw things at it as it stood waiting in my closet. We'd boo and hiss.

"It's the thing in the woods…" Rena would say. "The bad thing."

Mom hoists me onto the shower chair, and I try my best to cover myself up while Mom struggles to wash me without hitting my cast.

It's wrapped in a plastic bag for protection. I grab the washcloth and try to clean myself, but I'm off balance with the cast, and all I can think about is how this is all Dr. Jacoby's fault. Even though this moment of humiliation was really brought on by my foolishness.

In the book about my life, I decide, I'll definitely have to include this scene. It would be crucial for the low point. It would propel my story forward. You know, if this were the book, or even the movie version where some new kid actress would get her breakout role. And if Ben were there with me on the movie shoot, as the producer, he'd say, "Look at you, girl, changing lives." And we'd have the crew get us Pellegrino water with the bubbles stirred out, heavy ice, and a juicy twist of lime. Huzzah.

I stay silent as Rena stumbles into the bathroom, her hair a mess. "God, Mom, give Jenna a break. She's got skin under there. Or she used to."

"Very funny, Rena. If it weren't for your recent stunt—"

"God, Mom, people break legs," Rena retorts. "It does happen."

"That's true," I say. "See? Proof."

Mom just makes a face. This mom-ologue is going to be bad.

"I realize that, Rena. But answer me this: Do you think you are more likely or less likely to break a leg ice-skating when you are taking muscle relaxers and also happen to have cerebral palsy?" Mom's lips are pursed and her expression is sour.

"I didn't take my muscle relaxers, actually," I say. "Just to be clear."

"Yeah." Rena jumps in. "And we brought her skates. Julian was with her."

"I'm right here, Mom. If you want to be annoyed with anyone, be annoyed with me."

Mom looks me over. "Don't worry, I'm super annoyed with you as well. Turns out there's plenty to go around!"

She wraps me up then Hoyer lifts my ass onto the bed, throws my clothes on the bed, and leaves me to put on my bra and shirt. Then she retrieves huge-assed granny panties I've never seen before from my top drawer. Which irks me on so many levels.

"Don't make a face at me, young lady. These are the only kind that will go up over your cast easily."

I let her pull them up for me, and I cringe as she does.

"Of all the stupid things, deciding to climb out of the house in the middle of the night, for what? To go skate? For God's sakes. I thought you were smarter than that. I thought…" Here's the anger I knew would come. Finally. I try to leave my body a little bit. To think of a story that will lift me as she pulls a skirt on me, then puts one boot on my other foot.

"You could have broken your neck."

Ah. There it is. The "you could have broken your neck" part that Eric promised.

I breathe out. Breathe in. Breathe out. Breathe in. I try to imagine I'm flying, like I was when I was in the MRI tube. I try to feel the same things I felt that day. The breeze. The voice. The hand that brushed my hair back. Then stroked my cheek. The magic I'm always looking for. But there's nothing. Just me and the big mess I've made.

"Jenna, are you even listening to me?" Mom's tone is decidedly harsh until she realizes I've completely zoned out. "Jenna? Sweetie? Are you okay?"

"Yeah. Just a little dizzy." All of this being swung around is catching up to me.

"Maybe you should stay home?"

"I hate missing."

"Jenna?" Mom uses the soft *I-haven't-given-up-on-you* tone.

I just stare. It's like I'm exhausted from being showered. My body feels done. "I can't go to school," I say.

She nods. "Okay. Let's get you to bed."

I congratulate myself on dumbing down my expectations of myself and taking easier classes. It makes staying home easier, no doubt. But I let my mind drift over the essay I would have written for my AP Language midterm as Mom helps dress me and put me to bed. It would have been about the use of symbols in *The Scarlet Letter*. I would start off easy, talking about the letter A and how that symbol changes over the course of the novel. Then move to the meteor as a symbol, and finally, Pearl, herself, who is less of a child and more of a symbol of her mother's love.

I'm thinking about Mom and her love. How she's annoyed sometimes, downright furious at others, but how, no matter what I do or how I act, she still does love me.

. . .

I listen to the sounds of Rena getting ready and Mom rushing as I recover from my morning defeat. I hear Mom on the phone with

Dr. Rodriguez. She's got it on speaker, probably because she's busy getting my meds ready. And with Mom, speaker is pretty freaking loud. According to her, she's killed her hearing by listening to music with headphones turned up too high and now she can't hear.

"Yes. She's lethargic and kind of spaced…"

"Her body is telling her what she needs," Dr. Rodriguez responds. "Right now mostly she needs to rest and to heal."

Mom answers. "Yes. That makes sense."

So I guess I'm not dying. That's good news.

"I was hesitant to bring this up, but Jenna's rehabilitation needs may be more than what you can handle at home."

"What do you mean?"

My hearing goes into supersonic mode, but to no avail, because at this point Mom takes it off speaker.

I can still hear her responses, though. "I'm not sure about a rehab center. Isn't that kind of drastic?"

More of Dr. Rodriguez talking while I strain to read Mom's mood from a room away.

Then Mom. "I'll speak with her and her father, but I'm not sure it'll go over so well."

Dr. Rodriguez says something superintelligent and persuasive because then Mom says, "Well what would happen with her school?" and then the moment of understanding. "Oh. Okay. That might work."

And I think, hells to the no. There is no way on God's green earth I'll be going to a rehab center like our grandfather had to last year after his hip replacement. How could she make this decision without even talking to me? I text Uncle Steve.

We need to expedite our plans.

Why what's going on?

They are talking about sending
me away. To a rehab center.

We've got the paperwork completed
for medical emancipation.
I just have to file it.

Thanks.

I blow out a big breath. This is all too much. My body is aching. My muscles hurt, so of course I pretend for a second that I'm Jennifer. The one who isn't saddled with medical concerns or, God forbid, a trip to a rehab center. The one who is going off to college, having just graduated top of her grade after all her AP classes. I'd be so full of potential, bursting with possibilities. Maybe I'm taking the train out to school, so Julian drives me to the station. We park in the drop-off part of the parking lot. People are all around us and Julian looks so damned sad I can't even take it. He puts the car in park and then stares straight ahead. I put my hand on his. "It won't be that long." In my fantasy, even going to different colleges can't keep us apart.

We would sit there, me not wanting to leave, him not wanting me to go, but neither of us able to stop the ticking clock. If I don't leave soon, I'll be so tempted to chuck it all and follow him to his school, where he's gotten a spot on the hockey team. But then I'd realize that wouldn't be good for either of us. The Jennifer I would be would need to get back to my school, back to my life and my purpose.

So I'd hold his face in mine. I'd look into his eyes, hazel rimmed with brown, with the gold flames jutting out from the center. I would bring his lips closer to mine and everything else would stop existing. It would just be the air and the space between our lips, then the feel of his lips on mine, the explosion when my tongue presses against his. We'd be some kind of electric circuit, the power pulsing through us.

Our feelings would generate more feelings until there would be so many feelings there wouldn't be enough room in the world for them. And then my cell would beep. An alarm. Reminding me that I have to leave. And I'd pull my lips away from his. I'd feel the release of breath that would become air. He'd make a tiny moaning sound. A small complaint. And that would make me smile. "There will be more where that came from. In two short months."

And he'd pretend to push his head in with both of his hands. Like it was going to explode. And I'd laugh and kiss him again. Then turn away and open the door. And the sound of the door handle opening feels so real that my hand is still making that motion as Mom comes in and says, "Oh no, are you having spasms? Do you think it's a seizure?"

And I'd remember where I really am. Stuck in this house. In my bedroom, gathering my strength to do battle on the latest front.

I will not go to a rehab center.

"Let's get you back to bed. I know you're disappointed, that you wanted to go back to school, but it's going to be fine."

"Is that what you think I'm upset about? I heard what you and Dr. Rodriguez were talking about."

Mom helps smooth out the covers, then pulls them back. She's been doing this same routine for years.

It's like a calming rhythm, only this isn't the time to get calm.

"It was just a suggestion. I'm not saying we're going to do it."

"Right," I say, "because *we* don't get to decide. *I* do."

"Well, my dear, if you'd like to prove the doctor wrong, why don't you start resting now and hope that speeds the healing process?" She hands me a pill.

I take it, but make a mental note to check back in with Uncle Steve when I wake up. By the time Mom leaves the room, I feel these tiny places on my body heat up like they're being stung by a million bees. Then cool down. It feels like I'm flying, and I struggle to open my eyes.

But I can't, and I kind of don't care. It's such a relief not to be in my body anymore. So I let go and let myself be Jennifer on her way back to college. She's on the train, and she's tired and sad from already missing Julian. She closes her eyes and lets herself go. And then she is free and so am I. And it's so easy.

◦ ◦ ◦

Monday

7:25 A.M.

I think we should meet.

7:30 A.M.

I mean, we don't have to.
If you don't want to.

7:33 A.M.

Omg I made you mad.

8:40 A.M.

I'm sorry!

10:05 A.M.

Don't hate me!

11:13 A.M.

I'm sorry.

Home sick.

Just woke up.

Phew. I mean, I'm not glad you're sick,
but I thought you were mad at me.

I'm not mad.

So what do you think?

About?

About meeting.

Oh. That.

Yeah. That.

Well, I really like the way things are
going. You know, the way it is now.

And meeting would change that?

Maybe.

Why?

I don't know. It's just...

So meet me. Are you going to Hockey
Homecoming in a few weeks?

I've never gone before.

Well. The players wear our dirty
jerseys. Ok that doesn't sound
fun, but it's a tradition.

Okayyyyy

And the girls ask the guys to dance.

That's fun!

And if you go, you could ask me
to dance, and if you like the dance
you could tell me it's you.

No pressure. Smiley face emoji.

You're allowed to use the
real emojis if you like.

No. I like our system.

So? Hockey Homecoming?

Maybe. If you win the final
game with Danbury.

Deal!

Oh. And btw, I'll Febreze my jersey.

Hand over mouth feigning shock
emoji. Is that even allowed?

Is that even an emoji?

Yes.

Yes, it's allowed. And even if
it wasn't I'd do it for you.

Awww. Cutie pie emoji.

That one's made up.

Maybe, but they should have one.

Agree. Oh, and back at you.

TWENTY

For a smart girl, I continue to be shocked by how things play out in my life. Like how I believed, really believed, that my parents would listen to me since we had the "little talk" about my having more say in my medical decisions.

But somehow, two weeks after my accident, here we are in Dr. Rodriguez's office to discuss my rehabilitation. He's handed us each a brochure for the rehab center he's hoping to talk us into. "If you go to Brentwood, it would most likely be for a three- or four-week stay. We could wait until the cast comes off, place the baclofen pump, if you agree to that, before you went, and they could help you adjust to it there."

Mom looks at me as if it was all so reasonable. "What are you thinking?"

"I don't know."

Mom pulls up the calendar on her phone. "You get your cast off in three weeks. So you could go to Brentwood and be back in time for next semester."

"And what about the end of this semester?"

"We'll switch you to Hospital Homebound and you can finish online," Mom says.

My stomach sinks. No more English class with Julian.

Dr. Rodriguez scrolls through the Brentwood page on his iPad. "It says here that they have teachers at Brentwood to help also."

"So I miss all of winter break? With Eric?" My voice is shrill and shaky, and I know that's not helping me make my case. "Why can't I rehab here?"

"You could," Dr. Rodriguez says, "But at Brentwood you'd get daily PT. Here as an outpatient you'd only get two or three times a week at most."

"Why?"

"That's all insurance will cover," he says.

"Well, can't the trust pay the difference?" I ask. "I mean, isn't that what the money's for?"

"Yes, Jenna, but outpatient rehab isn't the same as inpatient. They have more tools inpatient. It's more intensive and also offers more healing treatments."

"So what do we think?" Mom says this like a salesperson trying to talk her customer into a big-ticket item that's really wrong for them—and she knows it.

"*We* would like time to think it over."

"How much time do we have?" Dad's faced forward, one hand on the arm of his chair and the other under his chin. He does this when he's hyperfocused on something. As in when Mom gets mad at him for working all night on a new product for a client. And in this moment, the thing he's hyperfocused on is me. Getting me better.

Dr. Rodriguez types onto his keyboard, looking at his computer screen. "Well, at this point, they have three beds open. Tomorrow they may have ten or none. It all depends."

"Have you sent people there before?" Dad asks.

"Yes. A few." Then to Mom and me. "They all did very well."

He's building his case. I need to build mine. "The thing is, it doesn't matter to me how many people have gone or how successful they've been." Mom's eyes practically bug out, but I keep going. "I'm not saying I'm not going to go, I'm only saying I want to think about it. That I want it to be *my* decision."

Dr. Rodriguez holds up his hand just in time to stop Dad's rebuttal. "Why don't you think about it for a day or two. Rehab will only work if Jenna buys in."

Dad stands up. Paces. This is going to be bad. All of the oxygen leaves the room as we wait for Dad's verdict. "No."

I surprise myself with an icy reply. "No?"

"We are your parents, Jenna. This is what you need." Then to Dr. Rodriguez. "What if we book her at rehab in three weeks and she decides not to go?"

Dr. Rodriguez says, "I don't want to take a space if she's not going to use it. In case someone else needs it."

Mom holds her hands up. "I think we should talk about this."

"I'm sorry. But I think this is nonnegotiable." Dad tries to soften the look on his face, but his words have done the damage. "It's for your own good. Make the appointment."

So the ride home is really silent. Mom keeps trying to check me in the mirror, but I'm too busy texting Uncle Steve.

It's worse than we thought. They
made the decision for me!

I'll meet you at the house after this.

Thank you.

You want me to bring the papers?

Yes. Unfort.

It'll be ok. OMW.

By the time we get home, Uncle Steve's car is parked in our driveway on the left side, which is the side Dad needs to pull into the garage. It seems tactical warfare is already at play in the Cohen household.

"What's he doing here?" Mom checks her phone and Dad's to see if they've missed a text or call from him.

"No idea." Dad parks. "Probably a slow day at work or something."

I detach my seat belt and open my door. Uncle Steve is by my side immediately. "Hello, niece-y." He kisses me on the cheek. The first thing I notice is that he's clean shaven.

"No beard?" I ask.

He winks. "Turns out I may have to go to court."

"What's up, Steve?" Dad walks ahead to unlock the door. "You parked on the wrong side of the driveway."

"My bad."

Dad looks like he's not buying it.

As we get inside, Mom helps us all unload our coats. "You'll stay for lunch? I think I have enough pasta salad for everyone. Plus there's leftover pizza."

Uncle Steve hangs up his coat, and I see he's wearing a suit. "I'm here for Jenna."

The room gets quiet. Mom and Dad may not know exactly what Uncle Steve is talking about, but I can see them putting it all together. Uncle Steve looking official in his court suit and no beard. Uncle Steve's words. He puts his hand in his inner pocket and pulls out a document in an envelope.

"Jenna?" Dad's voice is as tight as a guitar string.

Uncle Steve puts his arm around me. "Perhaps I should escort my client."

Dad shoots him a look. "That's great, Steve, let's encourage this entire deal."

"It's not a deal. It's actually called a motion." He helps me to the living room couch and drums his fingers on the outside of the envelope.

Mom puts her hands up. "We will all be civil. Underneath all of this, we are family."

Dad crosses his arms in front of his chest. I've seen him this pissed before. About Penn State football. About Eric's grades in middle school, before he turned himself around. About Rena's smart mouth. Never about me.

"So," Uncle Steve says, "my client, Jennifer Alden Cohen, would like to proclaim her rights to make her own medical decisions by filing for a medical emancipation."

"This is crap," Dad says.

"No. This is her right." Uncle Steve looks at me. "She is pursuing this action to assert her rights in deciding her medical care. This is in lieu of filing a living will, which would dictate in exquisite detail all of the possible morbid scenarios—which as her uncle, I would not like to be forced to do."

"God forbid!" Mom says.

"God forbid," Uncle Steve agrees.

Dad turns to me, face pleading. "Why wouldn't you want to try everything to help yourself? Why limit your potential?"

Uncle Steve looks at me, but the words I need are stuck. Not because of my cerebral palsy, but because I'm trying so hard not to cry. Dad's hand is fisted. I can't stop looking at that hand.

"We aren't forcing her to do anything, Steve," Mom says.

"She wants to decide for herself about rehab. And any future treatments."

"You don't even have kids." My dad's voice is strained. "You don't know what it's like."

Uncle Steve puts his arm around me. "If you think that I don't feel like your kids are my kids, you're mistaken. I love all three of your kids as if they were my own."

Mom, predictably, starts crying.

"We've made our needs known. Now the ball is in your court," Uncle Steve says.

"You didn't have to show up here in your court suit with your..." Dad points to Uncle Steve's pocket. "With your documents."

"He's my lawyer," I say. "He did what I paid him to do."

"Paid?" Now Dad can't help but smile a tiny bit.

"Yes. From my account."

Mom puts her hand up. "Jenna, are you scheduled for that baclofen class?"

"No."

"What if you do that? What if you sign up for the class and then we'll revisit this?"

Uncle Steve looks around the room, gauging the effects of Mom's offer. "Jenna?"

I nod, but a tear escapes, and I know if I speak I'll descend into full-on sobbing. Which pisses me right the hell off. Why can't emotions be something my system suppresses like it dulls the feeling in my hands by the end of the day? Why am I choking on all of this instead of standing tall?

"Okay," Uncle Steve says. "Let's look to see when they are offered."

"There's one in a week and a half. After school," Mom adds because she sees me start to balk.

Uncle Steve clears his throat.

"If she agrees," Mom says.

"Well if it's all worked out," Dad says, an edge to his voice.

Mom puts her hand on Dad's arm. "It's fine, David. We want Jenna to have a say. She should. It's her body."

"And we should have a say, also!"

"We do. But ultimately it's her decision." Mom holds up one of the photo albums she made for me. Mom's a photographer—gets paid serious money to take other people's pictures. She always said her family was her favorite subject. "I've been looking through these."

Dad says, "And…?"

"And Jenna has been through so many procedures. Procedures we decided—"

"We decided with the counsel of the doctors." Dad's got one finger raised like he's the one in court, testifying.

"Yes. Of course," Mom says, continuing. "But I remember there were times I wasn't sure if we should try something or not. It might ease my mind to know how she feels."

"She's a kid," Dad says. "She doesn't know what she wants."

"She's growing up."

Dad sighs. "Okay. Fine. We do the class. Together. Then we decide. Together."

Mom smiles. Looks at me. I try my best to smile. "I'll call Dr. Rodriguez and tell him we want to hold off for now."

Uncle Steve turns to me. "We okay with that plan, Jenna?"

I nod. But I'm not unaware that the entire convo between Mom and Dad happened as if I wasn't in the room. I want to point that out, but can't bring myself to do it. Uncle Steve slides my atomic bomb into his pocket. "Okay. Now let's talk about what you'll be serving for Hanukkah, assuming I'm still invited?"

Mom says, "I'm thinking honey cake."

Uncle Steve makes a face. "You wouldn't."

Mom laughs.

Steve leans forward, holding his tie down, and clears his throat. "My client requests chocolate torte."

"You'll be lucky if you get any cake whatsoever," Dad says, but he's using his teasing voice, so I know that, for now at least, my family is intact.

. . .

9:23 P.M.

Your biggest fear?

You mean in real life or like a
phobia or something?

Phobia.

The usual. Spiders. Any bugs, really.

Understandable.

You?

What's that fear of things living in holes?

Trypophobia?

Shiver.

Yeah. It's pretty creepy.

What about in real life?

That I won't get into college. That
I'll never figure my life out.

                        Everybody thinks that.

You're smart, though. So
you don't think it.

             You have no idea. I think it all the time.

              When I was little, it was like I could
              look ahead in time and know, just
              know that I'd be ok. I saw myself
              winning at life. You know?

Yeah. I do.

                    But now, I'm not sure of
                    anything anymore.

                    Let's run away.

Where should we go?

             I'm very into mountains these days.

I'm always into mountains.

Northeast? West Coast? Midwest?

Prettiest?

How could you choose just one?

Like books for me.

Let's go to Colorado.

For weed?

To ski.

I'm not very athletic.

Then North Carolina. To hike.

Slow hiking. With no packs.

We can stay in a cabin and you can read
or write or both. We can take small hikes
during the day and canoe on the lake.

Is it summer?

At this cabin, it always is. If
that's what you want.

                                Sometimes I like winter.

We could stay in by the fire.

                                And watch hockey.

Now that's a story I would
read. Or maybe we could find
something else to do?

                                Blushing emoji.

Gnite, Elsa. Sweet dreams.

                                Sweet dreams you too. About
                                the cabin in the woods.

TWENTY-ONE

Wednesday. It's exactly two days until the Hockey Homecoming dance. We won the final game in the series which means I've got to pay up on my deal with Julian and actually go. I've finally made it back to a somewhat normal routine. For the moment I've put off any talk of rehab centers, though my baclofen class is happening early next week. I've got my aide trailing behind me, and I'm in my wheelchair. Rena has fitted it with a leopard-print backing, because why the heck not? I'm moving forward, and isn't that the point anyway?

Back in English, I am all in. In my other classes, I keep up. It's not like it's hard, but the problem is, I'm worn down physically and emotionally. At home I stop doing the practice AP tests. It seems weird. And what's the point, anyway? I've got no future as an AP student. Every time I try to do something different, it ends badly.

At lunch, Ben sits with his classmates, and I sit with them and they make plans. And I don't. My only plan is to keep texting Julian, not just because it's Julian, but also because it's the only way I can escape from my life. The one I was given. The one my parents are in charge of. The one that was changed one day because some asshole doctor just couldn't focus. Medical malfeasance. The two worst words in the world. I never really minded the CP before I found out

about the malfeasance. It was always just how it was. Eric got weird
hair that never looks combed. Rena got horribly crooked teeth,
including a big fang that jutted out before she spent three and a half
years with braces on. And I got CP. The surgeries and therapies were
part of my life.

Until that day.

I usually don't text Julian at school, but I can't resist today.

C'mon. You going to the dance? We had
a deal.

I check to make sure he's not looking at me. He isn't. I write
back.

Yes.

The boy practically jumps out of his seat. I can see him lean
forward like he's in hockey-determination mode.

Woofreakinhoo!!!

I want to dance with you. Tell me you'll
dance with me.

I'm not a good dancer.

So we'll dance slow. I like slow
ones better, anyway.

                              Hold on, cowboy, let's take
                              this one step at a time...

You said you're going. I'm going
to live with that all day!

And I smile.

That's a big mistake, though, because that's the moment Ben's
eyes lock on mine. "Be careful." He points one of his french fries at
me, and his gaze doesn't waver. "You. Me. Strategy session later."

· · ·

After school Ben and I hold court in our game room. Mom brings a
tray of snacks.

Popcorn for Ben. Crackers with thin slices of sharp white cheddar cheese on top. Meanwhile Julian is blowing up my cell. And I'm
trying not to look at it.

"You are playing with fire, girl," Ben says. "What's your plan?"

"Honestly, this is the first time I've felt normal in forever. You.
Me. Movies. Can't we just keep it light?"

More texts.

Ben points. "The question is, can he?"

I shift my phone to silent. Then put it against my forehead. "I don't know. I don't know. I don't know." I hand it to Ben. "Advise me, oh wise one."

"Hmmm, let's see." He starts scrolling through our messages. "The boy likes to beg."

I reach for the phone and he holds it out of my reach while reading the texts out loud. "Oh, Elsa, won't you tell me who you are? It pains me. It…makes me swoon."

"He did *not* say that."

He stands on the couch. Literally stands so I can't get the phone.

"That's cheating! And me in a cast!"

Ben rubs one finger over his eyebrows, the same ones he claims are perfect even without any work. "I'm embellishing." His smile is huge and reaches his eyes, which makes me laugh, too. "A little."

Mom comes in carrying more snacks. Her eyes point to my cast. "Maybe take it a little easy?"

Ben slides back into his seat like a gentleman and hands me my phone. "Sorry, Mrs. Cohen."

She shines a big smile at him. "I'll just leave you two to it, but not too late. It's a school night."

"We have a late start tomorrow. Remember? PSAT for the sophomores."

"Ha! I did forget. Carry on."

The second she's out of the room I turn back to Ben. "So help me with my textual relationship."

Ben drinks some of the Coke that Mom only buys for him. We aren't allowed soda normally. Dr. Brown's for holidays, but nothing else. But anything for Ben.

"Welp…" Ben waves me along, gesturing with a celery stalk filled with peanut butter and raisins on top. Also one of Ben's faves that Mom makes just for him. God knows I can't chew those. "It feels like you're going to have to come clean at the dance."

My phone starts buzzing again.

Ben nods toward it. "Prince Charming?"

"I'm assuming."

"So let me get this straight, the boy is begging you to do God knows what and now you don't even want to hear from him anymore?"

"No. Of course I do, but I've got this unmasking-myself problem."

Ben puts a hand on my arm. "We'll figure it out."

I stare at Julian's texts. "So…how do I do it? How do I unmask myself?"

Ben grabs the remote from me and toggles until he gets to *A Cinderella Story*. "Relax, Elsa. Like any project, we just need research."

I take a bite of popcorn. "If you say so."

Ben lays his hand on my knee. "I say so."

We both sit back and watch the movie. No more texts from Julian. He must have figured out I was busy. Busy planning for how to deal with this next part. Mom comes in a couple of times to bring us more stuff to eat and drink, but really I think she just likes to see Ben and me hanging out.

Eventually, Ben says, "You know what I'm thinking? Maybe we watch *Cyrano*."

I make a face. Hate that movie. "We're that desperate?"

Ben grabs some Doritos. "We may be."

"But you'll figure it out?"

"Of course."

I stare at my cell.

Where are you, Elsa?

You don't want to meet me?

I only make it through ten minutes of *Cyrano* until I insist we switch to *Enchanted*.

"So?" I ask Ben. "What have we learned from our research?"

"Hmmm. I'm stumped. Not one of these will work. But damn, it was a fun afternoon. And I'm so glad I didn't even start on my AP Psych project, which, by the way, is due Friday."

"You said you'd help me."

"And help you, I will. The truth is you'll just have to come clean and hope for the best."

"Tell him? Gulp."

"Well, don't just spring it on the boy, but yeah. Tell him. Maybe he already knows. Maybe he suspects, at least."

I chew on an organic white cheddar cheese puff. "Maybe."

"Don't look so down, Elsa."

I make a face at him for using Julian's nickname for me. "I'm worried."

"Don't be. I've seen this movie before. Tell him at the dance. What could go wrong?" He shrugs.

I hit him. "You know whenever you say that, a whole lot of stuff goes wrong."

"Yeah. But that's what makes your story so much fun."

"I'm glad I can entertain you. Also, I'll be *so* gorgeous with this big ol' cast on." I smack my leg.

"You'll be gorgeous in navy lace." Ben picks at my hair. "Maybe we should look at a different cut?"

"What's wrong with my hair?"

"Nothing. Just maybe you should do a total makeover, really give the boy something to contemplate?"

"I don't know."

"I do. Go big or go home." He throws a chip into his mouth and presses play. He puts his arm around me. "Okay. One more movie."

· · ·

9:13 P.M.

So now I'm really worried.

What about?

What if you hate me.

Laughing so hard I'm crying emoji.
I know you. You don't know me. I'm
the one who should be worried.

It still feels scary. I've really gotten
used to these talks. You know?

                                        Yeah.

And we are so great together. Like this.

                              So maybe we shouldn't meet.

Nah. This story doesn't end this way.

                              So you like stories now?

What can I say? You've got me hooked.

                              Tell me, does this story have a
                              twisty ending? I like those.

No idea. But I have been thinking.

                                        About?

You. And me. Separately.
And also together.

                                   Confusing!

Well, we were talking about what we
wanted to be when we grow up and
I realized something about myself.

I like being outdoors. I like the woods. I
like plants and trees and animals. Dorky,
huh?

                                        Not dorky.

So I want to do something outdoors.
Park ranger or something. Does that
make me sound like I'm five years old?

                    I think it's nice. I could definitely see that.

I was worried you would
think it was stupid.

                              So now you're all solved and
                                    I'm still a big blank.

Really? I thought you'd want to
do something with books.

                         Whoa. How has that never occurred
                              to me? Like what, though?

Like a librarian?

Editor?

Maybe. Wow.

Writer?

Me, a writer? I'll think about it.

Since everything is going to
change when we meet, let's enjoy
a few more days of this.

Ok.

Shark week, yay or no?

I could do Jaws.

Now you ask me a question.

Starbucks or Dunkin.

Neither.

My heart.

But I'd gladly take you.

Heart emoji.

Is that for me or the coffee?

Both. Obviously. Smiley face.

New Year's Eve or Thanksgiving?

Both. If I got to spend them with you.

Heart emoji.

What color?

What color heart emoji?

Yes. It matters. Red hearts are for love,
yellow for friendship. Pink for innocence.

I didn't know you were such an expert.

Well, I am. And you're
stalling. What color?

Hmmm. I think blue.

What do blue hearts mean?

It means we'll see.

I'll take it. Blue heart emoji back at you.

TWENTY-TWO

Mom is bustling around, happier than I've seen her in ages. Both of her daughters are going to the Hockey Homecoming. I'm sort of surprised Rena wants to go; it's not usually her deal. But she slings an arm around me and says, "It's a family thing." So.

Rena's dressed in a maroon dress that has a sequined tank top and a ton of maroon tulle. Dad's going to freak when he sees her because it's pretty short. Mine is a two-piece navy lace dress. The top is embroidered with navy blue flowers and has sheer sleeves. The skirt is navy tulle, not as poofy as Rena's but just as short. Bad day for Dad, I guess. Rena is wearing heels, but I'm relegated to flats. At least they're supercute ones.

I try to pull my skirt down, to cover my scars, but Rena says, "Stop. You look amazing."

She maneuvers me into the bathroom. "Turn around, I don't want you to see until we're done. I'm thinking loose curls."

"Sounds perfect."

"You look so happy, Jenna. Like maybe you've got a secret or something?"

I'm just to tell her about Julian; it's really time she knows. But then Mom comes in and crosses her arms in front of her. She leans against the bathroom door. Smiles. This moment is just about perfect, so I don't mess with it.

Rena starts applying my makeup.

I fidget. "Can't I just see what..."

"Nope," she says. "I want to do a big reveal."

I set my cell to silent so Rena won't get suspicious about all the incoming messages. Part of me wants to tell her about Julian. Most of me thinks I should, especially since she'll be there when...if...I actually admit to Julian what's been going on.

"Sharon?" Dad calls from the other room.

Mom slides out of the room.

Rena moves my head to the position she needs it to be in to work her magic. "You know this dance is sort of reverse, right?"

"What?"

"The girls ask the guys to dance."

I know that, of course. So yeah, it's one of the things that is worrying me. But it also gives me a chance to talk to Julian. Alone. If I can figure out how to dance out of my wheelchair.

"So you going to ask anyone?" I ask her.

"Maybe." She smiles a little secret smile and now I wonder what she's keeping from me. I guess all will be revealed tonight when I see who she dances with.

"Look at me," Rena demands.

I do.

"Okay. Just a few finishing touches."

Then I remember Ben said I should do something drastic with my hair. I grab Rena's hand. "Hey."

"What?"

"I want bangs."

Her eyes light up. "Bangs would be perfect for your face." She grabs one of her style magazines from a pile that live on the bathroom counter and flips through the pages till she finds one with Ariana Grande in it sporting bangs. She holds it in front of my face. "Like this?"

"Yes." Ben's right, I *could* use a makeover. I need to be a different Jenna than the girl Julian considers Eric's little sister. I need to be sophisticated.

"I think we just have enough time," Rena says, "I'll keep them a little long in case we have to have you fixed professionally."

Rena bends, and her brown eyes zero in on my hair as she measures and snips. Her wrists jangle with the six bracelets she's got looped around them. She frames my face with her hands like she's taking a picture, measuring the ends she's snipped, and her thumb ring tickles me. Then Rena grabs my makeup bag, her graceful fingers plucking out the lip liner. I stare in the mirror at her nails, painted Sonia Kashuk's Stop Whining Maroon, as she brushes on the new MAC shade she got me at the mall last weekend just for this event.

"Awesome," she says. "It's so you."

"I trust you. One hundred percent."

"Okay. Don't look. I've got to get one more thing." She races to her room and comes running back with a tiara in her hand. "This is going to look amazing."

Suddenly it all gets to be too much, and I can't do it. I put my hands up. "No. People will think I'm—"

"That you're beautiful? Because you are."

"No. I'm—" Rena toggles the control on my wheelchair until I'm facing the mirror. "Wow."

I look…beautiful. The bangs are miraculously perfect and the tiara is glinting in the bathroom light, drawing attention to my face. My makeup is dark but not heavy; my lips are pouty thanks to the liner.

"Yeah," Rena agrees, "wow."

"But won't it look like I think I'm Homecoming Queen or something?"

"Nah. They don't even do that for this dance. It's Hockey Homecoming. Everything's different. I'm going to be wearing one too. Half the girls are."

I nod. "My kind of dance."

Rena smiles. "Mine, too."

Mom comes into the bathroom, sees my hair lying on the floor. Then she sees us and her face changes.

"Don't get all emotional, Mom," Rena says.

Mom wipes her eyes, then points to my hair on the white tile floor. "Who's going to clean up all of this mess?"

"Our ladies in waiting, of course," Rena says.

"Cinderella," I add.

"You two," Mom says. "Always colluding against me."

Colluding may be my favorite word.

Rena leans down and lets me wrap my arm around her, and she helps me stand on my one uncasted foot.

"Let me get your crutches," Mom says.

Rena harrumphs. "Those so doesn't go with her outfit. Not the vibe we're going for."

"But…"

"We are not entertaining buts at this point in the conversation," Rena continues, as she helps me maneuver toward the living room. It's not easy going with my huge cast. Mom trails behind us and calls to Dad, "David, make them…"

But when we are like this, there's no making us do anything. I realize I can't make it through the entire night without a wheelchair, but when I get to the living room, I see my small wheelchair is out and there is navy blue tulle and tinsel wrapped around the metal parts. It's so pretty that I can't even believe it.

Ben opens the front door and lets himself in. He's wearing a navy blue tuxedo and a crisp white shirt. He points to the wheelchair. "You like it?"

"I love it, guys. Thanks."

"No guys. All Rena's doing."

I shoot her a smile. Sister bonds transcend wheelchairs and able bodies and even imagined fairy tales. Sister bonds are weightless.

Friday

5:39 P.M.

Well, this is it.

Yeah.

You nervous?

Yup. You?

Yup. But you know what?
We shouldn't be.

Why?

Because I already know all about
you. Everything important.

Except my identity.

Except that.

Do you think this is smart,
meeting like this?

I don't think I'll be able to stand
it if I don't meet you. Smart
or not. It just feels right.

Doesn't it?

Yeah.

TWENTY-THREE

The gymnasium is completely transformed. Icicle art hangs everywhere, and little white lights blink from small fig trees placed around the room. There are white crystals in bowls, and there's even a big ice sculpture shaped like a hockey player.

It's crowded already and as we maneuver through the throng, I try to be super careful not to roll over everyone's feet. It's a little unnerving, but the music in the background is pleasantly distracting. The DJ is at the front of the room, his booth lit up, and the moment feels so big and beautiful that I almost cry. But there's also this giant knot in my stomach, a big ball of worry, and it makes it hard to breathe. Can I really tell Julian I'm the one texting him?

"Hey, going to say hello to some people. You good?" Rena checks in.

"Sure."

"You look gorgeous, Jenna," Rena says. Blows me two-handed kisses as she goes to join her friends.

Ben watches her walk away. "So...Rena doesn't know? Interesting."

"I'll probably tell her tonight. After. Whatever happens."

"Sure," Ben says with a smile.

"What are you all goofy about?"

He fake-wipes a tear. "My little girl is growing up."

I smack his arm.

"You want a little help with this next part?" Ben asks.

"Um. I'm not sure how you'll be able to help."

"You sure?" Ben asks, and pats his jacket. He pulls out a bottle of Coke. "How about some liquid courage?"

"Are you saying that's not Coke?"

"I said nothing of the sort. What I'm saying is that it might have a little something extra in it."

He passes it to me. My hands are somewhat crampy.

"Rum?"

"Yup. Classic combo. You get that buzz and that jolt at the same time."

"You think I should?"

"So you want to face Julian sober? No prob."

I swipe at the bottle, almost knock it to the ground. Ben captures it and, with his hand over my hand, offers me a sip. I cough a little as it burns my throat. It's not like I've never had alcohol. It's just that I've never drank in school. I take two more sips, then release my grip on the bottle and he retracts it.

"So who are you looking for tonight?" I ask him.

"Me?" He pulls up a chair from a nearby table. Sits. "I'm just here for fun. And as your chaperone."

I give him a look.

"Eric made me promise."

Just as he says that, the door opens and a crowd of hockey play-ers flood in, all in their jerseys because they won the Connecticut

Cup. Morgan and Neil each have dates, but the rest are flying solo. Julian doesn't even make it all the way across the room before Audra Bacon stops him.

I can tell by her body language—one hand out, leg bent, hopeful smile—that she's asking Julian to dance. I watch his face. He looks happy, I guess. And why shouldn't he be? Audra's got the straightest brown hair with red highlights, and when she moves it swishes behind her, a rippling shimmery bouncy curtain. She's also got a body that I'd kill for. Literally. And now that body is pressed against Julian's. My Julian's.

A slow song comes on, and I watch as they sort of sway to it. My eyes are filled with beautiful images of Audra and Julian until I'm believing their story way more than I'm believing ours.

"This was a stupid idea," I say. Breathe out. Sigh. I reach my hand out to Ben. "More?" He hands me the bottle.

"No worries." Ben leans his head against mine. "The boy is just getting started."

I take another sip as the song ends, and Julian backs away from Audra. She smiles, but I can tell it's a disappointed one. He slips his cell out of his pocket as he walks the perimeter of the room. My phone buzzes. I cradle it in my hand, hiding it from the rest of the world.

You here, Elsa?

I know I shouldn't be texting him here, right in the open, but I can't help it. The relief of having him leave her to try to find me makes me reckless.

Yes.

Where?

I watch as Julian scans the room, careful to slide my phone back into the little purse Rena gave me to use tonight. It keeps buzzing, and I wish I'd turned it off. Julian's teammate Nate stops Julian's forward progression. Nate is talking. Julian looks like he's trying to be interested, but his eyes keep darting to the room, to the kids dancing, the ones not dancing. He takes out his phone. My phone buzzes and I sneak a peek.

Tell me what you're wearing.

A dress.

Very funny. Give me
a hint? Color?

I gaze around the gym and see a few girls in navy blue dresses. None like mine but some navy blue-ers, for sure. But not enough; it would be a massive clue.

That's too easy.

Then tell me something about you.

Maybe you've already
danced with me?

I say a silent prayer that he doesn't fall for this—that he'll know that Audra is not his Elsa.

Nah. I don't think you're
wearing silver.

What color do you think I'm wearing?

Something less flashy.

Do you like flashy?

Nah. I like real.

And suddenly I feel so close to the boy that it's like my heart opens up and lets his words cradle my insides.

Cybil Matthews is the next one to him to dance. I watch helplessly as Julian puts his hands around her waist. Ben's hand goes on my shoulder. I reach for his bottle and drink a little more.

"How am I going to even get him over here, much less get him to dance with me? Also, how am I actually going to dance?"

"We talked about this. When you ask him, I'll make sure they play a slow one. I've already set that up."

"Still. With this…" I pat my cast.

"You can do it. You will."

I watch Julian extricate himself from his dance partner and pull out his cell.

Come on, Elsa. Tell me where

you are. Save me from another

meaningless dance.

My hand goes over my mouth to hide my smile. In the crowd, I spot Rena with a bunch of her friends. They each spread out and ask a boy to dance. Carla with Nate, Dara with Darren, and Rena ends with Chip, which seems to be happening more and more. Too much to be accidental or coincidental. My little sister is into a senior. This won't go over well with Dad, Uncle Steve, or Eric, but they won't hear about it from me. I'm no snitch.

This time it's a fast one. And I'm really glad that neither Carla or Dara ended up with Julian, because that would be another dance with another girl. When the song's done, Chip hugs Rena, and I feel happy for her. She smiles, and I'm sure in her circle getting a senior to dance with her is serious cred.

Julian texts again.

Come on. Where are you? I'll get on my

knees if that's what it takes.

And he does it. He gets on his knees right in the middle of the dance floor.

Is that what you want?

I start to laugh and too late I realize I'm not safely hidden away, reading these texts. I'm here. In the gymnasium. And Julian is looking right at me. I blush and fumble with my phone. "Crap," I say to Ben. "I've been spotted."

"Show me your cell."

"What?"

"Just do it. He has no idea what you're looking at. Could be a stupid cat meme."

Julian goes back to texting.

Will you ever ask me to dance?

"You can't react," Ben says. "He might be trying to see if it's you."

"I thought we wanted him to find out it's me," I argue.

"Yeah. Right. But not like that. You have to actually tell him."

I hand Ben my phone. "I can't be trusted. The boy is too cute."

"You're pathetic."

The unnerving sound of my cell vibrating in Ben's hand and not being able to check it is almost too much to take.

"He's good," Ben says. "Playing am I getting hot or cold?"

"Crap! Turn my ringer off." I gesture wildly like Rena does. "Oh my God. Put it on silent."

The guy I've crushed on forever is directly in front of me now, only two feet away and closing. He's got his hockey jersey on, of course, but I'm sure it's been sprayed with Febreze like he

promised. And he's got a bow tie around his neck. Not attached
to the shirt, just around his neck like one of those male exotic
dancers. I almost expect his clothes to be breakaway. I guess I'm
staring at him, waiting for that miracle to happen, because he
says, "Jenna?"

Ben elbows me into saying, "Oh. Sorry. I can't hear you." I point
around us. "It's so loud…"

Julian bends down a little, aims his words straight at me. "I said
you look amazing."

I blush like mad, and there's no stopping it.

Ben nudges me again because apparently being around Julian
like this is making me scared silent. For some reason, my hand goes
to my hair and I realize I'm actually twirling one of my curls when I
finally say, "Thanks."

Julian pulls up a chair. "Aren't you going to tell me I look good?"

I don't know if it's the dance or the rum and Coke or just Julian,
but I'm having so much fun. "You look good," I say.

He smiles like he and I are in on a secret joke. Then he leans
forward and shakes me off. "That's a mercy compliment if I've ever
heard one."

My turn to shake my head. "No. No. I mean it. You look…" I
point to his neck. "And the bow tie is a really great touch."

"I like to keep things classy."

"Well…obviously."

A crowd of girls converge behind us. Allison Riley, Stephanie
Johnson, LeeAnn Howlett. They're all in similar dresses—silver,
gold, hot pink. I'm glad that Rena talked me into wearing this one.

Ben pinches my arm. It's his signal for me to get this party started. I'm supposed to ask Julian to dance. Ben is supposed to slip the DJ a ten spot to put on something slow and sweet and long. The long part is essential, because I'm going to need more than the usual three minutes to get my courage up and my mouth working well enough to confess to the boy. I know this, but it's so much harder than when we practiced it at home. Ben insisted that the key to a good presentation is practice, but he definitely didn't factor in my stupid body, which freezes under pressure. Or my obvious performance anxiety. Ben clears his throat. I make myself say the first stupid thing that comes into my mind. An eloquent, "Are you having a good time?"

"Sure," Julian answers, "but I'm a little disappointed."

"What? The ice sculpture wasn't enough for you?" I'm finally starting to feel slightly more like myself with him now.

He smiles, his eyes skating to the floor. "Yeah. The ice sculpture is pretty cool."

"What more could you ask for?"

He lays his palm flat on my wheelchair. "Well, I was sort of wondering if you—"

Allison Riley taps Julian on the shoulder, apparently taking our body language and the fact that we are in deep conversation with each other as code for "please come up and disturb us." She asks, "Hey, you want to dance?"

My head is about to explode. I swear it'll do that right this second. Except Julian replies, "I'm sorry, Jenna just asked me."

I nod. Ben slips away, ready to hand the dude the money to play a slow, sweet, long song.

Allison backs up, slightly flustered, but that's nothing compared with the range of emotions I'm feeling. Happy that he asked me, of course, especially since girls are supposed to ask the guys. So maybe even extra happy about that. Flustered, because I'm supposed to come clean with him. Worried about the logistics.

Luckily, Julian takes charge while I'm pondering the exact number and order of movements I'd have to take to stand on my own.

He inspects my chair. "Wow. This is pretty tricked out, huh?"

"Rena did it."

"So are we going to…" He knows I don't usually even use my wheelchair, even with the cast, except when I'm tired. I have it because I promised Mom I wouldn't take any chances tonight—like dancing without my wheelchair. A promise I never intended to keep.

"No," I shake my head. "I don't need it."

Julian's hand lands on the armrest, and I swear my body heats up just from that closeness. He leans forward, his head near my chest, and searches for the brakes. They're already locked in place but telling him that would involve speaking, which his close proximity has rendered impossible.

"Oh. Okay. You're all set, I guess." He moves back sort of delicately, like he somehow just noticed that his face was practically in my chest, but he covers up with a sweet little smile. He extends his palm, all chivalrous. "Ready?"

I place my hand in his. His free hand goes to my waist, and he helps me stand.

"Do you need your crutches?"

They are hanging in a bag on the wheelchair handle. I want to say no, but that's not reality based. So I nod. He frees them from the bag and holds them out for me.

"Can I help you?"

I place my elbow in one of the crutches and Julian slips his arm around me, anchoring me to him as we walk toward the dance floor. He's got his palm flat against my back like he's guiding me and claiming me as his dance partner all at once. My heart warms at the thought that he's letting everyone know that I'm with him.

The music starts, and it's a slow one just like Ben promised. Julian's arms go around me, but I can't put mine around him because of the crutch.

"This isn't our first dance," Julian says.

"I know. I remember. When we were skating."

"We danced just like this." His attentiveness feels so sharp. "The skating part was fun. Until you fell."

"Right. That part wasn't so fun."

For some reason the mention of that fall puts my muscles on guard. Tiny points of tightness threaten to blossom into full-blown spasm. Julian senses something because he pulls me a little closer, closer than he was dancing with those other girls. Being so close to Julian makes me forget about my spastic muscles. It actually makes them soften and stand down. I send a silent thank-you prayer into the universe. This is going really well.

"I hope you don't mind the jersey," he says. "I had to do it right."

"I wouldn't have expected anything else. Eric would be proud."

Julian does a self-conscious little laugh, and I want to kick myself for bringing up my brother at a time like this.

"Can I tell you a secret?" he asks. His breath is warm against my ear in the nicest way and my body melts even closer against his.

"Yes." Even though the thought terrifies me.

"I've never met anyone like you, Jenna."

"I'm sure."

"I mean it. You are so fierce. So fun. When I knew we were moving back here, I was hoping I'd get to see you."

"We will always have *The Great Gatsby*." Why can't I stop making references to my alter ego? Am I insane?

"Yes, we will." His eyes sparkle. Actually sparkle. I feel like an idiot. He's having fun with me.

I swallow hard. My hands curl, gripping his jersey. I worry he'll be annoyed, but instead he presses up against me so our bodies lock. He's at least six inches taller than I am, but most of our parts align. I can feel my stomach against his. My chest against his. When he speaks, I feel his exhalations on my neck, tiny little pulses.

"I like dancing with you. I *really* like dancing with you. Even better off the ice." He pulls back so I can see his face. And that feels like such a sweet thing to do. Such an honest thing. Like he wants me to know how he really feels. "But I hate the way they this dance works. You know, if you don't bring someone, then girls keep asking you to dance."

"And that's a problem?" I ask.

"I'm not really good at all of that." And when I give him a questioning look he answers, "All the flirting and the playing games."

"You don't like games, says the hockey player."

His smile spreads the full length of his face. "Yeah. I like the hockey kinds of games, sure…"

"If you don't like to dance, why did you come?" I ask, feeling a little brave.

"I'm looking for someone."

This feels like an opening, a chance to tell him I'm the one who's been texting him. But this moment is so perfect and fun, I don't want to ruin it. And there's also this fear brewing inside me. What if he doesn't want to be with me like that? What if he laughs? What if he looks terrified when he finds out? Disgusted?

"Would it surprise you that I'm falling for someone I've never met?" he asks.

"You mean like a dating app or something?"

He laughs, and man, do I love that sound. Me making him happy. "Nah. Nothing like that. When I moved back, someone started texting me. Out of the blue."

"Well, I guess you've got me stumped now. And curious."

"I think it would be hard to stump you, Jenna Cohen."

I have the uncontrollable urge to clear my throat. Repeatedly. Like all of my feelings are stuck in there. "I don't know what you mean."

"Don't you?" He tips his head. I respond by curling up to him more. He makes a soft sound, like he's pulled in his breath and is holding it, and I feel like I could live an entire lifetime waiting for his breath to release. Can I measure my effect on the boy in how long it takes him to exhale? "Did you know I always wished I was as smart as you are?"

"You're smart."

"Not the kind of smart I'd like to be."

I push back so he can see my face. "Well, I always wished I was coordinated. Like you are."

"We are clichés…each wanting what the other one has. Like Daisy and Gatsby," he says. I can't help but smile. He does a little fist pump. "Score."

"I'm glad you're happy."

"I am, except for one thing. My mystery woman. The thing is," his voice sounds as tight as his body gets when he's about to hit the ice, "she's here."

I pretend to look around, more bought into this game than into coming clean with Julian. Who knew I'd like to play coy? "Oh. That's exciting, right?"

He nods. Smiles. "It is. And I have a plan for finding her."

I blush again and put my head on his shoulder. It seems like a bold move, but the music and the sound of his voice mesmerize me. And if this is all going to end in a second, I want the seconds just before to be amazing. Perfect.

"Is this okay?" I ask.

"More than okay." He moves his hand up higher on my back, his palm flat, but the tips of his fingers are curled into my back. When his fingers start moving in tiny circles, I get surprised and pull back.

"I'm sorry," Julian says.

"No it's fine, but aren't we supposed to be looking for your mystery woman?"

Julian puts his lips by my ear. "I almost forgot."

I pull back a little, trying to get hold of my emotions. "Tell me what you know about her, and maybe I can help you figure it out," I say, surprising myself with how much I'm enjoying this part, too. Conspiring with Julian is fun.

"Well, she's very smart," he says.

"That certainly narrows down a whole bunch of the kids here."

As I'm saying this, two of the players whip out Super Soakers and fire them at the ice sculpture.

Julian's body tightens, like he wants to join them.

"You want to go?" I ask, flicking my gaze over my shoulder in the general direction of the little hooligans.

"Nah. Having more fun with you. Also, back to what we were talking about."

"Right. Your mystery girl. Tell me more about her."

"She's funny. She's sweet. She's feisty."

"Wow. She's a lot to compete with."

"Are you competing?" He tips his head to wait for my response.

His question takes my breath away. I want to tell him: "Hell yeah, I'm competing." I've been competing with any girl who happens to enter his orbit. But that's not the kind of thing I can force out of my windpipe and through my mouth. That's the kind of admission that lodges in the back of my throat and stays stuck.

"I was wondering…" Julian pulls me closer, and it's amazing to me how soft my body can stay against him. How my body stops wanting to spasm or freak out or do anything harsh or stupid. It's a little miracle.

"What were you wondering?" I whisper.

"I was wondering if you know what position I play in hockey?"

"You know I do."

"That's right. You do. I'm a center. You know that."

I inch away from him, look at his face. He's amused, And I wonder what exactly he's amused about.

He pulls me right up against him so he can whisper in my ear. "So you know my line, me as center and Chip and Nate as my wingmen. Right?"

"Right," I whisper, although now my stomach contracts, and I feel the butterflies everyone always talks about. The butterflies I always thought were super clichéd, but here they are, inside me, making it hard to keep swaying. Or talking. Or breathing.

"Tonight, at Hockey Homecoming, I was supposed to meet my mystery girl. So, you know what I did?"

I shake my head.

"I brought my wingmen."

The song ends. I pull away, but he holds on, one cupped hand on my hip. His face is so intent, so excited looking, so damned beautiful, but I get what he's going to say.

His wingmen were there when we were texting.

And suddenly I know exactly how Cinderella felt when she was running down the stairs to escape the prince. Or more likely trying to keep the prince from finding out her true identity. That's the thing isn't it? That's what I'm keeping from him. Because it would suck if he turns me down. It would be worse if it's because I'm not perfectly built like he is. That's what I'm afraid of. That he will see me, really see me, and not want me.

His eyes haven't left my face. I feel them on me even as I cast mine downward. "Jenna, do you know what I mean about my wingmen?" His voice is soft as butter. "Jenna?"

"Yes," I say. "You weren't looking to see who was reading the texts. Chip and Nate were."

I'm caught. And all of a sudden, the enormity of what I've done, of what's going to happen next, is too much to bear. Is he angry with me? Disgusted? Amused, but not interested?

"Jenna?" He strokes my cheek, his voice as soft and sweet as his touch. His eyes promising good things. "Are you Elsa?"

I nod.

His lip turns up.

Then the lights go out.

TWENTY-FOUR

There's mayhem and shouting and cell phone flashlights strobing everywhere. Julian pulls me tight against his side, and I feel his muscles tense. He looks around. "It's a prank, I'm sure."

I laugh a little, relieved. "For a moment I thought I killed Hockey Homecoming." Really, I'm still wondering about the fallout from my big reveal. I mean, one slight smile does not a happy ending make.

Julian helps me forward, my crutches stabilizing me. "Let's get you back to your chair. If you get hurt tonight, your parents won't let me near you again."

His words hug me close. He wants to get near me again. That means something. Hope balloons in my chest. Could this be happening? Could Julian Van Beck really be into me? Me? Did we almost kiss? I swear it looked like he wanted to.

People are running and laughing and screaming. Marauding assailants have entered the gym, dressed in all black with masks pulled over their faces. Clown masks, *Scream* masks, mugger masks.

"Get the hell out of here," Chip screams at them.

Mr. Clooney, one of the chaperones, lurches forward, tries to grab one of them, and misses. Mrs. Walker gets one and rips the mask off just before the kid breaks away.

Julian says, "It's Danbury High. Revenge for the game."

Three of the Danbury players crouch down. I know what's going to happen before it even does. They pull their pants down and moon us. Cell phone cameras flash. My head gets filled with the bursts of white light, and I'm a little worried I'll have a seizure so I try not to look. Back at my table, where Ben has been sitting, Julian helps me into my chair. He puts my crutches on the arm rest.

A Danbury player squeezes between us, nearly plowing into me. Julian's face goes nuclear. He takes off after him with murder in his eyes, following his teammates who are chasing the Danbury players.

Ben stares after him, clapping. "Outstanding," he says and then whistles as our freshman goalie, Jason, chases the last of the Danbury guys out the door. I flinch as they plow past and aim my frustration at Ben.

"No. This is not good. Not. Good." I cross my hands in front of me. "They ruined everything."

The lights come blasting back on, which makes my eyes ache. I have to shield them. My pupils don't react to quick changes in light well, and I see dark spots everywhere.

Rena runs up to me. "Oh my God, did you see?"

Of course I did. Everyone did.

"Danbury was pissed about the game. I mean, I knew they were, but this…" She pushes my chair toward the gym exit, because with the craziness and mayhem I'd have a hard time maneuvering myself. "Did you see how mad our guys were? It's going to be a bad night."

"What do you mean?"

She leans close to my ear. "Retaliation," she whispers.

Ben clips along next to us, checking his cell the whole way. "I didn't get a decent shot."

Rena smacks him.

"What? We could've used it for a pie-throwing booth or something at our next carnival."

"Nice."

My head is throbbing. My eyes feel bloodshot. My mind is dizzy with all that just happened. Julian just asked me if I was Elsa. I just answered. And before he could respond, my world completely exploded, the room shattered instead. Now Julian and the other hockey players are out doing God knows what in some sort of revenge. Could hockey player revenge be good?

When we're out in the hall, I turn to Ben. "My phone?"

"Oh right, here." He fumbles around, patting his pockets. "Oh no."

"What?" My stomach falls.

"I'm not sure where it is."

"You have to find it!" What if Julian tries to reach me?

Ben races back toward the room gym. Mr. Wainscott blocks the entrance, but he moves aside to let my bestie go in, courtesy of all of Ben's contributions to our school. He's a golden boy, thankfully. Right now I need that influence. I need my phone back.

"Don't worry," Rena says. "He'll find it. Did you see how mad the hockey players got with this whole thing?"

"Yeah."

Kids rush by us. Rena's head twists and turns. "They're following our hockey players."

"How do you know?" I ask.

"Everyone's pulling out of the parking lot, fast. What do you think that means?"

"It means we need to find Ben."

"Right here," I hear him say from behind us. He comes around my chair and hands me my cell. Except the screen is cracked. "Sorry about that. I found it on the floor."

Rena grabs it, and I almost die right there. I really can't have my baby sister reading my texts with Julian. "Yeah. It's pretty smashed."

She gives it to me. I push the buttons, and I'm unable to get it to respond at all. My heart falls. No communication with Julian. And right when he asked me the big question. We hadn't even had a chance to talk about it. But he knew. He knew. And he didn't seem to be upset. He seemed interested. Happy. He looked like he wanted to kiss me. He talked like he wanted us to see each other. Like maybe he'd forgiven me for catfishing him. Those thoughts wrap themselves around my heart as Rena guides my chair to Ben's car.

I use my crutches to make my way to the front passenger side, where Rena helps me into my seat. Ben loads my wheelchair into the trunk, then comes around and gets in, starting the car.

Rena's working her phone. "Everyone's headed to Danbury High." She's breathless. "We should go too, don't you think?"

Ben's hands grip and ungrip the wheel. Then he turns to me. "We should probably go home. Right?"

And I'm so torn. Part of me wants to be there, making certain Julian is okay. But the other part wants to get home so I can use my iPad to send messages. We were interrupted at the worst possible time. I want to be ready to see what he has to say about all this. When he's done with this drama and ready to deal with *our* drama.

"Let's go to Danbury. See what's happening," Rena answers for me.

As we head toward Danbury, I'm sort of excited to be part of this entire deal. We pass through the Danbury town square and Rena points. "Turn right at the light."

It's not hard to see where we are going; there's a line of cars pulling into the high school ahead of us.

The trees blur by, and they conspire with the night sky to keep me in my head. I can almost believe that this is all part of a fantasy. But as we take the last turn toward the Danbury football field, I see my dreams literally go up in smoke. Our guys are on the grass and there are five fires climbing from the trash cans scattered around the perimeter.

"This is not good," I say. There are too many people.

Ben parks the car and turns the ignition off. Around us, other cars park. Kids pile out. Our kids. Their kids, too. Soon, it's a mob scene. My head swims, and I'm struggling. I can't think of a single book or movie where someone set fire to something and it ended well. Dread socks me in the stomach. "We shouldn't be here."

Ben nods and starts the car back up. "We'll just make things worse."

I turn to the back seat to tell Rena to put her seat belt back on, but she's got this look of incredulity on her face, and her hand grips the door handle like a threat.

"Our boys will fight harder if they're being watched. We all need to go home," I say, but she isn't listening. And even if she did, the others wouldn't.

"I have to go," she says. "I'll find a ride home." She climbs out of the car so fast neither Ben nor I can say anything to stop her.

The world goes in slow motion, and Ben turns the car back off. "This is not good," he says. "This is not good."

We've got to go after her. Only it's not that easy, given my huge-assed leg cast and my CP. Ben helps me get into my wheelchair, and I grab my crutches too; even though this is an ultrarich high school, I never know what kind of nonsense I'll find in terms of accessibility, which is insane considering it's nowhere near the 1950s anymore. The cold night air slices through me, but the fear of Rena getting hurt pushes me forward. Ben runs. I motor and steer toward the sidewalk.

"Where's the ramp?" I cry.

"Here, here." Ben points the flashlight from his phone on the ground, and I rough ride up and over the bump of a curb. I practically tip over, but Ben catches me. "Calm down, you're going to roll this thing."

Normally the idea would be hysterical, but right now everything feels so…desperate. The kids around us on the pavement race to the field. The night is freezing, and there's the sense of something dangerous in the air. I am powerless to stop Rena or Julian or any of it. I am powerless.

We pass a crowd of teens who must be from Danbury because they are in jeans and sweatshirts and winter coats while we are in our Homecoming clothes—definitely not made for the elements. Everyone's shouting.

There's a four-foot chain-link fence around the field and a row of hedges around that. If I'm going to get to the football field in this wheelchair, I'm going to have to go on the sidewalk and go all the way around. I watch the able-bodied kids climb the fence and urge my chair forward, but the battery is low on juice, and it's not as fast as it usually is—as fast as I need it to be. Ben jogs next to me.

"Do you see her?" I ask. He's got a much better view over the hedges than I do in my seated position.

He peeks above the bushes. "No. How could she have gotten away that fast?"

"It's her superpower."

I round the area where they take tickets and close in on the gates. My chair churns over the pavement, covered with blue paw prints for Danbury's mascot, the Wildcats. Our hockey players are on the football field, which looks like a cage now. The sound of cars screeching into the parking lot makes me jump. God, I hope it's the police.

Ben looks over his shoulder. "The Danbury players are here," he says. "We need to get Rena and go."

I couldn't agree more. I make it onto the track surrounding the field just in time to see the Danbury players propelling themselves over the fence. It's like a waterfall of anger. It doesn't take me long to find Julian. He's midfield. Bracing. His face is so angry, and I wonder why.

Ben points. "Found her."

Rena stands near us on the edge of the field, huddled with a group of girls who have their arms wrapped around themselves, shivering. There's one hockey player with them. Chip. Rena grabs him and talks to him so intently, I can feel the energy all the way over here. Julian locks eyes on me. I'm not exactly sure what emotions I expect to see, but I mostly see anger. He's mad at me for being here? Wait. What?

Julian takes Rena by the arm. "Say goodbye to Chip." His voice sounds like Eric's—protective. Firm. Nonnegotiable. Julian walks her over to Ben and me.

Dave and Nate come over all agitated. "Come on, man, we need everyone."

"Just a minute," Julian says. "I'll be there in a minute."

He bends down on one knee to talk to me. "I want to talk about tonight, but this isn't the place." His voice is all sharpness and rough edges, not the Julian voice I know. The grittiness gets to me and makes me nod.

"I get that. I'm sorry. We had to get her back." My eyes shoot to Rena, who is arguing with Chip again. It's so weird to see them together like that. How long has that been going on? "I didn't mean to upset you."

Julian's voice softens. "Please, I'm not mad. Just take Rena home."

Behind him, two of Danbury's players push one of ours. Julian's face tightens. I can see he needs to go, and I'm torn between wanting him to come with me and knowing he can't.

"Rena," I call in my big-sister voice. "Rena, we need to go. Now."

She shoots me a look filled with misery.

"Now."

Chip takes her hand. "Let's go," he says.

With Chip and Julian as our escorts out of the chaos, we are finally, finally heading toward the car. The wind cuts right through me. My teeth start to chatter.

"We gotta get you home," Julian urges.

"What's the matter, Van Beck?" a guy calls from behind us. "A little girl trouble?"

Another guy says, "Ooooh."

Julian ignores all of it and keeps walking next to me.

"What? You can't hear me now? So you're handicapped, too?"

The lights in the parking lot give enough illumination that I can see Julian's jaw clench. His fists tighten. I will Julian to stay calm, but his head whips around. "What's your problem, Anderson?"

Chip's meaty paw goes on Julian's shoulder. "He's just trying to get in your head."

Anderson jogs to get in front of us. "Leaving so soon?"

Julian's eyes stay on the ground. He stands in front of my chair, like a shield.

"Look, you crashed our dance, we crashed your field. We're even," Chip says.

Rena's eyes don't leave him the entire time he's talking. I squeeze her hand. Her breath fogs in front of her. I see her shiver, and I know it's not just from the cold.

One of Anderson's teammates catches up to us and throws his arm around him. "Let's call it. No harm. No foul."

Anderson spins. "We're going to let these guys get away with this?"

His teammate says, "We'll pay it back on the ice."

"We're going." Dave whips his finger around in the air to tell everyone to get moving. The Danbury players go back toward the field. The one with his arm around Anderson lugs him back toward the other players.

For a tiny second I believe this is all going to be all right. The guys were mad. They came here and retaliated. All is equal. All is cool.

I let go of the huge breath that was trapped inside my chest. We are almost all the way to the parking lot when I hear Anderson call. "Hey, Van Beck? You think you're better than I am?"

Julian keeps walking.

"I'm going to kick your ass next time we match up," Anderson screams.

"You do that," Julian shouts without turning around.

The car is about twenty feet away now. I push hard on the joystick that moves me forward as if my weakened electric wheelchair can outrun the trouble that's coming for us.

Anderson yells, "At least I'm not dating a crip."

Julian stops. I want to beg him to keep moving. To ignore the stupid comment. He's standing next to me. His breath is coming out heavy now. He looks at me, but it's like he's not seeing me. "Let's get you settled, Jenna," he says.

And I breathe again and inside that breath is this small light of hope. I stare at the stars in the sky and speak to God. I don't do this very often, but I need His help now. Please, God, please. Don't let Julian be hurt. Let us be okay.

We get to the car. Ben pops the trunk. I hop out of my chair, and Julian lowers me into the seat.

"Crap," Chip says. And I can tell he's having trouble folding my chair.

Tears run down my face. I shiver. This is going to turn bad. I know this. I've watched enough movies to know this. I've read enough books. I know this. I. Know. This.

Rena gets out of the car to help Chip. "It goes like this."

Please God. Please. I'd give anything, anything if this could be okay. I'd give up being one of the thirty-six saints. I'd give up everything. I'd give up Julian if everything could just be okay. If he could be.

"Start the car," Julian instructs.

But all of this is taking too long. Everything is moving so slow now. We are moving so slow. It starts to rain. Icy drops that send kids screaming to their cars.

The trunk slams.

Ben turns the key, and the car jumps to life. He flips the vents to high, so the heat will get to me.

"What's the matter? Truth hurts?" Anderson calls, and I hear the other Danbury players trying to calm him down.

Eric has always told me that hockey is filled with rivalry. Fueled by it, really. That "one man can only live if the other one dies" sort of rivalry. But this seems more than that. This feels dangerous. Hopeless, because I know that this Anderson person is not going to stop. Not until Julian takes the bait. I taste salt. We caused this by coming here.

Julian kneels. Our eyes meet, and in his gaze I can see the desire to hold on to this moment, to not be sucked into the insanity that's headed for him, but also the realization that he's not going to be able to. "Just go home," he says. "I'll text you later."

"I'm just saying it's kind of sick. You know?" Anderson is directly behind Julian now.

"Don't," I whisper. "It doesn't matter."

With the pad of his thumb, he wipes the tears off my face. He closes my thin wrap. "I had such a good time with you at the dance. I'm glad you came."

I grab his hand. "Let's leave together. Now. We can finish the night on our terms."

"If you're done with her, maybe I could have a go?" Anderson says. "Maybe when I'm done with her, she'll be able to walk right."

Julian's face tightens. I try to hold on to him, but he pulls his hand from mine, closes my door, and he's gone.

TWENTY-FIVE

The next few moments are a blur. I watch helplessly as Julian rears back and throws the first punch. It sends that Anderson kid stumbling backward. I hear it, too, the sound of fist against face. The grunt of the person hit. There's blood. So much blood. Chip tries to pull Julian back. Dave, too, but the Danbury players can't hold Anderson, either. A circle surrounds the boys, and I'm screaming and screaming.

Red and blue lights flash in the distance.

I hear a siren. Kids race for their cars. Tires screech. The world is spinning.

Ben throws his car into drive. We are moving. Away from Julian.

"Where are you going?" I bang on the dashboard. "Stop. We have to stop them."

"Police," Rena points at the four cop cars that now descend on the parking lot.

"They'll stop them," I say, mostly to myself. "They'll stop them."

A helicopter flies above us, spotlight sweeping the ground. The players break away and race in all different directions. I can't see if Julian is one of the guys who got away or if he's still on the ground. Someone is. An ambulance passes us on our way out of the high school, and I'm crying and Rena's crying and Ben is scared mute.

"That looked bad, didn't it?" I say. "I mean, an ambulance."

"It's probably protocol," Ben says.

Rena is working her phone like mad. "Shayna says they loaded one of the players in the ambulance. She isn't sure which one."

We pull into the driveway and Mom and Dad are outside. Mom has her arms folded in front of her, stamping in the cold to get warm. Dad is pacing. As Ben pulls into the driveway, they practically attack the car.

"Where've you been?" Dad demands.

"We've been texting you since we heard," Mom says.

"Heard what?" I ask. Eric taught me it's always useful to know what info they have before giving them more.

"About what they did at the dance. Which was over an hour ago. Where have you been?"

I hold up my smashed phone. "Sorry."

"Let's get you inside," Mom says. "You're freezing."

"I want to know where my daughters have been," Dad says, fuming, and I don't want Ben to be the recipient of his ire.

"Let's go inside, David," Mom says, "Then we can figure out who is to blame."

"It wasn't Ben's fault," I say, but my teeth are chattering, despite the blanket Mom's wrapped around me.

"We need to get you in the shower," Mom says. "You're too cold." And now she's crying and that just feels like the cherry on the sundae.

"I'll take her," Rena says. "I'll help her."

"I'll do it," Mom says, but Rena comes with us anyway.

"No shower," I say. "Just clothes." My body is numb from the cold. My heart is broken. I am broken. And I still have no idea how Julian is.

"Okay, sweetie. Let's get you into warm clothes."

I feel like a rag doll as Rena unzips me as Mom puts a sweatshirt over my head. Rena pulls thermal underwear on me over my cast. Together they help me to the bathroom and then to bed.

I put my hand out. "My phone."

"What could be so important?" Mom asks.

Rena sighs. "It's smashed," she reminds me and hands me my iPad. "You can use this in the meantime."

I curl up into as tight a ball as I can. Mom stays and rubs my back and arms until I'm not cold anymore. I fall into a deep cavern of sleep.

◈ ◈ ◈

When I wake up, I find that Rena crawled in bed with me like when we were little, and she's crying.

I try to get my mouth to move to ask what's wrong, but I'm so tired and freezing and fiery hot at the same time.

Rena rolls over. "Jenna? Are you awake?"

I nod.

"It's all my fault. It's all my fault."

"What?" I manage.

"Julian. He's been arrested. And it's all because of me. Because you had to come after me."

My mind is a swirling mess of pain. My lips are dry. So dry. My throat, too. And I'm on fire.

Rena must notice I'm not reacting to her confession or her angst, and she puts her hand on my forehead. "Oh my God, Jenna. You're burning up."

I want to ask her more about Julian. I want to tell her it isn't her fault. It doesn't matter what I want or what I think, because Rena's running out my bedroom, and I hear her frantic steps to go find Mom or Dad.

It's snowing outside. I feel the flakes land on me as they load me into the ambulance. Nothing seems real. Deep down I know this is probably just a cold or bronchitis, or even a slight bout of pneumonia. I've had that numerous times. But right now I am so tired and so cold and so numb to everything that it feels like this is the end.

The doors shut.

"Jenna, we are going to give you some fluids by IV," an EMT says. "You still with me?"

I nod.

"Nothing to worry about. A walk in the park."

I wonder if he realizes that a walk in the park would be difficult for me. I wonder if he knows how much he takes for granted. The ride goes by pretty quick. I remember that when we bought our house, Dad said a good hospital was close by. They didn't know I heard him say that, but I did. Who chooses a house by its proximity to a hospital? My parents did. Do. Because of me.

At the hospital, the doors swing open. My teeth are chattering even though I'm under a thermal blanket. I am moved down the hallway, into a triage unit, where I'm transferred to a bed.

Gary appears, and I'm grateful for the familiar face. "Here we go, darling. Here we go." He wheels me into my room. "Seems like you've won yourself a stay at our fine establishment." My eyes close. "Pneumonia. Bilateral. I appreciate your dedication."

He sets up my IVs, types a bunch of stuff into the computer, dispenses pills, and fills needles with magic medicine to put in my IV. Mom sits by my bed, a tissue crumpled in her hand. Gary puts his hand on her shoulder. "She's going to be just fine, Sharon. We got this."

Mom sniffles and nods. Her hand goes over his.

"We gotta take care of our girl," Gary says. "Let me just run and get some of those juices she likes."

The door shuts, and Mom starts in on me. "I just don't know what to say to you, Jenna. I know you all think you're immortal, like nothing can harm you. But I promise you, that's not true."

For a great moment, I forget all that's happened, all the misery, and I think of Rena and Eric. If they were here, they'd interrupt her and try to save me. I feel myself smile, and Mom scoffs.

"And Rena? She's worse than you are. Let me say this, in case you didn't get the memo: You two are grounded. For. Life."

I want to argue with her. I want to ask her if she was ever a teenager. If she ever felt the way Rena obviously does about Chip (who knew?) or how I feel about Julian. I want to scream at her for letting that stupid-assed doctor screw up my life so much that I could be used as a weapon against the boy I love. I want to flail and cry and throw every single person under the goddamn bus, but I'm so damned tired it's hard to stay awake, so I close my eyes and let myself sleep.

TWENTY-SIX

I'm half-awake when the door opens. "Jenna?" Rena's voice greets me.

I open my eyes fully.

She sits in the chair Mom usually occupies and holds my hand. "Hey. How are you feeling?"

"Okay," I lie. I feel like my chest is on fire. And that one syllable costs me a long, drawn-out coughing fit. Rena sits me up and pats my back until I finally stop.

"Well, maybe this will pick you up a little." She waves a bag in front of my face. "I got you a new phone."

I close my eyes and give her a throaty, "Thanks."

"Let me just get this set up for you. You still have the same password, right?"

"Right," I say. Then realize a second too late just what that means... Rena has my phone. With pictures that Ben must have taken of Julian and me when we were dancing. And the texts.

"Hey, this is a cute picture of you and Julian," Rena says.

I open my eyes and see her squinting at my phone, scrolling through the texts, I guess. I can't make my voice come out. I push the button to lift the head of my bed even though it makes me dizzy to do so.

"Jenna?" Rena's face looks all puzzled. "Are you and Julian…are you…"

I'm sitting completely upright, finally. From here I can get some breath. "I can explain…"

"You and Julian are a thing? And you didn't tell me?"

"It's not like that. Exactly."

She points the face of the phone at me. "It sure looks like it is." I can see disappointment in her face, and I want to fix it, but she's right. I didn't tell her. But also, she didn't tell me about Chip. So.

"Goes both ways, little sister," I manage to get out before going on another huge coughing fit.

She chews her cuticle. I swat at her hand. "Disgusting habit," we both say at the same time in the same Mom-voice. And the tension dissipates.

The door opens. Ben enters. "Hey sweets, what's the haps? You hear from Prince Charming?"

Rena fires her words at him. "What? You knew, too?"

Ben puts his hands up in surrender. "Come on, Rena. We're all friends here."

"So? *Have* you heard from him?" Rena asks me.

I stare at my new phone. I have twenty-one texts. I'd counted them this morning on the iPad. Twenty-one texts from Julian. "Looks like it."

Rena puts her hand out for my phone, when I won't relinquish it, she asks, "What does he say? How is he?"

"I haven't read them yet." I put the phone face down on the tray table and give her a "don't you dare" sort of look.

"Why won't you read them?" Ben asks.

"It would never have worked," I say. "It was stupid."

"Oh. We're doing this now, are we?" Ben says.

"Doing what?"

"Shooting this Julian thing in the foot because you're too scared to see if it could work out."

"That is not what I'm doing."

"No?" Rena asks. "The least you could do is read his texts."

"And what would the point of that be, exactly? He was just being polite. He doesn't want to date me because of my CP."

Ben points his finger at me. "Absurd."

"You saw how he acted when they teased him about me. You were there."

"I saw him coming to your defense," Ben says.

I lean back against the pillows and sigh. "But I didn't need him to do that. I didn't want him to do that. I wanted him to get in the car with us and drive off."

Ben cocks his head. "That's sweet, but maybe not exactly reality-based for hetero hockey players en masse. First rule of any situation is you've got to know your customer."

"Seriously, Jenna, you think Eric would have allowed those players to talk about you like that?" Rena's eyes are huge, and she's staring at me like she just can't believe I would do this. "He'd have been right there with Julian."

"I don't need anyone to fight my battles for me. I don't want anybody to fight on my behalf or because they feel sorry for me."

We are so busy arguing that the three of us don't hear the door open. We don't know Julian heard that last line until he says a very hoarse, "Is that what you think I was doing?" He's carrying a stupidly enormous stuffed purple bear that holds a heart balloon. His lip is split but now mostly healed, but there's still a glaring bruise around his eye and a cut above it. It's hard to keep track of time here, but I know it's been at least two days, maybe three. My phone is on the tray next to my bed. I glance at it and then back at him. I wish I was wearing normal clothes and didn't smell like a hospital.

Ben grabs Rena's arm. "We were just leaving."

Julian nods at them as they depart. Then he sits down, wincing a tiny bit as he does. When Rena came to visit me yesterday, she told me that Julian got three bruised ribs in the fight. "Hey," he says. "How are you feeling?"

"Okay."

"You worried a lot of people."

"I could say the same of you."

His hand goes to the area above his eye where the stitches are still held together with the butterfly bandage. "Yeah. I guess." He looks at my phone. "You never going to answer me?"

I lean back and cross my arms over my chest, feeling exposed. "I haven't read them."

"What?" His voice squeaks. "You never read my texts?" He shakes his head like he can't believe what I'm saying, then cradles it in his hands. "Can you tell me why?"

"I just got a new phone. The other one was smashed."

"So no other way to get your messages?"

I don't answer.

He stares at the ground for the longest time. When he looks up at me, his eyes are bright red. Like he's about to cry. I'm shocked to see that I have that much power over him. "Why?"

"I'm sorry," I say.

"You couldn't read the texts or didn't want to?"

"Couldn't. Not after what happened," I say.

"I didn't mean for it to get that bad." He gestures toward my phone. "If you'd read the texts, I told you that."

"I didn't want you to fight him because of me. There was no need. Unless..."

"Unless what?" There's an edge in his voice now that kind of kills me.

I don't know what to say. Which is a weird situation for me to be in. "I can't be with someone who is embarrassed to be with me."

"Who ever said that? Why would you even think that?"

"Admit it," I say. "It got to you when they said that about me. It embarrassed you." Maybe Rena's right, maybe Eric would've reacted the same way as Julian. But if there's any chance this is true, I need to end things now, before they even start.

Julian shakes his head. "You're wrong."

"No. I'm not. He got you mad because you don't want to admit that you're embarrassed by me. So you decided to act like a big hero, but really you're just a jerk."

Julian winces. I can tell that my words have hit their mark. "So that's it? You're just going to give up on me? On any possibility of us?"

I close my eyes. "Why do you even like me?"

"Because you're funny and smart and you're beautiful."

I open my eyes. "No, I'm not."

"You are. You've got these gorgeous eyes. And your hair…" He motions with his hands. "Your smile is the thing that gets me, though. And how you look at me when you and I get the same joke and no one else does." He stops. Takes a breath. "And I used to think you were nice."

"Used to?" The words lodge in my stomach like a rock. I gaze down at my hands, unable to look at him anymore. My own tears are finally forming.

"I guess we're done here." Julian pushes himself out of his chair. The echo of the door closing tells me all I need to know. He's gone. And he's not coming back. Was I right then, if he would leave so easily? Was he embarrassed of me? Or did I just blow it all?

Rena and Ben file back in but they can see I'm not in the mood to talk, so Ben gets in bed with me and Rena puts on *Into the Woods* because we both love that one. Me and my stupid fairy tales. I start to cough, and Rena jumps up. "I'll get you some more juice," she says, heading back out of the room.

Ben picks up my phone. "Are you sure you don't want to hear what the boy said?"

I pull Ben's arm back around me. "I can't. Not yet."

"Let me look at what he's written?"

"No. You'll tell me, and I don't want to know."

"The boy is hurting."

"He'll heal."

"But will we?" Ben asks.

"No," I say. "We will grow old and stay lonely and never marry.

We'll have no cats and no dogs and we will buy eggs in half cartons and half a loaf of bread."

"I'm sad for us." Ben lays back against my pillow with me. "But I'm glad we are sad together."

"Always."

The nurse comes in. Not Gary, unfortunately. This one is very businesslike and assesses the situation. She looks at Ben and shakes her head. "I believe it's time for you to go. Jenna needs her rest."

"I need my bestie," I complain, but it's hard to do it effectively because I'm exhausted. In fact, I'm almost asleep when Ben lifts off the bed, kisses me on the forehead, and puts my phone in my hand. "Think about it, sweets."

And then I'm alone. Alone to think about everything that's happened.

Eventually, my mind goes to Jennifer and what she would be like if she was the one in this position with Julian. I can see her walking on the street, her back held straight as a board. She's dressed in all black, wearing high-heeled boots. I stare at her shoes, like her walking in them is a miracle in and of itself. Like maybe she's a circus performer and these are her stilts. It's that amazing, because I could never do it.

She's magical, with her perfect posture, and she steals the breath right out of me. She's a force of nature. A gravitational field. She is an element. Fierce and strong and every single thing I wish I can be.

She feels eternal. And ethereal. Here and gone in the same breath. Like if other people looked at her, they'd see the bushes behind her. The houses she passed. But not her. To them she'd be the wind that blew. The rustle of the leaves. And a suggestion of something else. Something magical and important, but if they blinked she'd be completely gone.

Most of all, I'm struck by her confidence. How she carries herself so upright when she knows other people are watching. How she's so sure of her place in the world. Of the magic she carries with each step of her high heels.

And as I fall asleep, I think, I envy her.

Friday

9:45 P.M.

Hey. Are you ok?

I'm sorry about all of that.

Chip says I'm too much of a hothead. He's right.

Hope you are sleeping and we can talk tomorrow.

Gnite. Sweet dreams.

Saturday

11:10 A.M.

Are you there?

I know you're mad at me but I'm really scared. That guy is talking about pressing charges.

My parents are pissed.

Chip is pissed.

12:33 P.M.

I guess because you're not answering me, you are pretty pissed too.

It's not like me to fight like that.

I just couldn't let him talk about you like that.

I know I should've held my temper. And I get that I might have scared you.

But you have to know that's not me.

1:20 P.M.

You know me. I know you believe in
saints and magic, but I'm just a guy.

2:00 P.M.

Please answer me.

3:04 P.M.

OK. I'll leave you alone.

I'm here for you when you're ready. If you
ever are ready.

I was so happy at the dance and I know
I've ruined everything.

5:15 P.M.

OMG I heard you are in the hospital.

TWENTY-SEVEN

I spend the next morning staring at the screen of my television, not even paying attention to the show that's droning on. Mom comes in, takes a gander at the show, and says, "Didn't know you were so into deep-sea fishing. Hmmm. Good to know."

I turn the TV off and brace myself for more lecturing about how stupid I was to be out in the elements or how I never listen to her or do what I'm supposed to. But when I look at her face, really look at it, I see that she looks more sad than angry.

"How are you feeling? Better?" she asks.

"Yes."

"Good. Your doctor says you'll be released tomorrow. We have to keep up with the breathing treatments. You can't go back to school yet, but you are out of the woods." She smiles, but the sadness stays in her eyes and the edges of her mouth turn down. She opens her purse, the new one, the black Kate Spade briefcase-y one. The one Rena makes fun of, but I secretly love. She pulls out a file with papers in it. She opens the file, lays the papers out, flattens them with her hands. "I think we need to have a conversation. One that we should have had a long time ago, I guess."

"Mom?"

The papers look legal, but I can't read them.

"These are the papers from your settlement. The one right after you were born."

I sink back into my bed.

"Your Uncle Steve took care of this for us, as you apparently know."

A tear rolls down my face. This is the conversation I'd always wanted to have, but now all I want to do is stop it.

"Your father didn't want you to know about any of this. Still doesn't want you to know about any of this."

"Mom—"

She holds her hand flat and straight in the air. "No. It's time you knew."

"It doesn't matter."

She's not even paying attention to the tears that are streaming down her own face. "I was so excited about having you. Especially after we found out you were a girl. Not that I didn't love Eric, you know I do, but I was excited to have a daughter. And I wanted everything perfect for you."

"What does that have…"

Mom shifts in her chair and stares at her hands that hold the papers. "Not everything is in these, you know. It's not the whole story."

"What is the whole story, Mom?"

"Your father was working a lot. It wasn't his fault. We needed the money, and his job was very demanding. So, he took as many assignments as he could."

A knot forms in my stomach.

"I wanted your nursery finished. Dad and I fought. I was having a difficult pregnancy and was supposed to be on bed rest. But that night, I got it in my head that I wanted the wallpaper up. It was so stupid." Mom takes a shuddery breath. "I...I fell off the ladder. Dad came home and found me, and we rushed to the hospital." Mom's all-out crying now, just really going for it. "You were delivered after a difficult labor. No one could tell if it was the fall or the labor that caused your CP, and the doctor had insurance for this kind of thing...so... Even he admitted we'd need money for your care."

Mom's clutching the papers so hard now, and I can't breathe. I can't breathe.

"I knew there was a reason you didn't want to stay in AP classes. I never guessed you'd found out about the settlement. But I should have. And I should have told you all of this a long time ago so that you never felt like we lied to you, but I was scared and Dad said it didn't change anything anyway. But it was wrong. And I'm so sorry."

I'm so stuck on everything that she's said already that I barely hear the next words out of my mom's mouth.

"It was never the doctor's fault. It was mine."

TWENTY-EIGHT

I'm not really sure what I was supposed to say after Mom's confession, so I lie there and say nothing. For a few minutes we sit stone-cold silent. All the while I try to think of something to say. I will myself to say something, but I'm so busy choking on all of the anger inside of me.

Did it piss me off that Mom did something stupid, and this is why I was born like this? That's way too simple. I think I'm mainly angry that she never told me. But then this whole other conversation starts banging on the inside of my head and my heart. What if Mom hadn't been so stubborn? What if she'd waited for Dad? She is still like that, to this day. If she wants to do something, she just does it, no matter how it affects other people.

Something even deeper than a scream is building up inside me. It's dark and full and heavy. It breathes fire and wants me to shoot steam at Mom, like a rabid teakettle. And as angry as I am, as hurt as I feel, I still know that releasing that scream would be a bad thing.

So instead I grit my teeth and bite back the furious words.

Eventually Mom clears her throat and says, "I better check to see when they plan to send you home."

As soon as she leaves, I burrow the heels of my hands into my eye sockets and release the scream into my pillow. And the tears come. Free and easy and sloppy and horrifying.

Mom might have done this. *Mom*. Not Dr. Jacoby. It might not have been medical malfeasance after all—it could have been Mom and her inability to take no for an answer.

Then, because the universe really wants me to suck it, the door opens again, and Julian walks in. I bury my face in my hands and just sob. This is all too much.

His hand goes on my arm. "Jenna. Are you okay? What happened?"

I'm too busy trying to turn away from him, to keep him from seeing the horror show I've become. My eyes are dripping, my nose is dripping, God only knows what my mouth is doing, and he's here. Why is he here? I don't have much time to process any of this, because he pulls me close to him and lets me cry into his shoulder.

"Hey. Shh. It's okay."

I can barely breathe, and he keeps holding me and rocking me and rubbing my back, which I realize is exposed to the air, since I'm in—shoot me—a hospital gown. And I smell of hospital sick. And I'm not wearing a bra, so my boobs are free beneath the gown and pressed against the boy's chest, currently. None of this horror helps me stop crying.

Julian is holding me like this when the door opens again. Rena stands in the doorway, upset, and I wonder what the hell I've done to her to piss her off, too.

"Look," she says. "I know this all sucks. I know your life sucks, but our mother is out there breaking all the way down. They are thinking of sedating her. Dad is a mess. He and Uncle Steve got in another fight. And now, the boy you blew off is taking care of you. I just can't take it anymore."

"What—"

"Just because you have CP doesn't mean your life is one big telethon." And with that, she leaves. The line I once thought was funny and sarcastic is way too real.

Rena pops back in to land the final blow. "Oh, by the way, Mom told me to tell you they're keeping you another day." The door shuts, and I cry harder.

Julian stares at me. "What just happened?" he asks. "Why's Rena mad at you? What happened with your mom?"

I shake my head. No way I can get all of those words out.

Julian hands me my phone. "You can tell me later if you want. Okay?"

I nod, sniveling and trying to control my breathing.

"Let's get you cleaned up a little. You're kind of a mess." But he smiles as he says it.

Before I can protest or complain or tell him I'd rather be alone, Julian hops up and heads into the bathroom. He's back in an instant with a wet washcloth that he uses to wipe the tears off my face. He brushes my hair back off my face. "That's better."

I slow my breathing and look up at him. He still bears the marks from the fight, the line of stitches on his forehead above the purple bruise painted over his eye. His lip is still scabbed. What would it feel like to kiss him now? Would he make a noise if we kissed? A combination of small discomfort mixed with longing?

"Jenna," he says, "I know you're upset. I'm not even sure what about. So maybe the best thing, the nicest thing, would be for me to just leave you alone."

My heart cramps. Water leaks out of my eyes.

He looks at his hands and rubs the thumb of one hand over the back of the other. "But I just want to tell you," he says, his voice cracking, "I didn't mean to fight those guys. It just happened." He gives me an earnest stare. "I let them get to me."

And this is when words finally come. "Because you were embarrassed of me."

He stares at me like I've wounded him. "No, Jenna. Not that."

"Then what?"

"I was mad at you. So mad."

"Why?"

"Because I remember everything. I remember *you*. And if you liked me, why did you have to hide behind anonymous texts?"

"I didn't mean…"

"Couldn't you see how excited I was to see you when I came back? Didn't you think I felt the same way about you?"

"No," I say. "No. I thought you were too good for me."

His eyes get mad and his mouth turns down, and he shakes his head like he can't believe what I just said. "See? That's what I mean. I remember what you were like before, when we were kids. You were so adventurous. You always had so much fun. And I wanted that girl back." And now he's crying, too. "And when we ended up in the same class and then the texting…" His voice keeps breaking, and I know I've done this, I've hurt him this way. "Don't you remember before?"

And I do remember. We used to all play in the woods, me and Eric and Rena, and sometimes Julian. When we first moved in to the neighborhood, he was one of the boys on the bikes, but he soon became part of our crew. No matter what we were doing, we were always laughing, Julian and me. Right up until that day in seventh grade when he moved away.

Here, now, talking to Julian, I whisper, "I do remember. I do."

He nods.

I realize there is one question I need answered. "Did you know it was me? The texts?"

He wipes his nose with the back of his hand. "Not at first."

"When did you figure it out?"

"It was a few things. You didn't text or answer when you'd been hurt. That was suspicious. Then you said some things that reminded me of how we used to be."

"Yeah."

"And I looked up the thirty-six saints thing. It's Jewish mysticism."

"Yeah."

"So I figured that was another check in the it-could-be-Jenna column."

I nod.

"But I wasn't a hundred percent sure. Not until the dance."

I take a breath. Steel myself. "Did you want it to be me?"

His eyes are red and wounded. "Yes. I always did."

"And now?"

He blows out a breath. "I don't know."

I nod.

"I want the old Jenna back. The one who was texting me. The one who doesn't give up on herself."

My turn to breathe out heavy.

He holds out a hand. "You don't want to do that? You don't want to try again?"

"I don't think you know..."

"I do. I know all about you. You're one of the smart ones. You should be in the AP classes. You should be killing it GPA-wise, and all the colleges should be dying to offer you a free ride."

I shake my head. "That's not me. That's just who you think I am."

He stands up. Kisses me on the forehead. "You bring that Jenna back, the one I fell for in kindergarten, the one I told I was going to marry. Remember her? You bring her back, and I'm all in." He walks to the door, and I'm terrified that he's not going to even look back, but he does. "That Jenna is stronger than Mulan, prettier than Cinderella, and smarter than Belle."

I think of what Julian said about me being that girl he'd had a crush on in kindergarten. It's not like I didn't know on some level. For Julian and me, we are now and have always been part of each other's stories. The question is if we still can be.

The door shuts, and I'm left speechless and stunned.

TWENTY-NINE

I t's nighttime and the hospital is quiet like it gets. Visitors go home, and the sick and hurt are left to heal. My door opens, and I'm assuming it's one of my nurses. When I look up, I see Dad. He's holding two milkshakes.

"Mocha?" I ask.

"Your favorite."

He kisses me on the cheek, and that paired with the milkshake makes me believe he doesn't actually hate me, even though I would totally deserve that after how I treated Mom. He sits in the chair next to my bed and drinks some of his. We stay like this for a few minutes, and eventually he says, "Rough week for you, huh?"

"Understatement."

"We can talk about the Mom thing later, but aside from that, I think we've got Rena not speaking to you *and* Julian."

I throw myself back against my bed. "I do not want to talk with you about that."

"I think you're going to have to."

"No. I don't."

"Okay. Well, how about I tell you what I know and you can grunt or nod or whatever you feel like doing."

If Mom is known for her mom-ologues, Dad is known for his directives. Awesome.

"So, from what I hear, Julian attacked a Danbury hockey player because he said something unflattering about you after the big hockey dance."

"Hockey Homecoming."

"I stand corrected. It doesn't take a rocket scientist to figure out that you and Julian have something going."

I glare at him. "I really don't think that's a Dad kind of topic."

"Also it seems that your sister is also infatuated with a senior hockey player. Am I close?"

"I'm not going to rat out my sister."

Dad takes a long sip of his milkshake. "This is one of the moments I dreaded having two daughters. Excellent."

"Thanks for the pep talk, Dad."

"You don't need a pep talk from me." Dad drinks more milkshake. "It may surprise you to know, then, that Uncle Steve is representing Julian. Pro bono."

I throw my hands in the air. "Perfect. Why don't we make this a family affair?"

"Rena told me what happened. It was the least we could do." Dad wipes an invisible crumb off his jeans. "I have eyes, you know. And dads are like guard dogs around their girls. So, I've been watching every single guy who has come on your radar since you were born."

"Okay, but I don't know what that has to do with anything."

"Julian has been interested in you since you were little. You couldn't keep him away."

"So?"

"So, that means something, Jenna. You shouldn't discount a person's feelings because of a foolish mistake."

"It may surprise you to know that you don't get a vote in who I am friends with or date or—"

Dad continues as if I hadn't just stood up to him. "Julian? I like him. He's got to learn to control that temper, but I don't blame him for his actions. It shows he cares about you, and I like that."

"Maybe it shows that he's embarrassed of me."

"Ahhh... How convenient. This leads us into our next conversation."

The small bit of mocha shake I've ingested turns in my stomach. "Mom?"

"Yes. Eventually. But first, you. Do you know how beautiful you were when you were born?"

"Dad."

"You were this tiny little warrior baby. Like Wonder Woman."

"Dad..."

"We were terrified about how you came into this world. And..." Dad's voice breaks. "Then, when we found out you had cerebral palsy, your mother was so worried."

"But not you?"

"No. I saw in your eyes how fierce you were."

I take a sip of shake, trying to act like none of this is getting to me.

"Your mom made a terrible mistake, no question. And the thing is, we will never know if that's what caused your condition. But as far as I'm concerned, it doesn't matter."

"Because she's had to live with this my whole life? And because she's a wonderful mother?"

"Yes. Those things, too. But also, because you are now and have always been the Jenna you were supposed to be. Until you got mad. You've had your own temper tantrum for the last few months, and you're way smarter than that. So, I'm deciding right here, right now, that you are going to fix this. You are going to remember who you are inside. My sweet, beautiful, and incredibly kind daughter. Not to mention brilliant. And you are going to apologize to your mother. You are going to rip up that ridiculous agreement you forced Uncle Steve to write for you. If you want more control over your medical decisions, fine. You've got it, but not because you served us with legal papers."

"Is that all?" I ask.

"One more thing. You are going to assess your life and your behavior. And you are going to change."

"You're pretty sure of yourself."

"Yes. I am. But more than that, I'm sure of you. I love you, Jenna Cohen. Get a good night's sleep." He leans forward, kisses me on the forehead, and walks out.

People have been doing that a lot lately. The walking-out part.

And you know what? I kind of deserve it.

THIRTY

I spend the next hour trying to construct an email that makes sense and conveys everything I need to say to Mom. It takes me an inordinate number of tries, but I guess that's because it's a really hard subject, and I've got to dig super deep to get at all of the reasons I acted the way I did.

Here's what I come up with:

Dear Mom,

I owe you a huge apology after how I acted. Really how I've been acting for the past year. I should have come to you when I found out about the lawsuit and not jumped to conclusions about my condition. The thing is, when I saw that lawsuit, I was so angry. It's like all the feelings I'd pushed down or pushed away about how hard things are for me sometimes, all bubbled up and exploded.

I stopped trying in classes. I stopped being Dad's tough little girl. I just wanted to give up on myself. Maybe everyone feels that way in high school? And maybe a small part of me felt like it before and just didn't want to admit it. I believed in silly things like magic and saints and the possibility of everything being different one day. That day when

I found out about the settlement, I felt like all of that came crashing down.

You are the best mom ever. Not just saying. Rena and Eric and I won the parent lottery, for sure. We've always known that. And I am so lucky to have the two of them also. But that all starts with you and Dad. I know that. I've known plenty of kids with siblings that don't get along, with families not as close as ours is. Take Ben's, for example. His older brother has nothing to do with him, and his parents aren't much better.

The point is, I know you'd never do anything to hurt me. And without you, not only wouldn't I be here, but I wouldn't be the person I am today. And honestly, the entire anger at Dr. Jacoby thing was always a cop-out, anyway. I gave up on myself. I did that. And I want to fix it. I want to try the baclofen pump. As soon as they are willing to do it. And even if it means rehab because of my broken leg, I don't care. I'll do it.

I want you and Dad to help make my medical decisions, but I also want to have my feelings considered. I'm sorry that I hurt you and Dad with the Uncle Steve thing, but it wasn't his fault. It was mine. I just want to have a say in things that affect me.

Can we make up? I love you, and I am so so sorry.

Jenna

After I press send, I lie back. My phone is on my tray and a few minutes later, my email pings.

Jenna,

I'm sorry I didn't tell you the truth, either. I couldn't ask for a better daughter or a better little sister to Eric and big sister for Rena.

I will speak to the doctors about the baclofen pump, but I'm sure they'll want to wait for a few weeks until the pneumonia is completely gone.

Whatever happens, we will face this together. Dad and I are very proud of you.

I love you,

Mom

As I finish reading Mom's email I get a notification that I have a new email from BritCox@umass.edu. At first I can't remember who that person is. Then, oh! The girl in college with the baclofen pump success story.

I click on the message, which reads:

Hi there, Jenna! I'm so glad you reached out to me. I'd be happy to be your go-to person through this process (should you decide to go with the baclofen pump—and I totally recommend trying it bc it's changed my life!) and even if you don't do the pump and just want tips on college life, accessibility, etc.

About me: I am on the student government at UMass.

I run a differently abled group. (I hate the word disability even though I know some people in our community like it and use it.) I also work as a tutor in the writing lab, and am helping organize the dance marathon this year. College life is a lot, but it's so good. My CP has definitely made it more difficult, but I can honestly say I am living my best life. (I know that's super clichéd, but I'm going to allow it in this case because it's actually true.) Let's set a time to do virtual meetup and we can talk more. Finals are coming up in the next couple of weeks so maybe over winter break? Just let me know.

Whatever you decide, I'm rooting for you, Jenna.

Best,

Brittany

And just like that, my world gets a little bit lighter. I close my laptop and pick up my phone. I send a text to Rena.

Hey. Sorry I've been so dramatic and obnoxious lately. Sorry I made Mom upset. I sent her an email apology and she sent one back. I will try hard to be a better big sister and person.

It's ok. You've had a super sucky fall
and I know you were upset about Julian.
Which, btw, you never told me you liked
him and I feel stupid about that since
sisters are supposed to know everything!

I'm especially sorry I didn't tell
you about Julian. But to be fair,
you didn't tell me about Chip.

True.

Let's not be stupid with
each other anymore.

Btw, you're not allowed to date a senior.

Says who.

Says your big sister and your father
and I'm sure your brother!

We will discuss this further!

Count on it. ☺ Love you, baby sister.

Love you big sister.

Now all I have to do is deal with Julian. But I think I can make that quick.

You know how I said I believe in magic?

Yeah.

I believe in my heart that I can fix this. I can find the person I used to be. Is that stupid?

Nope.

Thanks for reminding me.

Red heart emoji.

Red? You skipped over purple and yellow and pink!

Happens.

Smiley face emoji. And all the other applicable emojis.

Which are?

Use your imagination. ☺

THIRTY-ONE

Three weeks after the pneumonia incident, I'm back in the hospital, this time for my baclofen pump. As they wheel me into the operating room, I think about all the times Mom took care of me when I was sick or hurt. I think about how she would always lay her hand on my forehead, checking me. And how my overly torqued muscles relaxed just at her touch because my body knew that I'd be okay as long as she was there with me.

There are already four people in the OR, all wearing scrubs and masks. "On three," a masked face says, and I'm transferred to the operating table. The door opens, and a nurse walks in. I know it won't be Gary this time. He doesn't do surgery. My body tenses.

Hands go on my head. "It's okay, Jenna. We're just getting started."

I think about my fantasy Garden of Eden. I think about all the Trees of Life I imagine are planted there. How they'd all be shaped by that person's life choices and experiences. I think that if I had a Tree of Life, it would be bent in ways tree bend, and that would be cool because everyone's trunks would show a little wear and tear. We'd all be leaning toward whatever sun we worshipped. My tree would be bent toward a certain hockey player's.

The oxygen mask goes over my face. "You comfortable, Jenna?"

I hate the feeling when your head is below your neck and you feel like you're choking, and I start to get panicky. I move my head.

A hand falls on my shoulder. "Can we get you something?"

The air feels tight and I want to tell them to scrap the whole thing, but instead I say, "My neck. Can we lift my neck?"

"Of course," the voice behind the mask says, and I feel my neck being lifted and something being placed under it. I feel the medicine they've given me in my IV loosen me, and I close my eyes. The sounds around me fade until I'm left alone with my thoughts.

Thoughts like how I'm more than my body, more than I ever gave myself credit for. If I am a tree in the Forest of Life, then I am here. I am eternal. These are the thoughts that swirl through my head as the doctor in front of me adjusts the straps on my oxygen mask and says, "Just a little gas to make you sleepy." A needle slips into the arm that's tied down to the bed.

"You're doing great, Jenna," my nurse encourages.

And I believe her. Soon her face blurs and then disappears, and I'm lifting out of my body. I hear a beeping, steady and strong, as my heart beats a different rhythm. I close my eyes all the way, and I pretend I'm floating higher and higher, until I am floating to the ceiling. I can look down on everyone and see all the people from up high. I want to reach out to them, but my arms are held down so I just watch. I am here, I think. I am here and you are there and suddenly everything seems to make sense. Everything fits together in a puzzle and I'm not sad about my body or what could have or should have been. I am just me. And that's enough.

My mind goes over everything that's happened in the last few weeks. It's a sad little montage, but from this distance it feel less awful and more inevitable. Maybe even forgivable.

"This is real." Jennifer's voice comes to me. "You are real. You are here. You are her. You are me."

And I think, I am *her*. I always have been.

I hear the sounds of waves crashing. I feel a breeze. Suddenly I'm back in Florida with Eric and Rena and Dad, and I'm crashing through the waves like his little Wonder Woman. I am flying like a mermaid.

"It's so *easy*..." Jennifer's voice is back. "You just have to be."

Soon I land on the beach and feel the sun warm my face. I open my eyes and see a white sun that doesn't hurt to look into. There are people playing Ring Around the Rosy all around me and the sand they kick up lands on my body, but it doesn't hurt or scratch.

"Well, look who's here," a voice says.

"She's awake," another one says.

Her voice lights up my insides with these tiny sparks that make me feel understood and loved.

Soft hands lift my head and lie it in a lap. I look up and see a woman with brown hair and a bright smile. "I'm going to stay with you for this next part." And I know she's one of the saints. Keeping me in balance. "You're doing very well, Jenna. Your body wants to heal. Rest and let it. Stay with us and let your body heal."

I want to ask her so many things, but my eyelids feel incredibly heavy and I let them close again. Hands fall over them, and the comforting pressure of those soft hands on my closed eyes promises a deep restorative sleep, and I'm so grateful. No spasms. No bad dreams. Only a sound, restful state. I embrace this feeling. It's been too long since I let go of all the bad and all the worry and all the pain. It feels like the right decision.

When I wake up after hours or weeks or months or years—it's all the same to me—I find two things on my hospital tray: a red rose and a Batman watch.

THIRTY-TWO

Everyone was slightly shocked when I chose to go to rehab straight from the hospital, but I felt like it was the best thing to do. It would give me time to work on my attitude. It would give Mom a break. And most of all, it would give me time to get stronger. To see what was possible.

Rehab is no joke. I found that out the first day I was here. They work you out hard, so hard that you can't wait to go to sleep at night. My first night here, I got a care package from Mom and Dad. The soft sugar cookies I like, new sleeping socks (I hate cold feet), and a letter from Rena.

Jenna,

Mom says I'm not allowed to call or text you when you're at rehab, that you're there to work and I am supposed to leave you alone. I wanted to tell you how proud I am of you. How incredibly awed I am by your strength.

Work hard and come home soon.

xoxo, Rena

These are the things that get me through. Especially since there have been very few texts from Julian. He told me before I left he was going to a hockey camp over winter break, and that we should both take this time to "get all beast." His words. I'm sure he's busy. But I also I wonder if he's over me? Has he moved on? Maybe he hasn't forgiven me for catfishing him. I take out his Batman watch.

My physical therapy assistant gets me set up for therapy. Each time the therapist tells me to lift my leg, I listen. I try not to brace. I try not to recruit other muscles to work for my underused ones, weak ones. It's hard, and sometimes I cry because it hurts so much it makes my head fill with stars, but I keep going. Jennifer's voice inside me reminds me, "You are her." And I believe I can be.

They've given me a schoolteacher named Mrs. Stein, who has short salt-and-pepper gray hair and dresses like she's working at a law firm. "Hello, Jenna," she says when I wheel myself into her office. "Let's see what we are going to do with you, shall we?"

I nod.

She pulls open a very thick file with my name on it and peers at her computer. She looks at me, back at the reports, and then back at the computer. "Hmmm." She clicks through the screens some more. Then says, "Strange."

I sit, ready to defend myself.

"I'm sort of confused," she says. "It seems like you were in all gifted classes, doing very well and then…"

"Then I sort of gave up on myself."

She takes her glasses off and smiles. Her red lipstick makes her teeth look so white and pretty. Her smile is like Mom's; part all-knowing and part hoping for better news. "That working for you?"

I laugh. "No."

"Well," she says as she claps her hands together. "Let's see what we can do about that. Because the good news, Jenna? You've got nothing but time to work here. No outside distractions." She types something into her computer. "No friends. No family. No boys."

I blush hot as if she's read my diary or something, even though I don't keep one. Still, this woman is way too observant for my own good. Except I'm ready to let her help me. I'm ready to help myself.

. . .

Every day is the same. I get up. Go to breakfast. Eat. Go to therapy. Go to the schoolroom. Go to the library. Eat lunch. Go to physical therapy. Go to the schoolroom. Eat dinner. Repeat.

By the end of the first week, I get something unexpected. A letter from Julian.

I rip it open. A picture falls out. It's of Julian, standing next to a sign that says Trail Magic.

Jenna,

Working hard at hockey camp so we took a day off to hike a portion of the Appalachian Trail and saw this. I've been thinking about you so much and this just felt like a sign or something (okay I KNOW it's an actual sign but also as the other kind of sign, too). Do you still believe in magic? Because I do. I do.

Julian

It's weird to get an actual letter. An email or text would have been quicker, but something about the permanence of the thing, the formality, and also the time it took to send it to me touches me and makes me hopeful.

I think about texting him that night. Like every night.

I'm not sure if I'm imagining it, but that night as I fall asleep I dream of him. And I can't wait to get back to see him. Even if he's over me. I hope he's not over me. But even if he is, I want to see him. I want to show him that I'm coming back. The Jenna I used to be is returning. Slowly. But no text can show him that. Only I can. In person. In five days when I come home.

THIRTY-THREE

I return home to a huge party. Just family. Plus Ben.

Eric's at school, but we Skype him. Uncle Steve, Aunt Betty, the little cousins, Rena, Mom, Dad, and me. Mom brings in food from an Italian restaurant I love. It means she doesn't have to cook or do much clean up.

Mom looks relaxed and calm.

"I'm scared to see him," I tell Ben.

He slings his arm around me. "It's a good kind of scared though, huh?"

"Is that a thing?"

"You ready for reentry?" Ben asks.

"As I'll ever be?"

Rena plops down next to me, a plate full of pasta. "It's going to be amazing," she says, framing my face with her hands. "Jenna Cohen, the sequel."

"The merchandising on that is going to be huge," Ben says.

Rena high fives him.

I simply sit and take it all in.

. . .

The next day Mom pulls up in front of the school. Rena is riding shotgun because she's trying to talk Mom into letting her stay late all of this week to work on the sets with Rocco. Some things never change.

Thanks to Hospital Homebound at the rehab center and Mrs. Stein's horrific work ethic, I've completed AP Psych and AP Lang semester one all in the span of a few weeks. Whew! Now I just have to play catch-up. Good thing I did some projects already on the sly.

Mom pulls up in our van. The door slides open. Rena rushes around to help me out. I've got a walking stick with me now and my crutches in a bag over my shoulder just in case. Rena walks next to me. I go in the normal entrance, not the shortcut one anymore.

Rena laughs. "Slow down, Jenna, it's not a race."

I adjust my stride, take normal-sized steps.

"Hey, Jenna, wait up," Kate, one of the girls from the AP classes, calls from behind us. "I heard you're back in class with us again. Cool."

Another girl, Selene, jogs to catch up. "Yeah. We can give you the lay of the land. Swanson? Terrible teacher. Leads? Better. Don't worry, you'll catch up."

Rena gives me her two-finger salute and is off with her friends.

Every single time I walk now, I feel the length of my gait. When we get to the courtyard I see a group of hockey players hanging around. I almost don't want to look, but I can't help it. I've been looking for that boy since kindergarten. But Julian is not there.

"You've got to get moving on your project for AP Psych. We're doing one on psychology awareness month. Maybe we can add you on," Kate says.

"She's spoken for," Ben says, showing up out of nowhere. "But thank you, anyway, Kate."

And somehow, I'm right back in my stride, like the Jennifer I always wanted to be. That's when I see Julian. His eyes do a slow crawl from the sidewalk in front of me and up until they land on my face.

"Hey," he says.

Kate looks at Selene, who looks at me. "We'll catch you inside." Ben goes with them.

"So," Julian says once we're alone. "You're back."

"I am."

"So..." he says. "You look like you're moving great."

"I'm doing pretty good," I say. "How's everything with..."

"Oh. The police? They dropped the charges."

I smile. "That's great."

"This isn't awkward at all," he says.

I nod, searching for something to say. "I got your letter!" I blurt.

His turn to smile. "Yeah, it was so cool. I saw the sign, and it felt like a sign, and I've said all of this before..."

"Yeah. Very cool."

"So," he says again.

"So."

The bell rings.

His eyes flit to the administrators trying to corral us toward our classes. "What does that mean? For us?" he asks.

"That depends."

"On what?"

"On whether or not you ask me out."

He looks at the ground. Then back up to me. That sexy but nervous grin on his face. "What are the odds you'll say yes?"

I lift the sleeve off my wrist. Expose his Batman watch. "I'd say pretty good."

Julian walks me to my new AP English class. "Mr. S. is going to miss you, you know."

"Aw. Poor Mr. S. He the only one?"

"Well, that Tommy seemed really into you, so…"

"Tommy, huh. Okay. Well, give him a kiss for me then."

"Not a chance."

Then, right in the middle of the hallway, Julian leans down and kisses me. My stomach flutters, and the feelings are so much bigger than the ones from that fantasy goodbye when I was Jennifer and I was leaving on the train.

"Get in here, girl," Ben calls from the classroom. "Saved you a seat."

Julian and I pull away from each other, and I send Ben an embarrassed grin. "Be right there."

Julian gives a little wave goodbye, and I stand there for another moment watching him leave, the feeling of his kiss still on my lips.

And for the first time, I realize my real life has far exceeded my fantasy one.

AUTHOR'S NOTE

Authors shouldn't love one of their books more than the others. I know this. But sometimes we can't help ourselves. (Shh…don't tell my other books.) The thing is, Jenna's voice came to me right away, but her story still took me ten years to write. Ten years is a long time to work on one book, but I felt like Jenna deserved my time and effort.

For me, this book wasn't about a kid with a disability. This book was about a girl who believed something about herself that wasn't true. Something that made her doubt herself and made her change the way she saw her future. Made her double down on wanting to make her own decisions, even when those decisions were not serving her. We all feel like that at times, though, right? We all think our ways out of things. We stop taking ballet because we didn't like the teacher. We stop playing the violin because we don't want to lug it around anymore. We put our manuscript away because someone (an editor, an agent, or a critique partner) didn't like it. There are so many ways we give up on ourselves.

Jenna's story is about how one girl gave up on herself and also how, when she wanted to help someone else, she found herself again. I think that's how those things work, too. I think when you do something for someone else, you end up benefiting even more than they do. To me, that's pretty cool.

I've been a speech language pathologist for thirty years, and have worked with many children and teens with cerebral palsy. This condition is different for every single person and everyone who has it has a different story to tell. This is just one of those stories. Jenna's story. I hope you like it.

ACKNOWLEDGMENTS

Every book has its own journey. This book took ten years from conception to print and went through many, many different versions. It also needed lots of people to help it along its way. I mean, so many people, that I'm certain I will inevitably forget to include someone in these acknowledgments. To those people I am sorry. It isn't that your contribution was unimportant. It's that my memory is faulty and ten years is a long time.

To start with, I need to thank my agent, Nicole Resciniti, for her tireless belief in me and my writing. We've been working together for almost five years now, and I can honestly say that with her tending my career, I have felt free to pursue the thing that means the most to me—the creation of books. For that I am eternally grateful.

I also have to thank my original editor, Annette Pollert-Morgan, who bought this book. And to the editor who has worked tirelessly on *It's My Life* to get it to its current state, thank you so much, Eliza Swift. You made this book better, more resonant, and more accessible. I am lucky to have all the people at Sourcebooks who help in immeasurable ways from acquisition to delivery and beyond. What a team!

As usual I have to thank my critique groups. The Tuesdays, of course, but also the Boca SCBWI group, the original Wellington

SCBWI group, the Boynton group, the PGAs, and the Palm Springs group. Early reads of a very different version of this book passed through Laen Ghiloni and David Case's hands and your input and friendship have been so appreciated.

I was lucky to have Lorin Oberweger take a peek at an early version of this and assist with story development. Her skill at finding the heart of story is something that influenced more than just this book, but my entire writing career. Thank you for being in my life.

To Joyce Sweeney, my mentor, friend, and faithful supporter. I cannot express how much you've shaped my writing world.

To Jonathan Rosen, Steven dos Santos, and Jill Nadler, each of you contributed so much to this book. You were faithful beta readers and more importantly, friends. I am always at a loss for how to fully thank you all. Maybe by my next book, I'll have worked that out. But the point is, you all believed in this book from the very beginning. Thank you all so much.

To Consuelo Kreider, who owned a pediatric therapy practice with me for years, thank you for all the lessons on the way. For always believing I was up to any challenge. For believing in the kids we worked with. That everyone has a right to live their best life.

Thank you to Marjetta Geerling for so many things, but in terms of this book, for setting me on my path to getting my MFA at Spalding University, where Beth Ann Bauman, one of my workshop leaders, helped me find my way when I was flailing. And to all of the workshop participants, thanks for helping me revise and revisit this book of my heart.

As to the people of my heart, much and eternal thanks to my

family, my husband, my children, and my nieces and nephews. To my sisters-in-law and my brother-in-law. My dogs. My brother and sister. You all are my world.

ABOUT THE AUTHOR

PHOTO © HANNAH MAYO
PHOTOGRAPHY

STACIE RAMEY learned to read at a very early age to escape the endless tormenting from her older siblings. She attended the University of Florida, where she majored in communication sciences, and Penn State, where she received a master of science degree in speech pathology. When she's not writing, she engages in Netflix wars with her children or beats her husband in Scrabble. She lives in Wellington, Florida, with her husband and their rescue dogs.

ALSO BY STACIE RAMEY

"A gripping novel that will tug on readers' heartstrings until the very end."

—BOOKLIST *on* THE SECRETS WE BURY

FIREreads
S #getbooklit

Your hub for the hottest young adult books!

Visit us online and sign up for our
newsletter at FIREreads.com

 @sourcebooksfire

 sourcebooksfire

t firereads.tumblr.com